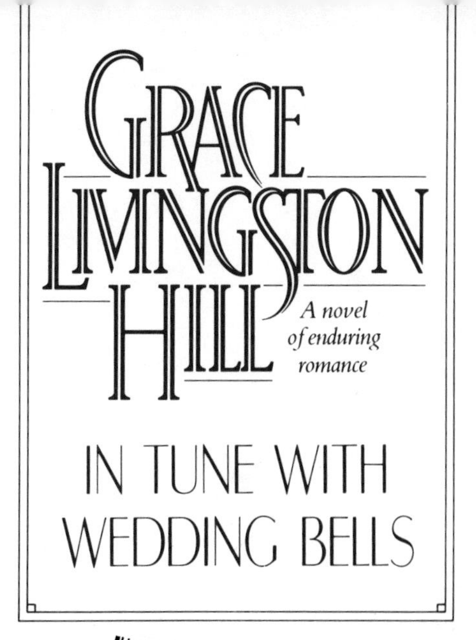
GRACE
LIVINGSTON
HILL
A novel
of enduring
romance
IN TUNE WITH
WEDDING BELLS

Tyndale House
Publishers, Inc.
Wheaton, Illinois

This Tyndale House book
by Grace Livingston Hill
contains the complete text
of the original hardcover edition.
NOT ONE WORD
HAS BEEN OMITTED.

Library of Congress Catalog Card Number 88-50911
ISBN 0-8423-1642-6

Reprinted by permission of Harper & Row, Publisher, Inc.
Cover illustration by Deborah L. Chabrian
Interior illustrations by Edward Martinez

Printed in the United States of America

95 94 93 92 91 90

10 9 8 7 6 5 4 3 2

IN TUNE WITH WEDDING BELLS

Tyndale House books by
Grace Livingston Hill
Check with your area bookstore
for these bestsellers.

COLLECTOR'S CHOICE SERIES
1 Christmas Bride
2 In Tune with Wedding Bells
3 Partners
4 Strange Proposal

LIVING BOOKS®
1 Where Two Ways Met
2 Bright Arrows
3 A Girl to Come Home To
77 The Ransom
78 Found Treasure
79 The Big Blue Soldier

CLASSICS SERIES
1 Crimson Roses
2 The Enchanted Barn
3 Happiness Hill
4 Patricia
5 Silver Wings

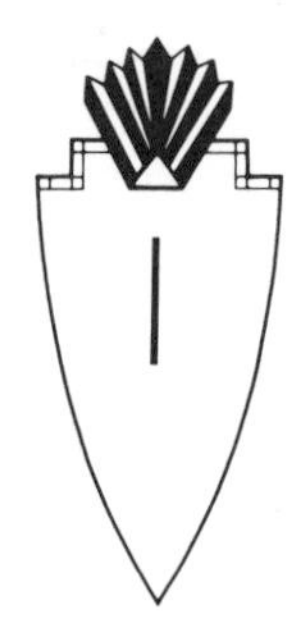

REUBEN Remington came out of the drafting room with his hands full of papers and blueprints, and walked the length of the big outer office toward the superintendent's room with a gay grin on his face, his pleasant lips puckered as with a suppressed whistle.

There was a spring in his step and a light in his eyes that was quite unwonted, and he glanced about in a friendly way toward the girls and men who were hard at work at their desks about him, which was quite different from his usual somber demeanor.

Reuben was tall and well built, with a grace in every movement that made people look after him as he went through a room, though his usual gravity prevented any of them from knowing him very well. He had red-gold hair that showed a tendency to curl if it was ever allowed to grow long enough to do so, and very blue eyes that looked as if they had a sunny light behind them. But he had always held his head so high, and kept such a veil of reticence over the blue of his eyes, that his fellow workers felt he was trying to be exclusive. He had been with the company now for almost three years and still they hadn't quite made him out. Of course he wasn't a mere member of the office force, and they did not have much contact with him, but they saw him often enough to make them curious. And sometimes at the lunch hour in the nearby resturants the girls talked him over. The men didn't need to. They were not so curious, and not so self-conscious. He was just another fellow working hard, and they were fairly friendly with him and let it go at that.

But there was something different today about Reuben as he walked across that room, and they all looked up and noticed it.

"What's got into our friend Mr. Gravity?" whispered Evelyn Howe to Wilda Murdock who was working at the next typewriter. "He looks as gay as a lark. See his eyes twinkle. He certainly is in high feather. He almost looks as if he might expect one to say 'good morning' to him. I wonder what's happened."

"Why, don't you know?" said Wilda, watching the young man furtively from her distance. "He's on vacation tomorrow. Going away somewhere. It's the first vacation he's had since he came here. The first year of course he didn't get any. They never do, starting, you know. And last year there was such a rush they needed him, and he stayed. He's that kind, you know. Always eating up work. Wanted the experience, I heard someone say. I wonder where he's going?"

"Probably home to his mother," said Evelyn. "That solemn kind are always mother-boys."

"No," said Wilda, shaking her head. "I heard his mother was dead. Ward Rand was talking to the superintendent one day and I overheard him say his father died when he was only a kid, and his mother just before he came here. Maybe that's what gave him such a grave look."

"Maybe he's got a girl somewhere," said Evelyn. "He's likely going to see her. Perhaps he's going to be married. That's likely it! That'll mean we'll have to scratch around and get a wedding present for him. Though I don't know why we should. He's not in our department, and he's never tried to be in the least friendly with us."

"He's awfully young, isn't he?" said Wilda.

"Oh, he's not so young as he looks, probably. Seems as if

he must be older that he looks to have accumulated all that dignity," said Evelyn folding circulars skillfully, and deftly sliding them into the stacks of envelopes she had just typed with addresses. "Have you got all your envelopes addressed, Wilda?"

"No, I've got another coupla-hundred. There! There he comes back! He didn't stay long this time. He's making business snappy. Say, I wonder if he might be going down to the shore to the house party the boss's daughter is giving this week end? I saw her talking to him the other day. Mr. Rand introduced them when I was in there taking dictation. I wouldn't put it past her to ask him. She's rather democratic, you know. And now since he's got this raise it brings him somewhat within her range."

"I wouldn't be surprised," said Evelyn grimly. "He's terribly good-looking of course. Watch him now. He walks like a prince, and Anise Glinden always was noted for getting good-looking men around her."

"Yes," said Wilda enviously. "She can get everything she wants. I suppose he wouldn't dare decline her invitation even if he did have another girl somewhere. He might lose his job if he did. They say she's awfully vindictive."

"Oh, maybe not!" said Evelyn wearily. "I've heard she's very pleasant sometimes. There! He's coming down this aisle. You better get to work, lady. Mr. Rand is with him, and he doesn't hesitate to jack us up if he thinks any of us is loafing on the job."

There was silence at once as the two men walked down the aisle past them, both rather preoccupied with their own conversation.

Then suddenly just ahead of them, the girl to the right, the third from the front of the room, slumped over her machine, her inert hands and arms sliding off the keyboard of her machine and drooping at her sides, her whole slim young body collapsing into unconsiousness.

Both men saw it at once, and both started toward her, but it was Reuben Remington who reached for her first and caught her as she was about to slide from her chair to the floor.

"Lay her down!" directed the manager coming nearer, and moving the chair out of the way. "Flat on her back. She's fainted. That will be best. Somebody bring some water. Quick!"

Half a dozen flew to obey the command, and the other girls started from their places and came nearer to see. But the manager waved them back.

"Give her room to breathe," he said sharply. "Call the doctor. He ought to be in his office at this hour."

"I just called," said one of the office boys. "He's busy. A man got hurt in the machine shop and he's dressing his cuts. They say he can't come just now."

"Well, get another doctor!" said the manager. "Where's Miss Stanton, the nurse? Isn't she around?"

"She's up in the infirmary helping doc," said the office boy in a reproving tone, as if he hadn't already thought of that possibility and acted on it.

"Well, hasn't anybody got a restorative? How about that aromatic ammonia you had around here the other day? Hasn't anybody got a flask or something?"

One of the girls produced a small bottle of aromatic ammonia and dousing it on a hankerchief, Reuben held it under the girl's nostrils.

The girls lips quivered and she drew a trembling breath as if it were almost too much effort, but the waxen eyelids remained closed, and the girl was far from conscious.

The manager watched her for an instant, and then he began to issue orders again.

"Telephone the nearest hospital. Tell them we need a nurse too. Tell them to send an ambulance and a doctor. We must get her to the hospital as soon as possible. Do any of you girls know where her people are to be found?"

"I don't think she has any people," volunteered Evelyn Howe.

"Yes, she has," said Wilda Murdock. "I heard her say she had a little brother."

"Somebody go look at the record; that ought to tell us something. She must have told who to call in case of acci-

dent when she registered. However, she'll have to go to the hospital in any case. We can't waste time. We can look up her people later. Who took this girl's registration?"

Suddenly the girl on the floor stirred, and her eyelids fluttered partly open. A troubled look passed over her face like a swift-moving cloud. Her pale lips formed a single word, though there seemed no voice behind it to make it audible.

Reuben was still on his knees beside her, wafting the handkerchief wet with ammonia before her face. He stooped a listening ear, watching the lips.

"No? Did you say 'no'?" he asked in a quiet tone.

The girl's eyes flew open for an instant, sad, pleading, anguished, and gave assent to his question.

"No, what?" asked Reuben.

"No hospital—" the pale lips uttered, the voice very faint, but vehement. "I *can't*—go. I'll—be—all—right—" and then her breath deserted her, and it looked as if she were about to pass out again.

"Here!" said Reuben, reaching toward a glass of water that someone had brought. "Take a sip of this," and he slipped his arm under her neck and lifted her head a little, holding the glass to her lips. She swallowed a few drops.

The manager gave a decided order for the hospital ambulance in a low tone, but the girl's hearing was quick now and she opened troubled eyes toward him, and shook her head.

"No!" she said faintly. "No!" But the manager gave his messenger a knowing nod and motioned him away, and then turned back and spoke to Reuben in a low tone.

"Would you have time before your train to stick around and see this girl located? I have an important conference with a man from Chicago in five minutes, and I ought to be in my office at once."

Reuben looked up with quick assent, and found the girl's troubled eyes upon him with pleading in them. He flashed her a reassuring smile, and laid her head gently down on the folded coat that Evelyn had slipped under her head.

"Of course you'll make them all understand that the company will be behind whatever seems best to be done," said the manager.

Reuben gave another grave nod of his head, and then wet the handkerchief with another douse of ammonia, and the girl seemed to gather in new strength from the breath of it.

"I—think—I could get up—now—" she said slowly.

"No!" said Reuben. "You're lying still till the nurse gets here. We don't want to take any chances." His voice was firmly kind, but there was a hint of smile in his eyes.

She studied him for a moment, and then, as she noticed that the group of observers were mostly gone, she steadied her voice and said softly:

"I'd like—to make you understand—" Her eyes were very pleading.

"Yes?" said Reuben. "I'll understand."

"I—couldn't go to the hospital!—" she went on. "I must go home! Put me in a taxi and I'll get home."

"Where is your home?" asked Reuben getting out a pencil and notebook swiftly from his breast pocket.

His tone was business like, and the girl murmured a street address gratefully. "Third floor, back," she said.

"Is there a telephone there?"

"No," she said sadly.

"Well, who is there? Any of your people?"

"Just—my little brother—" she said in a tone of anguish.

"Oh, don't worry!" said Reuben smiling. "He'll be all right. Boys always get along all right. I'll see that he understands and doesn't worry."

"But—" a wave of almost terror passed over the girl's white face, "but he's only five years old, and there isn't a thing in the room to eat!"

"Oh, that's different!" said Reuben, supressing an involuntary whistle. "Well, now don't you worry the least bit. I'll look after the kid. I give you my word of honor. Kids and I always get on. We'll be buddies till you get back."

"That's kind of you—" she murmured with an effort, "but I can't let you do that. You have your work. This is mine, and I must attend to it."

There was a sweet dignity about her even in her weakness that made Reuben look at her with respect.

"Well, but look here, sister, you are sick and not able to carry on just now. I'm sorry but I guess you'll have to trust me."

"Oh, it isn't that!" said the girl desperately. "You don't understand. He's only five, and you have a big job here. You can't leave your job and look after my brother all day!"

"Well, you see, sister, I happen to be going on vacation tomorrow, a whole month, and I'll have plenty of leisure on my hands. Besides, who looks after him while you are off at work?"

"I take him to the Day Nursery before I come. They bring him back at five."

"That sounds easy enough, and if worse comes to worst I guess I'm as good as a day nursery any day. Now look here, sister, when did you have your lunch?"

"She didn't go to lunch today," said Evelyn Howe who was standing by. "She hardly ever does."

"I'm never hungry at noontime," said the girl on the floor apologetically.

"I thought so," ejaculated Reuben under his breath. "Look here, sister, that's no way to look after a little brother. A dead sister isn't much protection against the world. Now listen; this has got to stop right here, and you've got to get fit to carry on your job. Sammy," to the office boy across the aisle, "run down to the resturant hot foot, before that ambulance gets here, and bring me up a cup of hot tea and some toast. Or would you rather have coffee?" He turned to the sick girl, but she shook her head. "Tea," she said breathlessly.

"All right, Sammy, tea it is, and maybe a glass of milk, and make it snappy. It's on the boss. He put me in charge."

The girl gasped and looked troubled.

"I—mustn't—lose my job!" she said desperately.

"I give you my word you won't lose your job for this," said Reuben with a restful smile. "Boys, what's the matter with bringing in that little couch from the rest room?"

The girl put on a look of protest, but the two young men hurried away and presently returned with a small couch from the nearby rest room. Reuben promptly lifted the girl upon it. The tray was on hand almost at once, and Reuben lifted the girl's head and held the cup of hot tea for her to drink.

A few swallows and the color began to steal slowly back to her white face. Reuben knelt there beside the couch feeding her bits of toast.

While she was eating the hall door swung open and a doctor and nurse entered, followed by two orderlies carrying a stretcher, but the girl was lying with her face away from the door and did not see them until they were upon her.

"Oh!" she said, sitting up suddenly as she recognized what they were, "I don't need a doctor. I'm quite all right now. I—shouldn't have tried to work so long—without food."

"No, that never pays," said the doctor's grave voice. "Lie down, won't you, till I see what condition your heart is in. Nurse, get the temperature, and pulse." The girl fell back on the couch with a look of despair as the doctor got out his stethoscope and made his examination. The typists in the big office ceased their copying and went quietly at some other service for the moment. It was very still in the big room, while the workers watched furtively the quiet girl who had come among them so unobtrusively, a few months before.

It was all over very quickly, and the girl was transferred to the stretcher, the orderlies lifting it and carrying her from the office. Then behind the swinging doors that shut her out from them all their tongues began to buzz.

"Well, I thought there was something queer about her, her color was so pasty," said Norah Whately. "I wonder what she's saving money for?"

"Didn't you hear her?" said Peg Howard. "She's got a young brother to support, I suppose. Poor thing! If she'd been a little less closemouthed we might have helped her some."

But out in the hall waiting for the freight elevator the girl on the stretcher was much excited. By a supreme effort she lifted herself to a sitting posture, then tried to stand, till the interne gently pressed her back to the cot again.

"Lady, you must lie still if you don't want to pass out on the way to the hospital."

"But—I must—go—home. I cannot leave—my little—brother alone! He will not under—stand!"

Her breath was very short. She could scarcely make her words heard. Except for her excitement she would not have been able to speak above a whisper.

"Now look here, girlie!" said the handsome young interne, holding her firmly down to her cot, and speaking with command in his voice, "this gentleman here is going to look after that brother of yours, and everything is going to be all right. You've got to go to the hospital at once, see?" and he smiled amiably at her.

She gave him a frightened look and her glance hurried around the group beside her till she found Reuben. So eagerly her eyes spoke to him that he answered her at once by stepping to her side, stooping to speak in a low tone.

"It's all right, sister," he said reassuringly. "I've got the address, 1017 N. Fresco Street, third floor, back. Is that right? And the boy's name is Noel Guthrie? Is he there now? Not till 5:15?"

Reuben glanced at his watch.

"Then I'll have to go with you to the hospital and see you located first," he said thoughtfully. "Does he always come promptly?"

She shook her head. "Sometimes not till six. But he'll have no supper. I was going to get the supper on my way home. But I have to stop at the desk and get my pay envelope. Oh!" and she fell back on the cot in despair. "Oh, I must go to the desk! I haven't *any* money!"

The girls had brought her coat and hat from the cloak room, and her purse from the desk drawer before she left the office, and now she opened her purse wildly and began to feel frantically for the quarter she thought she had left to pay for Noel's day at the nursery.

"That's all right, Miss Guthrie," said Reuben, "I'll see to

that. But you must have money of course. Sammy," turning to the office boy who was still in evidence, "run down to Mr. Ensigner and ask for Miss Guthrie's pay envelope. Meet us at the freight elevator door right away."

Then Reuben turned back to the girl as the elevator arrived, and smiled gravely down at her.

"It's all right, Miss Guthrie. Sam will bring your envelope, and as for the boy's supper I'll look after that. Would you feel better if I went right away to the Day Nursery and called for your brother?"

"No," gasped the girl, "they wouldn't give him to you. I've told them never to let anybody else have him."

"Where is this Day Nursery, girlie?" asked the interne. "Down on Third Street? Because we could stop and pick him up now, if that will make you feel any better. They'll give him to us if they see you."

"Oh! Will you do that?" the girl's face fairly bloomed with relief. "Oh, you are very kind. He would be terribly frightened if I didn't explain to him." There were tears of relief on her face.

"Okay, girlie, we'll do that little thing!" said the gay young interne, and he motioned to the orderlies to lift the stretcher. Then he turned to Reuben as they went into the elevator, and said a few words in a low tone to him, and Reuben bowed gravely.

Sam was on hand as the elevator arrived at the first floor, produced the pay envelope in good order, and Reuben handed it over to the girl quietly and helped her put it in her purse.

"Now," he said as he left her in the ambulance, "we're off for the Day Nursery! Don't you worry! I'll be seeing you, and I'll take good care of the kid!"

Then he slipped around and rode in the front seat with the driver. This was the first opportunity he had since he picked up that girl in the aisle ahead of him, to realize just what all this was going to mean.

For a month past, since ever he had been told he was to

have a month's vacation, Reuben Remington had been happily looking forward to it. A respite at last from the hard grind of work!

Not that he didn't like the work. He did. Even when his mother died and dashed all his bright hopes of making a happy home for her, he had been glad and thankful for that hard work, and had plunged himself into it with all his soul that he might forget that she was gone. It had helped him to concentrate on something besides himself, and his own loneliness. And especially since he had begun to succeed in what he was trying to do. Since the men who were immediately over him had commended him, at first charily, and at last unqualifiedly, and had recommended him for a rise in his position, he had reveled in his job, reaching out even higher, more ambitiously. Not that there was any especial reason to rise any more now his mother was gone, and there was no immediate friend or relative to care. It was just that he wanted to do the thing he had set out to do, he wanted to justify his promises to his mother.

But as the days had hurried on, bringing him only more and more duties with no let-up in view, he had grown weary. He had sometimes tried to think ahead and see what it was all about.

Undoubtedly he could make friends, and perhaps now was the time he needed them. He had supposed they would come when there was time for them, and he had been willing to wait. He had gotten in the habit of hoarding his strength, because he had felt that was his only capital, and what leisure he had he had filled with reading and study, because there were courses that he had not had opportunity to study deeply in college, and he felt his lack in them now. He had never been in the habit of playing since his high school days. There had always been something important to do, although back in his mind there had always been an indefinable longing for it; he was always promising himself that the day would come when good times would be his again, just as they had been when he was a child and had a father and mother to think for him and provide needful amusement.

But now suddenly he was up against a vacation, and that ought to mean a good time. He was breathless with the thought of it, wondering what he was going to do with it.

Should he take up the time in travel? He had saved his salary, such part of it as had not been needed for his exceedingly modest maintenance, with a view to a pleasant interval when the time should come. Should he travel and see some of the country's notable sights? Great buildings and bridges, and feats of engineering? He had enough for a limited amount of that without making himself penniless. And of course such sight-seeing as that would be along the line of his business, and would be valuable to his work. But somehow he shrank from a vacation that had a business reason. He wanted something entirely different. He sensed that he was getting into a rut and needed to get out and meet people, to develop along new lines. In fact Mr. Rand had told him that one day when he had been asking him questions about his ambitions and plans. He hadn't thought much of it at the time. It had seemed to him always that Mr. Rand was a very worldly man, and his advice was to be taken with care along such lines. His standards and ideals would be so different from the ideals and standards of Reuben's father and mother that he regarded them with question. Reuben hadn't got so far yet from his family traditions that he wanted to give them up entirely. Perhaps all the more because he missed his family, and his native surroundings. So he had not swallowed Mr. Rand's suggestion whole, and here he was, up against a real vacation at last, and with no place to go.

Oh, of course there were places. There were mountains and shores, and attractive cruises, and resorts for amusement, but none of them so far had quite clinched with Reuben.

Just recently something had come, quite new and bewildering. Anise Glinden, the peppy smart daughter of Mr. Glinden, the head of the firm, had come to his office, bursting in upon his quiet busy hours most unexpectedly. He hadn't known her very well before. She had been away to college, with summers abroad, and had just recently appeared on the scene, a full-fledged college graduate, with a coming-out party in the offing, and society waiting breathlessly to receive her and absorb her. She wore the latest thing in garments, and her face was illuminated brilliantly, her hair a shining helmet, her voice breezy, nonchalant, impudent. He hadn't considered her at all as being in the world where he lived and moved and was expecting to have his being for some years to come.

But she had breezed into his office and addressed him with all the familiarity of one who had a right to give him orders.

"Oh, Reuben!" she had said without waiting for him to greet her. "Dad says you're having a vacation next week. Beginning when?"

Reuben looked up with a smile and something of sunny anticipation in his eyes, and answered laconically:

"Tomorrow!"

"Grand!" said Anise. "That just suits my plans!" Her face was gaily radiant.

Reuben watched her in astonishment.

"Your plans?" he questioned with quick amazement. What did that mean? Was she planning to get his job away for someone else? Was she going to try to put one of her sophisticated friends in his place? The amusement went out of his glance and a look of gravity lurked in his eyes.

"Yes," said Anise. "I hope you hadn't any ironclad plans of your own, because if you do you have to change them, see? What were you planning to do? Where were you going?"

Faced suddenly with this question Reuben was at a loss what to say.

"Why—I—I wasn't quite sure about the whole of the time," he said hesitantly. "There are several places I want to go, and people I have to see."

"Well, you can just call them all up and tell them you're not coming, because *I* want you!" she announced, as if that settled the question.

"You want me?" said Reuben, dumbfounded. Was he not to have a vacation after all? Did this pampered daughter of his boss think she could absorb his vacation and make him work at something for her? What was the idea? He frowned

and lifted his chin a bit haughtily, with a memory of the old Remington self-respect and pride in his glance.

"Yes," said the girl, "I've planned it all out. I'm having a house party down at the shore, Glindenwold, out on our island, you know. You've heard of it, of course. It's going to be all kinds of a gay time and I want you for one of our house guests. I've got it all planned and you simply can't get out of it, even if you want to, for you would just upset everything. And besides when you see Glindenwold you wouldn't want to, for it's swell. I know you'll be crazy about it. We have our own swimming pool and our own little theater, and all kinds of sports! There isn't a thing you can name we haven't got!" she declared proudly. "And we're going to put on some thrilling plays this summer. Amateur, you know, and that's where you come in. I want you to take the part of the hero in the next play, opposite me. I know you'll be great! I want you to come right down and start rehearsing. We've got a professional coach of course, but you're just the type I want. I thought we could get a start before anybody else comes around."

Reuben grinned.

"A play! Me? Oh no! Not me!" said Reuben decidedly. And then he laughed.

The girl looked bewildered.

"Now listen!" she said and then she dropped into the chair his stenographer had vacated just before she came in.

Reuben listened, and studied her. This was an entirely new contact for him. His had been a simple Christian home. Except for occasional high class patrons whom he had to confer with when the manager was out he did not know this kind of human being at all. And even with patrons he was in a position to feel confident; with them he could almost dictate about matters that were altogether familiar to himself, and not so familiar to them. Now the order was reversed. He was dealing with matters about which he literally knew nothing except by hearsay, and the girl he was talking with was an expert in the ways of the world. It all amused him very much. He listened and grinned. And when at last after a voluble plea she came to a momentary pause he shook his head.

"No!" he said decidedly. "I couldn't! I wouldn't belong!"

"But you have to," she said with an engaging earnestness, "because *I want* it!" There was a childlike naivete about her that was hard to deny. Was it genuine simplicity? He studied her, perplexed for an instant, but shook his head again.

"Impossible!" he said smiling. "I tell you I wouldn't belong in an atmosphere like that," and there was a ring of positiveness about his voice that annoyed her, for she drew her imperious eyebrows down.

"Now, what nonsense!" she said haughtily. "You mean clothes, of course, but you wouldn't worry about that. I have two brothers about your size. They will lend you anything you need. They have slews of garments down there of any style you could possibly demand. And—besides—if *I* ask you, you *do* belong!"

He looked at her for a moment with an impersonal smile, and then suddenly grew grave.

"I'm sorry," he said pleasantly. "It's not a matter of clothes. But the whole thing is quite out of the question."

A man arrived by appointment just then and she had to leave him but that was not the end. For the rest of the day she had appeared unexpectedly a number of times and renewed the subject, until finally she just took it for granted that he was coming, no matter how often he declined, and went on with her plans, telling him what to do and where to meet her; telling him who would be there that he ought to meet for the sake of business, even if not for his own sake, until like the continual dropping that wears the stone, he actually found himself considering the possibility of going.

What if she was right and he ought to get out and get acquainted with other kinds of people? What would his family have said to that?

Long ago when he was a little boy his mother used to have a question she would put to him when they were considering a perplexity. She would say, "What do you think God would say if you were to ask His advice?" and that somehow always settled the matter the way his own conscience had already tentatively settled it. But since he had been out in the world, his mother gone, and no one to suggest submitting a matter to God—a God that so many people nowadays didn't seem to believe in—Reuben had gotten into the habit instead of saying, "I wonder what dad and mother would say about it?" Because it had been a settled fact in his mind that dad and mother used always to think what God would think. And he was pretty well decided that neither God nor his mother would pick out this special girl to conduct his venture into an alien world.

And yet, he wasn't a kid any longer, and he could surely stand a few hours of contact with a world that wasn't his own. And it wasn't as if he couldn't leave when he chose, always provided he didn't accept a part in that fool play. And *of course* he *wouldn't* do that! And then, quite the most important of all the phases of the matter was that this was his boss's daughter who was asking him, and he wasn't at all sure but it might affect his job if he didn't go—at least for a short time.

So he had almost decided he would take in a brief stay at Glindenwold. Well, anyway, he would go long enough to look over the land and see how it lay.

And now, how was this affair of the moment going to fit in?

He couldn't of course get through this in time to go to Glindenwold tonight. That was what Anise Glinden had wanted. She was planning to have the first rehearsal of the play tonight. She had told him he might watch it the first night and be all ready to get to work on it for the next day. She would have a young actor come out to take the part she wanted him to take, just for one night and let him see how simple and easy it was.

Perhaps it was just as well that he shouldn't be able to go tonight, then they would start without him and she wouldn't be harping on his taking part. Besides he needed to see just what this was and not get tied up to something that he would hate.

He couldn't go tonight, even though she had suggested

driving by his boarding place and picking him up in her car. This girl in the ambulance would not be out of the hospital in time for him to go, and he had promised to take care of the kid. What could he do but telephone Miss Glinden that he wouldn't be down until tomorrow?

Then the ambulance whirled skillfully around the corner into a side street and brought up before a large gloomy tenement, which bore the signs in one dreary window, "Day Nursery," and the driver stopped his car.

"Make it snappy!" he said to Reuben, as he swung down to the irregular old brick sidewalk.

Reuben nodded and hurried up the wooden steps. He didn't care much about this part of his job, but he had promised, and he could still see the anguish in the eyes of the sick girl.

He glanced nervously back toward the ambulance, wondering if she could see out, but he saw she could not. As he hastily turned back he caught a glimpse of a quickly gathering group of neighborhood children, assembling in a semicircle, in various stages of dirt and squalor, staring eagerly to see who was inside the ambulance, or who was to go to be taken away from their vicinity.

Then the door was opened by a large fat woman with a sullen mouth, a frown on her brow, and a cross, sick baby in her arms. She eyed the ambulance with irritation, and brought her insolent eyes to bear on the intruder. Reuben stepped within and closed the door behind him. He didn't wish any more witnesses to this incident than were necessary.

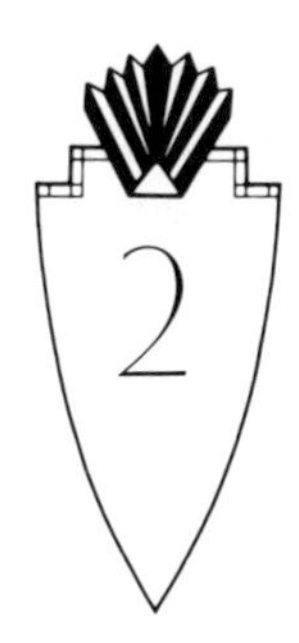

REUBEN had a glimpse of large gloomy double rooms, absolutely bare except for a row of dilapidated iron cribs, a few chairs that didn't match, and a couple of low tables at the far end.

As he told the matron what he wanted he stepped within the front room, and was instantly aware of eyes, baby eyes, staring at him, and wailing young voices crying out with disappointment. Their mothers had not come and they were weary to death of this dreary place, and this desolate woman who had charge. It struck a pang to Reuben's heart. He didn't analyze it at the time, but afterward the scene hung like a pall over the day. How he would have liked to set all those babies free and put them into a big meadow with daisies and buttercups, and butterflies, and birds singing high in the trees, and make the little hearts happy.

His eyes quickly searched the rooms, and then he saw the boy Noel!

He was sitting at one of the low tables with a box of crayons before him, and a small sheet of paper on which he had been drawing. He had large dark eyes that instantly reminded him of the girl out in the ambulance. They had the same quality of hopelessness, and helplessness.

"I have come after Noel Guthrie," he said, raising his voice a trifle, and the boy at the little table instantly arose, his eyes wide with question, fear trembling behind the whiteness of his face.

The large woman stepped closer and spoke arrogantly.

"Well, I can't letcha have him without a written order from his sister. She wouldn't leave him be here onlyless I should promus that," she said. "It's a lotta fool nonsense, o' course, b'cause who would wantta steal a young one from a place like this? But I give my word, an' I gotta keep it! B'sides, she ain't paid her quarter fer today. He general'y brings his quarter every morning, but he didn't have none taday, 'r else he lost it!"

The boy gave a look of protest, but Reuben handed out the quarter he held in his hand.

"Here's the quarter," he said, "and if you want to see his sister you'll have to step outside and speak to her. She's in the ambulance, and isn't able to get up and come in. She was taken sick while she was working,"

There was a dignity about Reuben's voice that somewhat awed the woman, but she gave a twist to her mouth and there was a canniness in her eyes.

"Well, I gotta go out and see ef she's thar first," she said, and turning toward a crib that already held an occupant asleep she thumped the sick baby down from her arms, who promptly began to protest in loud screams of anger. The other baby woke up and added his voice to the song, and over the duet the woman shouted out to Noel who was standing there clasping and unclasping his hands in agitated excitement.

"Noll, you stay right where you are, d'ya year? Don'tcha dare stir till I get back!"

"But I must go to my sister!" said the boy in a low, firm tone. "She wants me!" and he walked forward determinedly.

The woman strode over to him and jerked him back by the shoulder, setting him down hard on the chair from which he had arisen, and adding a stinging slap on his cheek.

"Now, you *set there!* D'ya *hear?* An' don'tcha stir till I come back, ur I'll smack ya good, an' you know what that means!"

The boy quivered and turned white, and two large tears

rolled down his cheeks, but he sat still, one great look of anguish turned upon Reuben as he followed the woman.

"I'll be right back for you, kid," said Reuben, and stepped outside.

The woman had already gone to the door at the back of the ambulance and demanded entrance, and the interne, seeing how things were, flung the door open for an instant. The matron assumed an attitude of investigation, with three neighbors in the offing getting a front seat at the show.

"Yes, that's her allrighty!" she said, nodding back at Reuben. "I'd know her anywhere, even without her hat. Aw, ain't it awful! How white she looks! What's the matter of her? Ya think she's goin' ta die, do ya?" She cast an eye at the glaring doctor. "Now ain't that a pity!"

"That'll be all!" said the doctor getting out of the ambulance and taking the woman with a firm grip by the arm. "You get in your house there and send that child out at once or we'll have a policeman here in short order."

"Oh, ya don't say so!" said the woman. "Who crowned you, I'd like to know? Quit shovin' me! I gotta find out what she wants I should do with the kid. She made me promus I wouldn't give him ta nobody. Say, Miss Gutry, don'tcha want I should keep Nollie till ya git well an' cum back? I won't charge y but fifty cents extra fer day an' night, an' then ya ken hev yer mind at rest. The gentlemon give me the quarter, so it'll be siventy-foive per day from now on."

"No!" said Gillian excitedly. "Bring my brother here right away! I want to see him at once!" and then she dropped back on her pillow and her breath was almost gone.

"Here he is!" said Reuben quietly. "Say hello to your sister, Noel!" For Reuben had gone back with three strides to the house, had gathered the boy up in his arms, and now brought him out and held him up for the sister to see.

"I'm here Gillian!" called Noel. "Hello, Gillian. I'm all right! Don't be sick, Gillian! I'm here, and I'll take care of you! Gillian—!"

But everything had faded out and turned black for Gillian, and she didn't answer.

"Let's go!" said the doctor. He shoved the big woman aside, slid into his place and closed the door. Reuben, with the boy still in his arms, swung up into the front seat. The bell clanged, the children and neighborhood people scattered hastily while the great white wagon rolled down the street and around the corner and out of sight.

But inside the doctor and the nurse were working hard.

"I guess we shouldn't have risked that," said the doctor under his breath.

Reuben on the front seat with the small frightened boy in his lap held him close because he was trembling like a leaf. Presently he lifted a scared little face and asked in a shaky voice, "Is—my—sister—going—ta die, man?"

"Oh, no," said Reuben with a confidence he was far from feeling. "She's going to the hospital to get well."

"But they do die when these white wagons with bells come to the houses. There was one came last week for a little baby at the nursery where I stayed."

"Well, your sister isn't going to die, not now. She's going to get well and take care of you."

"But what will I do? Will I have to go back and stay—with—that—awful—woman? I don't like her! She'll smack me, I know! She said she would! And it—hurts—something—awful!"

"No, you don't have to go back to her, not ever again!" said Reuben. "You're done with her!" and he hugged the child closer.

The boy was still for a moment and then he asked with anxious eyes:

"Then do I go to the hospital, too?"

"No," said Reuben, "you're not sick so you couldn't go to the hospital. We're just going in a minute to see that your sister gets a nice room and is all right, you know, and then you're coming to visit me, till your sister gets well and can come home."

The child looked up anxoiusly and studied his face, and Reuben turned on his pleasant grin for the little fellow.

"We're going to have a grand time together, fella," he said reassuringly.

"I don't—*know* you—very well—yet," said the boy hesitantly, "but—I think—I like you—pretty well!"

"Fine!" said Reuben heartily. "And I like you too, so don't worry now. We'll have to be pretty quiet when we get out, but I guess you'll understand. Your sister needs to have things rather quiet. And you know there are lots of other sick people in a hospital, so we'll just be as still as can be while we stay."

The boy bowed gravely.

"And can I see Gillian again?"

"Well, that will depend on what the doctor says. If she's awake perhaps you can, but if she's asleep we'll have to let her sleep."

The child nodded gravely.

"Awright!" he said with a sigh of disappointment, and Reuben's heart ached for him. At that minute he had no memory of Anise Glinden, or the play he was supposed to be in that evening. And in two hours more the Glinden car would perhaps be waiting for him at his rooming place. But he had other things to attend to now.

No one was noticing the man and the little boy when the ambulance finally drew up at the entrance to the hospital. They got out and stood at one side while the stretcher was lifted out and carried in, and they followed the white face on the cot with awe in their hearts. The girl's eyes were closed again, and she did not appear to be breathing.

"Is—that—my Gillian?" whispered the child, lifting his small shy hand and pointing with a half raised index finger.

Reuben looked down at the great eyes with plain terror written in them, and tried to smile, but somehow his own heart was afraid for that still young face that did not even hold anguish now in its whiteness. He nodded and hoped his assent didn't carry too much of his own uncertainty.

Noel put down his hand and grasped tighter the man's hand that held his.

"Is—she—asleep?" He murmured half audibly.

Reuben nodded again, and held the little hand the closer with a comforting warmth.

Solemnly they followed to the big elevator door that stood open.

"Private, or semi-private?" asked the orderly impersonally, looking at Reuben.

"Private!" said Reuben quickly, realizing that this was something he had not thought about, but feeling that it ought to be private of course, whether the house would stand for it or not. Something in the memory of that girl's anguished eyes seemed to cry out for privacy.

The elevator man, ready to start, looked down at Noel with withering glance.

"Children not allowed," he muttered toward Reuben who was still holding him by the hand.

The doctor who had come with them spoke crisply.

"It's all right this time, Anderson, it's *necessary.*"

"He's supposed ta set over there on the bench," said Anderson speaking under orders.

Noel's quick ears heard, and he gave one wild frightened glance toward the indicated bench, and then lifted appealing eyes to the doctor. Reuben saw that slow silent tears were flooding down the boy's white cheeks.

"No!" said the doctor. "We may need him! The lady was afraid for him!"

The elevator man set his lips disagreeably, but started the car moving upward, and Noel gripped Reuben's hand as if his very life depended on it.

Reuben looked down at the earnest little face with wonder, the great eyes lifted up and watching the car going up, startled, speculative, concerned, as if he himself had great responsibility about it all. Studying the child the young man marveled at the beauty of that young face. No wonder the sister was concerned about the beautiful baby. And yet he wasn't a baby, just the lingering outlines of the helplessness of infancy, with a dawning apprehension of the great things of life.

Reuben had not had much contact with childhood. He had no brothers and sisters of his own, no living young relatives on his side of the family, no touch with little children anywhere to have given him experience of how lovely a child can be, and he looked with almost awe, and wondered what kind of task this one was likely to be, this task he had accepted for himself with such alacrity. And yet, of course it wouldn't last long. Likely the girl would soon be all right, and take over her brother again.

But then he glanced toward the white face on the stretcher again and it was so deathlike in its pallor that he caught his breath with dismay. Was it possible that this was no mere collapse from weariness and lack of food? Could it be that it had been going on too long and the girl would never rally? And if so what would be his responsibility? Would there be relatives and friends who would step in if they were notified and take the boy? And if so where would he find them? Would there be a way to reach them? Would the office perhaps have some data that would help in locating them? If not, what would become of the boy? He looked down into those clear young troubled eyes, and felt sure that if anything like that happened he would never break his promise to the girl whose anguished eyes had pled with him.

His grasp on the little hand tightened as the elevator stopped and the steel door swung back, and the small hand responded quickly to the friendly clasp. Reuben looked down and smiled, and a sad little semblance of a smile responded on the quivering young lips. A sudden thrill went to Reuben's heart. What a dear little wise young soul, so frightened and so lonely, yet so brave!

They were at the floor now, and the patient was wheeled out and down the hall, the little procession following. Another nurse appeared. The doctor murmured an order and a door was opened.

"You and the kid wait there in the reception room," said the doctor. "I'll call you if you're needed."

Reuben led the boy into a small room furnished with comfortable chairs and tables and much-used magazines.

The boy obediently sat down on the edge of a low chair with his eyes fixed on Reuben.

"What—is the matter—wif Gillian?" he asked in a hoarse little voice. "Is she deaded?" There was pain and knowledge and great trepidation in his tone.

"Oh, no," said Reuben cheerfully, sincerely hoping that he was telling the truth. "She fainted in the office, and the manager thought she ought to see a doctor to be sure she was all right. We hope she'll be better now in a few minutes. You see she didn't go out and get her lunch. She was busy. I guess that made her faint. She must have been hungry."

The boy shook his head.

"She's never hungry," he said in his grave precise tone, the tone of a child who has been exclusively with older people. "She—always—gives—me half her part of—suppah! She says she's not hungry."

"Yes?" said Reuben thoughtfully, reading more between the lines than the boy knew. "Well, what did you have for breakfast this morning? Do you remember?" He felt like a contemptible spy asking such questions, but somehow he had to find out the worst.

The boy nodded.

"We had—oatmeal! The last there was in the box. Gillian gave me all the milk. She said—she didn't want any."

"Did you have enough?" Reuben looked at the boy keenly and the color crept into the thin white cheeks.

"Oh, it was—awright!" he answered diffidently.

So, there was loyalty, too, in the sweet strong soul of the boy. He was scarcely more than a baby, and yet he was like that!

"Well, and then, you get your lunch at that nursery home?" he went on pursuing the subject.

The boy nodded.

"I'm *s'posed* to," he said with a sigh.

"What do they have for lunch there?" said Reuben, half idly watching the child, wondering just what should be the next procedure. *Supper?* And where should he take him? To his rooming house? There was no extra bed in his one room and he couldn't put this mere baby in another room by himself. It was going to be complicated. So he asked Noel, "What did you eat today?"

The child averted his eyes shamedly, and the color stole up into the thin white cheeks again.

"I *did*unt!" he said, half defiantly.

"You didn't eat *any*thing?" exclaimed Reuben, sitting up straight and looking at him perplexedly. "Look here now, why not? Do you want to get sick like your sister?"

"I couldn't eat ut!" he said still defiantly. "It was old cabbage an' bread. Old dry bread and cabbage with a lotta grease on it, and it makes me sick every time I eat it!"

"Why, you poor child! Why didn't you tell the woman you couldn't eat it?"

"I did! But she said I couldn't be too choosey there! I hadta eat what was set before me or go hungry! But I told her I wasn't hungry."

The young lips were pursed together and the big eyes were lifted bravely. "I didn't want any of their old lunch!"

"Well, you must be terribly hungry now," said Reuben distressedly. "I'd better go out and get you something right away."

"No!" said the boy with quick alarm in his face. "I—want—my Gillian! Can't I see my Gillian?" and suddenly two great crystal tears stood for an instant in his beautiful eyes, and then brimmed over and rolled slowly down his cheeks.

"Hold everything!" said a voice from the doorway, and there was the house doctor just entering from the hall.

Reuben and the boy looked up startled.

"You dropped something, kid!" said the doctor. "Didn't you know it? Two big fat ones! Where are they? Can't you find them? I saw them fall on the floor."

The boy looked down puzzled for an instant, and then he looked up with sudden understanding, and burst into a little nervous laugh, and Reuben and the doctor joined in.

"Now, that's better!" said the doctor with approval. "So, tell me what's all this about? Don't you know they don't allow children here?"

The child's lip quivered and his eyes were instantly full of earnest pleading.

"I want my Gillian!" he said, young anguish in his voice. "She is my sister, and I bringed her here because she was sick. I'm not children!" There was indignant and mature resentment in his tone.

"Oh, you're not? I see. You came in the capacity of protector! Is that it? Well, then, you're the young man I'm looking for! Your sister wants to see you. But, first, before you go in I've got to talk to you."

The earnest little face was at instant attention.

"I'm the doctor that is taking care of Gillian, you see, and you've got to obey me. Do you understand?"

The boy bowed his head gravely.

"Yessir!"

"Your sister has been pretty sick. I think she's going to be better now. But you mustn't do anything to excite her. Do you know what excite means?"

"Yessir! It means not talk loud nor cry!"

"Okay!" said the doctor winking at Reuben. "I think you'll do. Now, listen! You go in there and smile at her. Can you smile?"

Noel struggled with two more tears that appeared in the offing, and managed a watery twisted little smile.

"Okay, kid! You'll do! Now you just go stand by the bed in there and smile at Gillian, and say hello, and then if she smiles back you can step softly near the bed and throw her a kiss and say good night. Understand?"

"Sure!" said Noel. Then he reached out and took Reuben's hand in his and walked solemnly down the hall, stopping at the door where they had left Gillian.

The boy's eyes sought the bed and the white face on the pillow with the closed eyes.

"Hello, Gillian!" he said with almost bated breath, and a yearning look in his wide eyes, half awe, half fear.

The girl opened her eyes and looked at the little boy, great relief coming into her tired face, a light in her eyes that almost overcame the utter lassitude that had been there but the moment before. The smile that came was like a ray of sunshine to the frightened child.

"Noel!" her weak voice managed. "Are—you—all—right?"

The boy's eagerness shone out now above the anxiety.

"Sure, Gillian. We be awright." Then he stepped closer and laid his young lips tenderly against her forehead.

"S'long, Gillian. I come again! You get well!" His words were very low as if he hoped the doctor wouldn't hear that he had said more than he had been told. He smiled, and waved his gallant little hand, stepping back.

But Reuben stepped nearer for an instant, and spoke clearly.

"I'll take care of him as if he were my own," he said. "You needn't worry for an instant!"

There was a smile on the girl's lips before the great weariness blotted it out again, and the eyelids closed with a quiver.

Reuben led the boy away quickly and silently, his heart shaken with fear. She looked so gray and very tired, as if perhaps only Heaven could rest her. His hand gripped the small one in his with a tender protecting reassurance, and the little boy looked up and smiled sadly as if almost he understood.

Silently they trod the marble halls, the boy trying to keep step with the man, a sense of great importance upon him, and for the first time perhaps a question of what might be coming next?

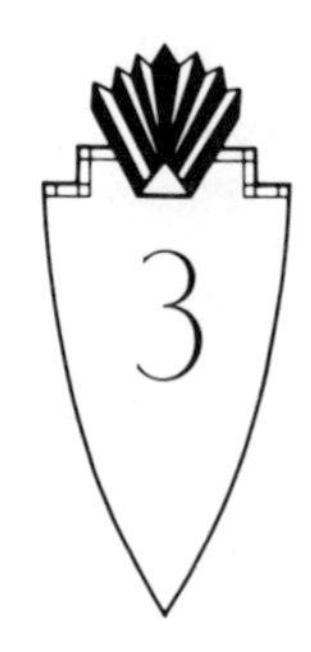

"AND now, where do you want to go?" said Reuben looking down at the boy as they came out of the great door and went down the stone steps to the sidewalk.

"To my home?" said the boy with a sigh. The words were a question. "It will be lonely in my home without my Gillian."

"Yes, of course," said Reuben. "Too lonely! I couldn't let you stay there alone of course. I promised her I would take care of you. And besides, we haven't got the key. We couldn't get in, you know."

"Oh, yes *I* have got a key," said the wise youngster. "I always carry my key on a little chain around my neck," and he began to fumble inside the shabby little gingham collar, and brought out a key attached to a small chain.

"Oh!" said Reuben. "Well, now, that's interesting. I wonder what's the idea of you wearing that?"

"Why, my Gillian said sometimes that woman brings me home a little too soon, or something might have happened to keep her later than usual. She didn't want me to have to stay outside in the hall. There are sometimes some unpleasant people who come up those stairs, and Gillian wanted me to go inside and lock the door." He explained it very earnestly, quite soberly.

Reuben was startled.

"I see!" he said, but marveled at the fears and burdens this young girl must have been carrying for this engaging young brother.

"Well, anyway," said Reuben, "I don't think we'd better go there tonight, do you? It would be better for us to be nearer the hospital. Your sister might want to call us up for something, or send some word to us. I think we should be quite near by."

"Oh!" said the child thoughtfully. "And have you got a home near by? Could we go there?"

"No, but there is a hotel just across the street in this block. I thought we might go there for tonight, and then see how things are in the morning."

"Oh! But isn't a hotel very expensive?" He asked the question with a wise manner as if he had come up against that hindrance a number of times.

"Sometimes," said Reuben kindly, "but I don't think that matters when we are doing things for Gillian, does it?"

"But it will worry Gillian when she has to pay it," said the child anxiously. "She hasn't much money! And there'll be all that doctor's bill. They are very expensive. Gillian and I had a hard time getting the doctor paid after our mother died!" and he sighed deeply as if a great burden had suddenly come to rest again upon his small shoulders.

"Oh, but you don't have to pay this, you know. The office pays all your sister's bills. Doctor and hospital and nurse. Mr. Rand told me the company would attend to all the cost."

The wise eyes studied his face a moment, a look of relief in them.

"That was nice!" he said with a sigh of satisfaction. "But then that wouldn't be *me,* you know. I don't belong to the office. I think I'd better go back to my home tonight. I don't mind—not *very* much."

"No," said Reuben, "I couldn't let you go back there alone. Didn't you hear me promise your sister that I would stay with you until she got well? You're my guest, you know. You are visiting me. And guests don't have to pay board."

"Don't they? Only just boarders?"

"That's right. And you are my guest till your sister gets well and able to plan things for you again."

He considered that a moment.

"Do you think Gillian will think that's all right?" he asked seriously.

"I'm sure she will. She would be sure I would do that or she wouldn't have trusted me to take care of you. Now, you put everything like that out of your head and just trust me, and we'll have a nice time visiting together."

But the child's face was still serious.

"You, see, Gillian was planning to get me a new suit. She said this one was getting very shabby. Now I suppose we'll have to wait for that a long time!" and he sighed. "But I don't mind," he added with a little crooked smile. "It's only that she's ashamed because I'm her brother and she doesn't want people to think she doesn't take care of me. Maybe she wouldn't think I looked right to go to a hotel." He looked down at his shabby little self anxiously.

"Oh, you are quite all right for tonight and we'll talk that over a little later and see if we can't work out a way for you to earn a new suit yourself somehow. There might be ways perhaps. Anyway, we'll think about it. And now, the first thing we must do is to go and get some supper. I'm terribly hungry. How about you?"

Noel's eyes shone with eagerness and he nodded his head vigorously.

"So, what do you want? What do you like best?"

"Soup is the cheapest, isn't it? Or maybe a glass of milk."

"But you are my guest, now, and you mustn't think about how much things cost. That is my lookout. You are visiting me, and I won't suggest anything I can't pay for!"

"Have you got much monies?" asked the child wonderingly.

"I've got all I need."

"My! Isn't that nice!"

"Here we are!" said Reuben, leading the boy into the hotel

and stopping at the desk to register and secure a room. "Now, shall we go upstairs and wash our hands and faces before we eat?"

Wonderingly the child followed him into the elevator.

"I've been in a nelevator before," he said softly. "Out in Chicago, before we came here."

"Well, when we get time you'll have to tell me all about it," said Reuben.

Five minutes later they went down to the dining room and Reuben ordered vegetable soup as the first course, with stewed chicken, little round biscuits, a glass of milk and ice cream to follow. The child looked at each new dish with large eyes of wonder, tested each delicately, and ate slowly to make the most of it lest he might never get such a meal again. After his first ravenous hunger had been appeased he looked up and smiled gratefully. Finally as he put down the glass of milk after a long delicious drink of its richness, he looked up at Reuben and smilied again.

"I wish—my Gillian—could—have some—of these!" he said, wistfully. "Couldn't I please take some over to her? I've had plenty now, and I'd like to give her some."

"Oh, they will be giving her plenty over at the hospital. Didn't you see the nurse bring in a tray just as we were coming out? I think that was a bowl of soup for Gillian."

The child's face lit up with joy.

"Just like mine?" he asked joyously.

"Why, yes, I think it was something like yours."

Then the little boy laughed out softly, and after that went to work and carefully ate every crumb of every portion that was given him.

When they had finished Reuben led the boy into a men's furnishing shop that occupied one of the big windows in the front of the hotel.

"We've got to get some pajamas, you know," he explained to the boy. "We came away without our suitcases."

"Oh," said the boy, "I have pajamas. Gillian made me a pair out of an old dress of hers with blue stripes in it."

"Well, we'll save those for another time. Here are some. Which do you like best? The ones with the red binding, or the green?"

"Red," said Noel as if it were a most momentous decision.

While the man was wrapping the two pairs of pajamas, Reuben was looking around.

"There!" he said. "There is a little suit I believe would about fit you, and we might need it before we have time to get to yours. These are cheap. We'd better get a couple."

"Oh, but— " said the boy with new trouble in his eyes again.

"You're my guest, you know," reassured Reuben. "In eastern lands I believe it's sometimes the fashion for a man to furnish garments for his guests."

The worry suddenly bloomed into a smile on the boy's face.

"Why, that's like the Bible!" he said.

"How is that?" asked Reuben in astonishment.

"Why, don't you know, there was a man that came to the party without the wedding garment on? Gillian often reads me that story. Don't you remember it?"

Reuben puckered his brows.

"Why, yes, I think I must have heard it," he said, "Let's see, what happened? I don't remember it all. What did he do? Didn't he know it was a wedding he was coming to?"

"Oh, I guess he did, but it was just like you said. The man that gave the party furnished the garment, only this man hadn't put it on. He just came in with his own clothes on and went around, and the man that gave the party had to have his servants put him out because he wouldn't put on the beautiful garment that was furnished. That's the way it is in Heaven, you know. We can't go there without the white linen robe of Christ's righteousness about us to cover all our sins. We haven't got any goodness of our own, just sins. So we have to have Christ's righteousness."

"Oh! Yes, I see!" said Reuben greatly astounded. Where had this child learned his wisdom? He somehow felt rebuked, but he didn't exactly know why. This was something he would have to think about. Did that girl teach her brother all this, or had he learned it at a Sunday school? It was most remarkable.

The man came with the package then. Reuben added a few toilet articles, and then they went up to their room.

"Now, how about a bath?"

"That would be good."

Reuben threw open the door of the well-appointed bathroom and the child surveyed it with satisfaction.

"A tub and a shower, *both!*" he remarked. "We had a shower once when I was a little boy, before my mother died. I sort of remember it."

So Reuben inducted him into the mysteries of the bathroom and Noel spattered and splashed around to his heart's content, and seemed greatly delighted with it. Then after a good rubdown of the slender little body Noel put on the new pajamas and came to stand by one of the two single beds.

"Two beds!" said the child gleefully. "That is yours and this is mine!"

"Yes," said Reuben, "jump in and see how yours fits."

Noel giggled.

"How it *fits!*" he laughed. "That is funny! How a bed fits! Oh, I must tell Gillian that!"

"Well, jump in! You must be sleepy. This has been a long day."

"But we haven't prayed," said Noel with a bright look.

"Haven't *what?*" asked Reuben perplexed.

"We haven't said our prayers," explained Noel. "Don't you say your prayers?"

"Oh! Why yes, of course!" he answered quickly in a half embarrassed tone. It had been some years since Reuben had remembered prayers. "Let's see, what do we say? 'Now I lay me'?"

"Oh, no," said Noel, shaking his head solemnly, "you're too old for that, and I'm too old too. That's only for babies! I haven't said that in a long time. I really *pray.* Ask God for things, and tell Him things. Now, I'll kneel down here, and you kneel beside me, that's the way Gillian and I do. Now, you take hold of my hand. It's easier that way. It doesn't seem so lonesome. Now, I'll pray first and then you pray, and put in all the things I forgot. That's the way Gillian does."

The curly head went down on the bedside, and the small hand nestled in the young man's unaccustomed grasp, and the boy began:

"Dear Heavenly Father, I didn't know what You were going to do today when they came after me at the nursery, and I was feeling so bad and sick because of that old greasy cabbage. And I was so frightened at that ambulance, because so many people die when they take them in those. But I thank You, dear Heavenly Father, that You sent a nice man after me, and he has taken care of me, and we had a nice dinner. I am glad You are taking care of my dear Gillian and giving her something to eat too, and won't You please make her well quick! Help me to be good and brave, and not to be scared. And take care of this nice man and don't let us spend too much money, so Gillian will have to work overtime and get sick again. I thank You for the pajamas, and the new suits, and the toothbrush, 'cause my other one has the bristles out and hurts. And please bless dear Gillian, and bless my new friend, and give him a nice wedding garment, and show him how to put it on. And make me a good boy. For Jesus' sake, Amen."

There was a great silence then, and Reuben felt he had to pray, but it seemed to him the hardest thing he had ever tried to do. He grasped the little hand, clutched it firmly and cleared his throat.

"Dear Heavenly Father—" He wondered if he had a right to call God that? But he mustn't let the boy know there was any doubt. He had been very much touched about the child praying for a wedding garment for him. He felt he ought to do something about it but he didn't know what.

"We thank Thee that we—that even a child may come to Thee with everything—all his troubles and all his joys. We ask Thee to bless the dear sick sister, and help her to get well quickly. We ask Thee to take care of Noel and help him to be happy while he is with me. We—I don't feel as if I knew how to pray aright, but I'm asking You to teach me, and help me to be a fit guide for this boy, and let me have a wedding garment too. And now will You be with the doctor and teach him how to cure the sick sister, and show the nurse what to do for her. For Christ's sake, Amen."

There was a great embarrassment upon Reuben as he got up from his knees, but the little boy was scrambling into the soft bed, and snuggling down happily, a smile on his lips.

"Shall we telephone over to the hospital and see how Gillian is?" asked Reuben, to cover his embarrassment.

The child's eyes shone.

So Reuben got the nurse on the phone and asked her a few questions.

Then he turned to Noel.

"She says your sister is sleeping, and is as well as they could expect. Her pulse is steadier. She ate her soup, and had a cup of tea before she went to sleep. The doctor was in to see her just now, and said he would come in again after midnight. So now, Noel, we'd better get some sleep."

"Yes," said Noel sweetly. "We'll leave her with God to watch over her, and maybe in the morning she'll be weller."

So Reuben turned out the light and got into his bed, marveling at the things that had happened to make up his strange day.

And now indeed he had time to consider Anise Glinden, and the play he was supposed to have been in this evening. Perhaps even now it was about to start, and he hadn't so much as had time to telephone her. What would she think of him? Well, he would have to call her up in the morning and explain. But just how was he going to explain? Would she consider his reasons for not coming to Glindenwold sufficient? Well, and suppose she didn't? The time had gone by, anyway, and what could he do about it? Was his job on such a very slender footing that the indignation of a silly girl with very red lips and long curly eyelashes could endanger it? Perhaps it would be as well to find out.

And anyway why was she of more importance than the white-faced girl in the hospital room he had been set to look after?

And why should he have to explain to her anyway? Just tell her that some matters of personal interest were preventing him from giving attention to other things for the time being.

And then there was that western trip he had thought about and written about several times in his letters to two old college friends, Ted Whitney and Gart Medford. He had asked them if they would care to go along in case he decided for it, but had as yet no word from them. As he drifted off to sleep his mind was busy with the thought of airplanes, and transcontinental trains. Tomorrow morning he must definitely either put this matter out of his plan or decide whether he cared to go west alone.

When he awoke in the morning, however, it was all hazy in his mind. He was bewildered for an instant over being in a strange room, and looking over to the other bed where the beautiful boy lay with his soft curls tumbled away from his fine brow, and the long curly lashes shading the white cheek, it all came back to him how he happened to be here taking care of a little stranger waif, with complications blocking his path in every direction against his greatly anticipated vacation.

Then suddenly he heard a soft little quivering sigh, almost like a sob, and looking quickly across to the other bed he saw that the young face was wet with tears, and more were slowly stealing out from under those dark lashes and flowing silently down, until his face was fairly drenched. His lips were quivering and the small hands outside the coverlet were clenched with the effort to keep back the sobs that were all too evidently getting the better of the child.

"Oh, I say, fella, are you awake?" he asked engagingly.

The small figure tightened alertly, the young throat worked convulsively, swallowing down the tears, the face turned for an instant away from him, and a small hand came up quickly and mopped away the tears onto the pillowcase.

"Yes-sir!" he gulped, "I'm awake!" The words trembled out dejectedly.

"Well—say, old top, what's the trouble? Why the tears? Feel bad anywhere?"

"N-n-o-ss-i-r!" A forced cheerfulness came to the front.

"Well, then what's the idea? Why the depression?"

There was silence for an instant while the young soldier got control again.

"Oh, nothing!" he said with an attempt at nonchalance. "I-I j-j-just had a b-b-bad dream!" and his lip quivered again. "I dreamed—my Gillian—was g-g-gone! And—w-w-when I w-w-waked up this was a s-s-strange room!" The boy buried his head in the pillow and his small shoulders shook convulsively.

Reuben swung himself out of bed and went and sat on the side of the other bed beside the boy, gathering him into a strong comforting embrace.

"Yes, I see, old fellow," he said soothingly. "I've had dreams like that sometimes too. It's tough! But you see, fella, you just forgot for a minute and were kind of startled. It wasn't real at all. I wouldn't waste any suffering over that. You know your sister is over at the hospital, and we are going to call up pretty soon and see how she is. Remember that?"

The boy looked at him with troubled, sober eyes, and finally nodded.

"Well," said Reuben, "suppose we call right now and see if that nurse is awake yet. Would you like that?"

The boy nodded solemnly as if he were almost afraid of that phone call, but he rolled over and sat up alertly. Reuben as he walked over to the telephone found he had much the same feeling of fear in his heart that the boy evidently had.

"All right, here goes!" he said with a kindly wink at the child, who smiled gravely back through his shadow of anxiety.

Reuben got the hospital, and the little boy lay trembling and waited while he went through the formalities of getting the nurse.

Then came the nurse's voice, clear, almost cheerful. Noel could hear it even across the room.

"Yes, Mr. Remington. Yes, this is Miss Guthrie's nurse. Yes, she's had a fairly comfortable night. Yes, the doctor came in a little after midnight again. He said her pulse was a trifle steadier."

"Then she's no worse?" questioned Remington almost sharply.

"N-no! I wouldn't say she was worse," said the nurse in her formal tone. Of course the nurse was not supposed to give out information.

"What time will the doctor be there?"

"He usually comes in about eleven o'clock."

"Very well, I'll try to be over there at that time," said Reuben, and hung up.

So! The problems were no nearer an immediate solution than they had been. His way was simply blocked!

Then the anxious little face caught his eye and he smiled.

"Cheerio!" he said. "At least she's no worse. Let's get in shape to go out and get some work done before it's time to go to the hospital again."

"Work?" said Noel with quick interest. "I didn't know we had work to do. What do we do? Get our breakfast? But there isn't any stove in this room, is there? And we didn't buy anything to cook. Sometimes my sister cooks an egg over the gas burner. But we haven't got any gas burner. And if we had we haven't got any egg."

Reuben's eyes smarted at the thought of all the makeshifts poverty had brought to the life of this child and his brave young sister, but he only laughed.

"No, we don't have to cook breakfast. We'll go down to the resturant for that. But afterwards I've got to go to the office for a few minutes to look after some mail and be sure the man who is taking my place while I am away understands just what he has to do. We'll have to hurry, for I may find more to be done than I thought and I must allow time enough."

"Oh!" said the child in a small lonesome voice. "And will I stay here, or do I have to go to the day nursery?"

"No," said Reuben cheerily, "no more of that day nursery for you, lad, not if the court knows herself, and she thinks she does."

"What do you mean, 'the court knows'?" said the child with a look of terror in his eyes. "Do I have to go to court? I haven't done anything naughty, have I?" His lips were trembling again.

Poor baby! What experiences he must have been through to have ideas about such sinister matters.

"Oh, no!" laughed Reuben. "I meant 'not if I know what I'm doing.' I was referring to myself as a court that was going to keep you safely away from such places any more. And no, you don't have to stay here alone. Of course it would be an all-right place for you to stay if you *had* to, for a little while, but I wouldn't want you to be lonesome, especially just now while you are worried about your sister. No sir! We're going to do things together, old man. I thought perhaps you'd like to go down to my office and see how it looks there, and you could sit in a big leather chair and look at a picture book while I'm busy. We'll stop at a book store and get one on the way. Will you like that?"

"Oh yes!" said the child with a relieved smile and a sigh of content.

"Well, into the shower then, and see how quickly you can get dressed!" said the young man.

And soon the two were on their way into a new day.

THERE was orange juice, oatmeal with real cream on it and sugar, bacon and two eggs apiece, and a glass of milk for breakfast. It was unheard of in Noel's small life. At least if it had ever been it was so long ago he had almost forgotten such affluence.

When he was half through his oatmeal he paused and looked at Reuben.

"Will my sister have some of this?" he asked anxiously. "Because if she wouldn't I would like to divide with her."

"Oh, yes," Reuben assured him, "she will have a nice breakfast. Everything that the doctor thinks she ought to eat. And she will be so glad that you are having a nice breakfast too."

The boy looked at him thoughtfully as if he understood more than his years warranted.

"Yes," he said pensively with a sigh. "She's always that way."

They bought the picture book which had stories in large print three-letter words, and Noel sat in a great green leather chair in the office by a window and enjoyed it while Reuben went at the pile of mail that was lying on his desk, and talked things over with his new assistant. It was very still in the room, till all at once the door opened briskly and Anise Glinden walked in.

"Well, upon my word!" she said haughtily, "so you're here, are you? Is this where you have hidden yourself all night?"

"Oh, good morning!" said Reuben looking up with a hastily summoned smile. "No, I haven't been here all night. I just arrived and I'm trying to beat time with this mail before I have to go to an appointment. I meant to telephone you later and explain my absence last night. I didn't want to disturb you so early this morning. Sorry I wasn't able to come but I hoped you would understand that something unforseen had prevented me."

"Yes," said Anise disagreeably, "I understood. I understood perfectly that you did not *mean* to come. After practically promising me you would be there, and after I took the trouble to secure a fine actor to take that part, that you might understand fully what it was I wanted you to do, you failed me! Miserably failed me! I—you—" Her eyes swept the room and rested with startled dislike on the astonished young face that watched her.

"Who is that child? Can't you send him out of here? I want to talk to you. What right has he in an office? Run away, little boy. We're busy here now!"

"No!" said Reuben firmly, gravely. "He is waiting for me. Sit still, Noel!" he said to the boy with a reassuring smile. Then turning back to the girl, "I'm sorry but I really won't have time to talk now. I must get these letters ready for the morning mail before I leave. I certainly regret that I inconvenienced you, but I thought I had made it quite plain from the first that even if I came I could not possibly act in a play, no matter how many perfect actors I had the privilege of watching. I am not an actor and I do not want to be one. Couldn't you induce the actor to take the part permanently? And then perhaps I can find time to run down some evening and see the play. I can't promise just how soon that will be, for some matters have come up that demand my attention at once, and I cannot tell how long they are going to take."

"But I thought they said this was your vacation!" pouted the angry girl. "Why are you bothering with letters now?"

"Yes, but these letters did not arrive yesterday as they were expected to do, and they must be answered by return mail. It happens that I am the only one who knows the answers to some of the questions they ask, so before I go I must see that they are on their way."

He reached out his hand and touched the button on his desk calling his secretary.

"The other matter which may detain me for some time even in my vacation time is personal and unavoidable. Now I do hope you will pardon me. My secretary has come to take the dictation, and I don't suppose you will particularly enjoy listening to that. But I shall let you know if things adjust themselves so that I can take the pleasure of accepting your invitation."

Anise looked up and glared at the quiet elderly woman who entered with her notebook and pencil, and then with her head up haughtily, fairly flouted out of the room, much to the relief of the small boy who was greatly shaken by the conversation that had been going on.

Mr. Rand came in just as Reuben finished dictating and was getting ready to leave.

"Good morning, Reuben. I'm glad I caught you. I thought you would like to see this letter from Avison Brothers before you left. Thought you would enjoy having your mind at rest about them. After all the hard work you did on that case it's nice to know it has come out as we hoped and everything is ready to go forward now."

"Oh!" said Reuben with relief, "that's good. I was wondering about that this morning. Yes, I'm glad to know about it. Thank you."

He glanced through the letter, while the manager watched him, thinking again as he had thought a number of times before how fortunate they were to have found such a young man. He seemed to be working right into the plans of the house wonderfully. He personally was going to miss him while he was away. But he certainly deserved a vacation, for he was about the hardest worker they had.

Reuben handed back the letter and Rand started toward the door, then suddenly turned back.

"Oh, by the way, how is that girl that you took to the hospital? Is she all right? Was it just a simple faint? Though I noticed she wasn't in her place at her desk this morning. I hope you assured her that she could take a good rest if she needed it."

"Oh, yes," said Reuben. "I was planning to stop in your office and speak to you about it. She's still in the hospital. I am due there now in a few minutes to meet the doctor and see what he says about her. No, I don't think it was just a simple faint. I'm afraid it's a case of undernourishment, and living on simple nerve, though I can tell you better after I've had a talk with the doctor. I'll call you up around noon and let you know just how things are. But I'm afraid it's not such a simple case."

Rand puckered his brows with a worried air.

"I'm afraid she's been working too hard," he said. "She's that type. She's been asking for overtime work, just seems to eat it up. She's done a lot of extra work for me too, and that reminds me, I have a check for her for some extra work she's been doing for me evenings. I meant to give it to her this morning. I wonder if you would take it to her? She might need it for something. Of course you'll explain that we will look after the doctor and hospital expenses. That's all provided for in her hospitalization, you know. But there might be other needs, and I'd like her to get this right away if possible. I have an idea she has somebody dependent upon her, and that may worry her."

"She has," said Reuben. "Her small brother. Here he is. I'm taking him to see her."

Mr. Rand looked at Noel in surprise.

"You mean this little fellow? Why, he's a mere child! That must be a heavy responsibility."

"Yes, I think it must have been. Noel, this is Mr. Rand. I expect you've heard your sister speak about him, haven't you?"

Noel arose respectfully and looked at Mr. Rand, solemnly searching his face.

"Yes sir!" he said.

"H'm! Looks like his sister, doesn't he? Acts like her too! Well, I'm very glad to have seen him. It's good of you to take him to the hospital. He seems to know he's in good hands. Well, Reuben, if you'll be kind enough to stop at my office when you come down I'll give you that check!"

Reuben promised, and the manager hurried away.

"He's nice!" said Noel with a sigh of satisfaction, as Reuben went about gathering up some papers and putting them in his brief case to take with him.

"Yes," said Reuben. "He's very nice."

It was silent in the room while Reuben searched in his desk drawer for some more papers he would need, and then suddenly Noel brought out another thought:

"My Gillian likes to work for him. He never is cross."

"That's right!" smiled Reuben. "He is always pleasant. I like to work for him too."

"Do you work for him?" asked Noel with a look of surprise in his big eyes.

"Oh, yes," said Reuben with a smile. "I work for him too."

"Oh!" said Noel thoughtfully. And when Reuben looked up again he saw the child studying him.

They went down presently to the next floor and stopped at Rand's office.

Rand looked down at Noel as they were leaving.

"You take good care of that sister of yours, young man!" said Rand with a smile, and Noel looked up with his sweetest smile and answered clearly:

"Yes, thank you, I will."

Mr. Rand gave an astonished look at the child again, and then winked at Reuben.

"He's all right!" he said with a grin, and then watched Noel as he walked sedately along by Reuben's side.

"Some boy!" he murmured to himself as he turned back to his office, and was glad in his heart that he had made Gillian's check a little larger than he had at first intended.

Meantime, in her father's office, Anise Glinden was storming about and sneering at Reuben Remington, wondering why her father had him working for him, and declaring that she wished he would dismiss him.

At last her father, quite accustomed to ignoring such familiar pranks from his spoiled daughter, caught a phrase or two of what she was saying, and swung around on his office chair to face her.

"What's this? What's all this about, Anise? You want one of the best men we have in this whole outfit dismissed because he has displeased you? Just what have you got to do with this business, Anise, except to spend the money it makes. Did you suppose we carried on this business for the purpose of providing puppets and playboys for your shows? Think again, young lady! Why should you presume to pick out a man like Reuben Remington and want to turn him into a good-for-nothing actor? Lay off him, girl, and get some sense into your head! Though goodness knows it's the first time you ever picked out a real man to work on. But I'm not going to have him spoiled even to please you, baby! What's he done that you should get so furious at him?"

"Why, he's practically ruined all my plans for the next week or two by refusing to get into our play, in a part where he just exactly fits, and he has the effrontery to lie about it. His excuse is that he has work to do that he can't leave. Though he's on vacation, and admits it. He says something has come up that had made it impossible for him to come down right away, and he doesn't tell me what it is, nor excuse himself in the least. He's just awfully *awfully* rude about it. When I asked him what was hindering him he said it was personal private matters, shut his lips like a steel trap, and not another word out of him. I knew he was lying all the time."

"That'll be about all out of you, girl!" said her father. "That young man doesn't lie, and if he said he had important business, then he had important business, I'll wager. He has the biggest sense of duty and honor of any young man I know, and I won't hear a word against him. So pick up your powder puffs and your silly gloves and folderols and go on your childish way. Find another playboy to tag you around. You won't get Reuben Remington, I'm sure of that, unless his conscience says it's all right. I only wish there was any hope of your getting a man like that for a friend. Though I'd be sorry for him if you did! You're not good enough for him, and that's a fact, my child! Now, run along. I'm busy and I have to work to keep the money flowing in to finance all your foolish notions!"

So Anise went pouting out of her father's office, and after scouting around to see if Reuben was still in the building, presently discovered that he had left without looking her up again to make his peace with her. That was something she could hardly forgive, because she wasn't used to being treated that way.

Reuben and Noel arrived in the hospital a little before the doctor.

Reuben could see that the child was in a tremor of anxiety again, solemnly watching every person that came through the hall, listening fearsomely to every sound, snuffing terror in the pungent scent of the air.

The doctor found them in the little reception room where they had waited the night before. There was no one else in the room so they could talk freely.

"She is better! Yes, she is decidedly better," he said breezily with a smile toward the anxious child who was watching him with incredulous, doubting eyes. "But—I wanted to talk to you. How well do you know this little lady?"

He fixed his eyes on Reuben, studying him keenly. "Suppose we step out into the hall a moment."

Noel dropped into a chair with a white look coming around his lips, as if he sensed there was more than they were telling him.

Reuben smiled at him as they went out.

"Now," said the doctor again, "how well do you know her?"

"Not very well," said Reuben with a grave expression. "I've seen her in the office occasionally. I know she has the reputation of being a steady, conscientious worker."

"So I should judge," said the doctor nodding. "But is there

anyone else of the office force who knows her better? Anyone with whom she has been intimate? One in whom she would confide?"

"I'm afraid not," said Reuben. "She has a reticent nature, and her habit was to hurry home from work to this child whom she had to leave in a most unsatisfactory day nursery during the day. It just happened that I was around when she fainted, and the chief had an important conference with a man from Chicago, so he asked me to get her to the hospital and see that she was all right. It developed on the way that she was frantic about the boy, for there was no one to look after him, and nothing in their apartment to eat till she got there. We picked him up and brought him along. I promised to look after the boy till she was better.

"I see," said the doctor looking deep into the other man's eyes, studying him with a keen understanding of human nature. "Well, that being the case, are you going to be good enough to go a little farther and be a friend to the girl too? For she desperately needs someone."

Reuben lifted startled eyes.

"Is—she— Isn't she—going to get well?"

"I didn't say that," said the doctor with an impatient movement of his sensitive hand. "The point is this. She needs someone who can be a friend and help. She's got something on her mind and we can't seem to find out what it is. Do you think you might try? By virtue of being the boy's protector? If it's lack of money perhaps something can be done. It it's something else it must be either eliminated, or overcome, one of the two, and I'd like to know which. It would help immensely in solving the problem. Hasn't the poor girl any family living?"

"I judge not, from what the child says," said Reuben.

"Well, we've got to be sure, and find them if there is. *Somebody* has *got* to help!"

"I'll do my best," said Reuben earnestly, "but what shall I do? Is she conscious? Is she able to talk?"

"Well, yes, a little, if it could be done in a quiet, reasonable tone and spirit."

"All right," said Reuben, "I'll try. But suppose you tell me a little more about the possibilities of this thing. Is there any likelihood of her getting well? And how long will it be before she can go back to work, if at all?"

"Oh, yes, she can go back to work as soon as she is strong enough. How long that will be depends largely upon herself. She's got to stop worrying, and she's got to eat and build herself up. She's just about on the point of starvation. She's got to the place where she doesn't care to eat. How much of that is due to anxiety I can't be sure. That's what I want you to find out. If you can break through that shy reserve you may save a life."

Reuben lifted eyes that showed he had a deep sense of what a responsibility that would be.

"Do you want me to go now?" he asked.

"Yes, if you will. Don't keep her talking too long. Not more than ten or fifteen minutes at first. Then she ought to have some nourishment. But I'll be back here in twenty minutes and get your report. By the way, what about the child? Will he stay here while you are gone?"

"I think so." Reuben looked toward Noel and met his questioning gaze. Noel couldn't hear what was being said, but his eyes had followed the two into the hall, and he knew something momentous was being discussed.

Reuben stepped over to him, and spoke so that the doctor could hear.

"Fella, would you mind sitting right here while I go into the room and speak to Gillian a few minutes? Mr. Rand sent her some messages and a check that I think will make her feel happier, and I'd better tell them to her first before you go in. Then afterward the doctor thinks when he comes back you can go in and speak to her."

The child's face lighted with a great gladness.

"Awright!" he said resignedly, and settled back in a deep chair, with his picture book in his lap, though he did not offer to open it.

The doctor smiled his approval.

"Fine, son. You're a real man. Now don't you worry. We'll both be back in less than half an hour."

Noel put his head back against the chair cushion and closed his eyes. But to look at him not even the doctor would likely suspect that he was praying, putting his dear Gillian into the care of his Heavenly Father.

"Some kid, that is!" said the doctor as he walked to the door of the patient's room with Reuben. Then he opened the door and Reuben went in.

GILLIAN turned bright tortured eyes toward Reuben as he came into the room. She seemed such a frail child as she lay there in the hospital bed, so tired and harrassed. Reuben's heart went out in pity for her.

Then he saw that her eyes were looking beyond him toward the door, and he knew at once that she was thinking of the little brother.

"Good morning!" he said cheerily. "I hope you're feeling a little better. Noel and I have been thinking a lot about you. Noel is sitting out in the little reception room with a picture book, waiting till the doctor says he may come in. He's quite all right, and happy as a lark except for being anxious for you to get well. We're having a grand time together and I'm enjoying it a lot. I would have brought him in with me, but I wanted to have a little talk with you first. Mr. Rand sent some messages and a check he said he owed you. I thought perhaps that would come in comfortably now somewhere."

Reuben put Mr. Rand's envelope into the thin white hand.

"Oh, thank you!" said the girl. "Mr. Rand is always very kind. And it is so good of you to take care of Noel. I'm very sorry to have made you so much trouble. I'm much better now, and quite able to take my brother off your hands. If you'll just help me to persuade the doctor to let me get up today. The nurse won't let me stir. She's taken my clothing away. She says I'm not strong enough yet to go back to work. But she doesn't know me. I'm used to working whether I feel well or not, and I simply *must* get back to my job. I couldn't afford to lose it!"

There came a frantic look in her eyes at the thought.

"Well, now, put that idea out of your head at once!" said Reuben. "There isn't the slightest danger of your losing your job. Mr. Rand told me to assure you that you were to stay here as long as the doctor felt it would be good for you, and that even after that you were to take as much time as you need to get really well and strong again. The firm appreciates your work, and your job will be waiting for you when you return."

"Oh, that's very kind of him," said the girl. But she said it almost wearily. "I do appreciate that. But you see, that isn't the only thing. I couldn't afford to lose my salary just now. I have my little brother to care for, and I've just succeeded in paying off the last of our mother's funeral expenses, so our resources are very low. I simply must go back to work today."

"Now, my friend," said Reuben with his pleasant voice tuned low to soothing quality, and his boyish smile turned on, "you don't need to worry about your brother. He's my guest and we are having the time of our lives. I'm quite alone in the city, you know, for I haven't been here long enough to have made a host of friends, and I'm just enjoying that boy. I'll be delighted to have him with me as long as you can trust him to me, so that's not a matter to be considered at present."

Reuben was watching her face intently, to see if the shadow was lifted by what he was saying, but it was still there in the back of those anguished eyes. She was polite and grateful for his care of Noel; it relieved the present situation immensely, he could see. But there was, as the doctor had said, something beyond even that, something that he was sent in here to find out.

"But now, I know I mustn't stay too long," he said, "so I'd better be getting at what I came to say before the nurse sends me away with my errand unfulfilled. Would you be willing to consider me a friend, and be very frank with me?"

The big questioning eyes, so like the little brother's eyes, gave him a startled look.

"Why, yes, certainly. You have been a wonderful friend in our need."

"Well, I'm glad you feel that way. Now may I feel that I can ask a few personal questions without being considered as intruding into your private affairs?"

"Of—course—" Her lips faltered as she spoke and her eyes held a new kind of terror, mingled almost with haughtiness.

"All right then. These are questions that any friend would have to know the answer to in order to be able to help you intelligently. First, is there someone, some dear friend or relative, either in this city or away, who would have a right to know that you are not well and are carrying a heavy burden?"

The eyes took on a guarded look.

"No," she said firmly. "No, no one!"

Reuben felt that he had got nowhere so far.

"Your brother told me that your mother was dead," he said, trying to make casual talk to cover what might have been an embarrassing pause. "And your father, is he gone too?"

"Yes," said Gillian sadly. "Mother died a couple of years ago, and father when Noel was a baby." She was quite impersonal in her tone, as if it were only a matter of form to answer him.

"And you have no brothers or sisters except Noel?"

"Nobody but us two."

"Well, excuse me, but isn't there perhaps an uncle or aunt, or some close friend you would like to have notified, who would perhaps come and cheer you up a little?"

"No!" she said sharply. "Oh, no, *please!"*

He looked at her astonished that his question should so stir her.

"Excuse me," he said. "I didn't mean to worry you. I only felt there was something that is troubling you, and we don't seem to have any way of getting at it, and removing it so that you can get well. Now believe me, I'm only asking these questions for your good. The doctor feels your mind must be at ease or you can't possibly get up and go to work again. You don't want to die and leave that little boy alone, do you?"

She put her hands up to her face in a quick motion as if to shield herself from a blow.

"Oh, no!" she said with a shiver of horror. "No, but—*I won't!* I'm not as sick as that. I guess I didn't eat enough."

"Well, but listen. Human flesh can't stand everything, no matter how willing a sacrifice it is. You have got to keep well for your brother's sake, even if you don't care to live for your own sake. You have a responsibility you cannot shirk. And you are carrying some kind of a worry that makes your heart have to do extra duty. The doctor says that extra burden *must* be lifted if you are to get well. Suppose you just put your pride aside and treat me as a friend. Tell me what it is that is troubling you, and I'll pledge my word to do my best to help get that burden out of the way. Come now, tell me. Is it a broken heart? Is there someone you love who has disappointed you?"

Suddenly Gillian laughed, almost hysterically.

"No!" she said decidedly and laughed again.

Reuben began to laugh with her.

"That's good!" he said. "I'm glad it's not that, because it would have been a delicate matter to arrange, perhaps, if it had been that. I didn't really think it was, you know, because you don't look like a lovelorn maiden!" And then he laughed again.

"But you see," he went on sobering down as he saw her struggling to brush away some tears that had appeared, "you see I am determined to find out what it is that stands in the way of your quick recovery, and if I can't win your confidence I'll have to find some other way, just for the sake of the grand little kid you love. You see when I first started this business it was because Mr. Rand asked me to look out for you for the company, but after I got to know Noel I had another reason. He's a great kid and deserves a happy life, and if I can do anything to make it so I intend to do it. But of course you can hinder me a lot if you won't open up and tell me what is the matter, and it's no use your saying it's nothing, because both the doctor and I know that isn't true."

Gillian let a shy smile come through her tears now.

"Thank you," she murmured. "It's good to know you really like my little brother, and you certainly have been wonderful— I suppose I'd better tell you what has frightened me."

"That's the talk!" said Reuben. "I'll try to be worthy of your trust."

"You'll probably think I'm awfully silly, but—it's that—I'm fearfully *afraid* of something."

"Afraid? Afraid of what?" asked Reuben, trying to talk calmly, soothingly.

"Of something happening to Noel!"

"But why would you think anything would happen to Noel? What would you think *could* happen to Noel? I am certainly interested to know of any danger threatening him, and will do my best to protect him. But one has to understand to do much in a line like that."

"Yes, I'll tell you," said Gillian catching her breath. "It's our uncle. That is, he isn't really an uncle. My grandfather on father's side married a widow with one son long before he ever met my grandmother. She died when they had been married only a short time, and the boy went to live with her people. Then grandfather married again and my father was born. He and mother were very happy when they married and we had a happy home. We never saw father's stepbrother as he was living away out west. And after our father died we lost track of him entirely. Until our mother's health began to fail, and then one day he turned up and pretended to be very much interested in us. He knew that our father had been successful in a business way, and he offered to take charge of things for mother. That wasn't necessary, as father had arranged everything in trust for us. But Uncle Mason hung around and would offer to go to the office and get mother's dividends when they were due and all that. Mother didn't like it but finally was so sick she had to let him go for once. I was rather young then, and of course in school, but mother used to talk to me about the business arrangements, and told me that if anything happened to her, when I was of age I was to look out for things myself and take care of Noel."

Gillian was panting for breath as she talked, and now the nurse came up and gave her a spoonful of medicine.

"Take it easy, little girl," she whispered. "I'll go and get you some orange juice, and then you'll feel better."

"I'm all right," said the girl wearily. "There isn't much more to tell. Uncle Mason stayed around till mother died. After the funeral he called me one day and handed me over fifty dollars. He said something had happened to our investments, and that was all there was left. He said that I would have to get out and get a job. He was looking around for one for me, and when it came I'd better do the best I could, for he couldn't afford to look after me. As for Noel—he called him 'that brat'—he said he couldn't support him. He was going back to his home in the west pretty soon and he wanted to get everything settled up. So he was going to take Noel the very next day and put him in an orphanage, and then I wouldn't be hampered with him."

Gillian suddenly broke down and wept, her frail shoulders shaking at the memory. Reuben put out a comforting hand and laid it softly on the tumbled brown curls.

"You poor little girl!" he said softly.

Gillian was still instantly, and in a moment she lifted her tear-stained face, giving him a sad little wintry smile, and then went quickly on with her tale.

"That night I took Noel and ran away out of the house while he was asleep. I went as far as I dared on the fifty dollars and then I hunted up one of father's old friends and asked him for a job. He was old and sick, and not in business any more. He didn't live long after that, but he wrote a note to Mr. Glinden and I got my job. I had studied stenography and typing when I was in school, and I knew I could do good work. Mother saw to it that I had that. So I got the job, and we've been getting along till now, only sometimes I've been afraid Uncle Mason would turn up. You see there was a big doctor's bill for mother, and he didn't pay it. He said I'd have to pay it. So I've been saving and now it's all paid. Only there hasn't been much over for Noel and me. But if Uncle Mason has heard that I'm making money enough so I've paid that big doctor's bill, maybe he'll come around and claim half my money or something, and if he does he'll send Noel away to an orphanage. I'm sure he will!"

Reuben reached out and gathered her two little cold hands in both his own warm ones.

"There, dear friend, don't you think of such a thing again! That isn't possible now, because you have plenty of strong true friends who would take your part, and look after you and that dear child as if they were their own. *I* certainly will, and so I know would Mr. Rand and Mr. Glinden. They are both good men. And if anyone tried to molest you or Noel we would all rise up and protect you, and you mustn't be afraid any more. Will you promise me you won't?"

She looked up from her imprisoned hands and faced him through her tears.

"Oh, that is good of you, but I couldn't have people put to all that trouble to take care of us! I must do it myself! And I wouldn't want you to tell anybody about my family affairs, please! You promised, you know! I've trusted you!"

There was sweet pleading in her eyes, and he was instantly reminded of the boy Noel. Two dear children, they were. His heart was stirred within him. He was filled with a sudden longing to gather up this poor burdened tired little girl and take her to some quiet lovely homeplace where she wouldn't have to worry any more. He was startled at his own feelings. He had never felt so about any girl before, not even the girl out in his old home town whose books he used to carry home from high school, and who used to root for him when he was on the high school football team. But he had sense enough not to show how he was stirred. Of course it was only pity for her suffering, he told himself.

So he spoke reassuringly, pressing her hands with a comforting touch.

"Why of course not!" he said. "I wouldn't think of mentioning it, unless of course it became a matter of averting some calamity from either Noel or yourself. In that case I am sure you wouldn't want a little pride to stand in the way of doing everything I could for you both."

"Of course not!" she said softly, submissively.

"But I don't anticipate any such happening," he said quite cheerfully. "However, before we leave this unpleasant subject, so that I shall always be wise enough to help you if needed, suppose you give me the name and address of that uncle. Also the address where you lived when he was with you and your mother was alive. I want her full name and your father's too. It is just as well I should know those things in case there ever comes a time when I shall need them."

He got out his pencil and notebook with a businesslike air and Gillian roused herself to give the needed data. The very act of doing something like her ordinary every day work in the office seemed to calm her troubled spirits.

"One thing more," said Reuben as he closed his notebook. "Have you ever communicated with your Trust Company that was supposed to handle your finances?"

"No," she said apathetically. "I was afraid to. I thought they might tell my uncle where I was, and then he would come and make me go back and take the job he was getting me, and send Noel to an orphanage."

Reuben was still for a moment, then he asked:

"Are you quite *sure* your uncle always told the truth?"

"Oh!" said Gillian, "I don't know. I suppose he did. Yet my mother never trusted him. But I didn't dare take any chances."

"Do you happen to know whether he had any papers giving him the right to handle your mother's money?"

"Yes, I think once she wrote a note to the bank asking them to give him the money. Perhaps other times. I couldn't be sure."

"And did he ever give you any money after your mother died except that fifty dollars before you came away?"

Gillian shook her head.

"No, but he had told me he would have to handle our money for us until I was of age. That was the day after my mother died."

"And that was how long ago?"

"Almost two years. I will be of age in December."

"And you never did anything about it?"

She looked up surprised.

"What was there I could have done? I wouldn't have dared go back there."

"Suppose you give me the name of that Trust Company. Can you remember it? And the address? It might be useful sometime. But don't worry. I won't do anything that might reveal your whereabouts to your uncle."

She gave him the address half fearfully.

"But I wish you wouldn't bother about that!" she added pleadingly. "I don't need money now Mr. Rand has sent this nice check. I'm sure he's given me more than the work was worth."

"Don't worry! I'm sure he hasn't, and don't think any more about this matter now. Here comes your orange juice, and soon the doctor will be back. After that I can bring Noel in to see you, but you must be very quiet and rested or the doctor will think you're having too much excitement." He smiled pleasantly and went out as the nurse came over to the bed with the orange juice.

The doctor was in the reception room with Noel having a friendly talk, and discovering a good many things for himself that went to make up the background of his puzzling patient. He turned to Reuben as he came in with a knowing look.

"Well, sir, how did you make out? What do you think of my patient?"

Reuben saw the quick look of fear dart into Noel's eyes, and let his own smile blaze forth reassuringly:

"Why, she seems quite a little improved, doesn't she? Yes, we had a pleasant talk, and I think I have some light on the matter. I believe she is expecting you to come in and say whether this young man can visit her. She is very eager to see him of course."

Noel's smile lighted his face and he looked anxiously at the doctor.

The doctor smiled down at him.

"All right, young man, you win. I'll go in and give her the once-over right away, and then you can see your sister while Mr. Remington and I have a bit of conversation."

The doctor left them and Reuben looked down to find the child's eyes fixed earnestly upon him, as if he were reading the thoughts of his guardian.

"Is my Gillian—all—right?" he murmured in a whisper.

"She's doing very nicely," said Reuben. "I don't think you need to worry. I think she's going to be better very soon. Now you be gentle when you go in, and don't get excited, you know. We don't want to get on her nerves. She's just beginning to get a little rested."

"I will," said the boy eagerly. "C-c-can I ask her if she had nice oatmeal and soup and things?"

"Oh yes, I don't think that will do any harm. But you know the doctor may have ordered some different things for her from what you have. He may think she needs them."

He looked grave at that and presently said, "I see!"

Then the door opened and the doctor summoned him.

It was a beautiful sight to see the boy as he entered the sick room, stepping softly lest he make a noise, his cheeks bright with a lovely pink flush, and his eyes like two stars, his hands outspread to balance himself. Reuben found himself watching him as if he were his own, and being proud of him. Such a little, wise, loving, manly baby!

In the middle of the room he stood poised looking radiantly at his sister.

"Hi, Gillian!" he said sweetly. "Are you awright?"

And Gillian's eyes were filled with quick tears of joy, her lips in loving smiles.

"Hi, Noel!" she answered feebly.

The doctor and Reuben gave each other a quick look and stepped out into the hall together.

"Great kid, isn't he?" the doctor said, and then drew Reuben back into the reception room. "Well, Mr. Remington, did you find out anything?"

"Yes," said Reuben. "We had a fairly plain talk. I discovered a miserable old reprobate of a step-uncle who turned up just before the girl's mother died, bullied her into letting him handle her money for her after she was too sick to go to the bank for her own check, and then after the mother died has been tormenting the girl out of her senses, threatening to send Noel to an orphanage. The girl was in such terror of him that she took the boy and ran away in the night, and has been living in fear ever since she came here lest something would happen to the boy. The uncle told her that the money their father had left in trust for them was all gone, the investments had failed, and that fifty dollars he gave her was all she would ever get. I don't imagine there was much perhaps, but I wouldn't be surprised if the old bum made away with it himself. The girl was too frightened ever to go back or even write to the Trust Company and investigate. She lives in stark terror that the old sinner may turn up on any corner, and snatch her brother from her."

"Poor child!" said the doctor. "I don't wonder! Were you able to calm her?"

"Oh, I hope so. I told her she had a lot of friends here who would protect her. Of course I mean to investigate more fully and see what can be done to frighten the old reprobate, or put him somewhere so that he can't molest her. If he's meddled with their money, even though it may be but a small amount, we'll have some ground for having him arrested. But meantime, what do you think of her? When can she go back to work? She is wild to go. Insists that she must, and is hard to help because she is exceedingly proud."

"I see! Of course! They evidently come of fine stock. Well, thanks, Mr. Remington, you've cleared the atmosphere a little and perhaps there'll be more to discover. If you find it convenient drop in again toward night, and maintain your friendliness. Perhaps she'll give us more light, and you can give her further assurance of her security. Now about her stay here. I think she should remain at least a week where I can see her every day and she can have proper care and rest and the right food. Then if she could go to the country or the shore somewhere, with maybe a nurse along, that would be the thing for her. That'll run into money of course. You'd better find out what the company will do for her. Or there might be a quiet place where she could board, and where the boy could be near by and see her every day. But that too might involve too much anxiety for her. I don't suppose you are at liberty more than briefly, of course. We'll have to think it over and talk it over. Meantime, can you carry on, or make some arrangement for the boy for a few days? I suppose you have to be going back to your office soon."

"This is my vacation," said Reuben quietly. "I have a month and I'll stick around as long as I'm needed."

The doctor eyed him with admiration.

"But that's no vacation, Mr. Remington. You've been great to look after them. You deserve a good time and a swell rest."

Reuben grinned.

"What *is* a vacation?" he said. "Doing what you please and getting all worn out trying to have a good time, or forgetting yourself and trying to rest somebody else? I'm not sure. Maybe I'll try it out and see what comes of it. However that is, I'm sticking while I'm needed."

The doctor reached out his hand and grasped Reuben's, his eyes alight.

"Congratulations!" he said heartily. "You seem to be a real person. I haven't met so many."

"Thanks!" said Reuben. "And now, when do you want us to appear again? Sometime this afternoon? Or have we done enough damage to the patient for one day?"

"Come in around five a few minutes, and give her a comfortable feeling for the night. I don't think she had much real sleep last night. It looked to me as if she had been doing a lot of worrying. Get her mind off her troubles if you can."

"I'll try," said Reuben thoughtfully, and then he went back to the patient's room, with orders not to stay much longer this time.

There was an almost happy look on Gillian's lips as she lay there listening to her small brother. As Reuben opened the door he heard the young voice chirping gently and clearly.

"No, Gillian, I didn't forget to pray. We prayed together,

just like you and I always do. Reuben prays *very* nicely."

Reuben paused with the door barely unlatched to get the reaction of the sister, wondering if he ought to wait just a little before entering.

"Noel, my dear, do you mean that Mr. Remington prayed with you? You shouldn't call him Reuben. That's not respectful. You should call him Mr. Remington."

"But he *said* I was to call him Reuben," answered the boy firmly. "He said I was used to being a brother to somebody, and we would feel more at home with each other if I had somebody to be a brother to, so he told me to call him Reuben!"

Then Reuben swung into the room.

"That's right, Miss Guthrie. Have you any objection to that? I thought we'd get along easier that way." Reuben was grinning in a pleasant friendly way, and Gillian's white cheecks flushed a little.

"Why, no," she said, "if you think it is all right. I just thought it didn't sound very respectful."

"Well, I don't think there is much danger of this boy ever being disrespectful. We are too good pals now for that. If he ever gets disrespectful we'll go back to 'mister.' How's that, kid?"

Noel grinned.

"Okay!" he said.

"So, that's settled," said Reuben. "And now, I think there are a few questions I ought to ask. The first is, would you like us to go to your room and get anything for you? You had to come here rather in haste. I thought you might enjoy having your own hairbrush or something."

"Oh, thank you, that's very kind. I would like— But no, that's foolish. I can get along until the doctor lets me get up. I had my little comb in my hand bag. I'm sure he'll let me go home this evening, and then I thought by tomorrow, or the next day at most, I could go back to my work."

"Sorry," said Reuben, "but that's not on the cards for you yet, my friend. We're following the doctor, not your own eagerness to get back to work. So, if you don't mind my entering your room with your brother we can easily bring anything you want. And by the way, here's the next question. For how long did you take that room? Was it a monthly contract and do you have to pay from month to month, or did you pay ahead?"

Her cheeks flushed and then paled again.

"Oh, that's one of the things I was worrying about," she said in a low tone, "I pay by the week, and there's a payment due today, and that's a reason why I *must* go home tonight."

"I thought so," said Reuben. "Well, now just put that out of your head. I'll look after that till you are able to look after things for yourself. I have an idea we can find a better place for you."

"No," said Gillian, "you can't, not that I can afford. I've looked everywhere."

"Well, don't worry about that. I'll see that the rent is paid this morning for another week at least. And now what was that you were wishing you could have? Could Noel find it for you? I can recognize you wouldn't want a strange man racketing around in your room." He smiled genially, and Gillian thanked him with her eyes for understanding.

"And would there perhaps be some message about your work in the office you might want to send to somebody who knew about it?"

"Yes," said Gillian with a sudden look of utter weariness around her mouth. "The letter I was writing was a very important one. I had promised that it should be taken to Mr. Moore in time for him to sign it and get it off in the morning mail. I should have attended to it last night. I could have asked the nurse to telephone. But I didn't remember it till just a few minutes ago, and I hoped the doctor was going to let me get up and go. I wanted to get it off myself because Mr. Moore was very particular about some of the phraseology, and maybe not all of them could read my notes. They were taken in a great hurry."

"I imagine that's already been taken care of," said Reuben.

"Mr. Moore isn't one to let things go, and he would of course have heard of your illness. But just in care, I'll telephone at once and make sure. Anything else?"

"No, I think not. It was the last letter on my notebook. Evelyn Howe could finish it. She's used to my shorthand."

"All right. I'll straighten that out at once. I'll go down to the booth in the office. I have some calls of my own to put in too. It may take me ten or fifteen minutes, and in the meantime, fella, I'll park you here. Can you be depended on not to talk too much nor get your sister excited?"

"Sure!" said Noel with an important light in his face.

So Reuben went down to the public telephone, and the sister and brother looked at each other with a sweet radiance in their faces.

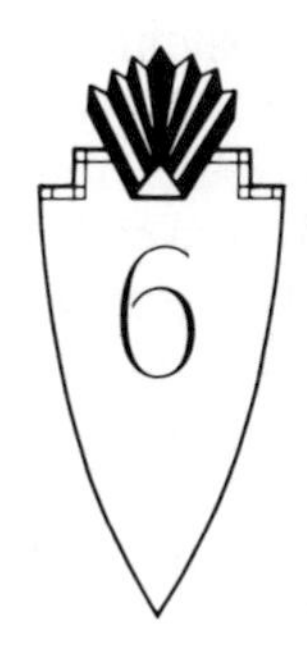

REUBEN called up the office first and found as he expected that Gillian's letters had all been carefully attended to. Then he got long distance and called a firm of detectives in New York with whom he had had some contacts before in looking up matters for the company.

"That you, Ted? Good morning. This is Reuben Remington. I'm calling you to see if you can get a line on a man named Mason Albee, who used to live out west and two years ago came to stay—" There followed all the details of address and movements he had been able to get in his brief talk with Gillian. "This is strictly confidential, of course. I want to know where the man is now, and what have been his movements in the past two years, especially under what conditions he is now living. If you can find out where he gets his money, that is important. I'll be calling you later, perhaps late this evening. Yes, and at what hour? Or tomorrow mid-morning? What will be most convenient? I would appreciate haste, even if the details have to be filled in later. Whereabouts and financial state matter most now. All right, Ted, I'll be calling you, and I'll send you a check as soon as you send me the memoranda. All right, Ted. Nice to hear your voice again."

After he had hung up he sat in the booth for a minute or

two thinking. Should he or should he not follow up a thought that had just come to him? Well, it wouldn't do any harm to find out if it was possible, in case it should be advisable. Why shouldn't he give Aunt Ettie a call? He hadn't written to the poor old soul in almost a year, and it would please her tremendously to have a few minutes' talk. She was getting old of course. Why, she might not even be alive yet. She had sent her usual birthday card last November, and a Christmas card at the holidays, but he hadn't heard from her since. It certainly would be a good idea to telephone her, even if it had nothing to do with the present problem. She had been a good faithful nurse, and a sort of mother-servant in the old home when he was a boy. She deserved a little attention from him. Now that his mother was gone there was likely no one to think of her. She lived with her old sister, but the sister was grumpy. He could remember hearing about that.

With sudden impulse he took up the receiver again and called the number. He couldn't forget that. He had known it ever since he was a child. Poor old Aunt Ettie! How she used to enjoy the thought that her family had a phone and could call her any time they wanted to. Not that they seemed to want to very often, but it was nice to know it was there. He smiled at the memory of her kindly face while he waited for the answer to his ring.

He had about decided that she wasn't at home, and his impulse had been ill-advised, when he heard the receiver taken down and a brisk voice answered "Hello!" It was Aunt Ettie! There was no mistake, and she didn't seem to have changed a mite! Her voice was just as young as ever.

"Is that you, Aunt Ettie?" he shouted joyously, just as he used to when he came home from school years ago.

"Well! My word! Ef that isn't Reuben! Where are you, Reubie? My! It's good to hear your voice again. I thought you'd entirely forgot me! How are you, boy?"

"Forgotten you, Aunt Ettie? Why, how could I do that? I've been a busy man since I saw you last, but I was just thinking about you, and I took it into my head to call you up and see if you were all right. How I wish I could have run in to see you instead of just talking to you across distance. I'd just love to run in and say: 'How about a little snack, Aunt Ettie? What have you got?' the way I used to do. And you always had a big plate full of crullers, or a huge pan of cinnamon buns, or a great dish of baked beans. My how good they used to taste! I could appreciate them now after these years of boarding houses and resturants. What have you got in the house this morning, Aunt Ettie?"

"Oh, gingerbread with whipped cream, baked apples and fresh brown bread, and the first green apple pie of the season!"

"Hurrah! Aunt Ettie, I'm almost persuaded to rent me a plane and fly up to Maine and have me some. Wish I could. I can't of course just now. But sometime maybe!"

"Well—I wisht you could," said the old lady sadly, "but I know that's all wishes. You won't come!"

"Well, maybe I will surprise you sometime, who knows?"

"Oh yeah?" came the answer.

"You haven't changed much, have you, Aunt Ettie? But say, how about taking a little vacation yourself? How are you these days? Feeling pretty well?"

"Yeah, I'm all right. Been straightening out things and getting in shape. Thinking of renting a room. It's kinda lonesome all by myself since Ellen's gone."

"Oh, Aunt Ettie! Is your sister Ellen gone?"

"Yeah. She passed on last week. I was going ta write ye sometime soon and tell ye, but I ben cleaning up and getting the room ready in case I was ta find somebody I was willing ta hev around all the time."

"Well, I should think that might be a good idea, if you insist on staying away off up there out of the world. But why don't you rent that whole place and come down into the real world? I might even be able to buy me a house sometime and let you be housekeeper."

"Deary me! Now ain't that something!" she said in a pleased voice. "A-course I know ya don't mean it. But say! I did hev an offer ta sell me place a few days ago. Yes, I really did! Wha'd'ya think o' that? Only I figgered, where would I go? I'm too old to begin all over again."

"Why, I think that would be fine," said Reuben pondering a plan. "Say, Aunt Ettie, how about trying it out for the summer to see if you would like it? Can't you rent your house with the privilege of buying at the end of the season, if you decide to sell? I've been thinking of renting a little cottage at the shore, or somewhere in the mountains near by. If I had you to run it I believe I would. Of course I couldn't be there much myself, probably, but I could run down week ends now and then. And I know a young girl who is desperately in need of rest. She works for our firm, and she's got a little brother dependent upon her, about the age I was when you first came to our house, and that kid needs to get out in the open. He's pale as a lily, and a great little kid! If I thought I could get you to come for a while I'd try and persuade them to come and take a bit of rest. The girl thinks she ought to go back to work right away, but if she does the doctor says she won't last long. She fainted in our office the other day, and she's not been eating enough nor resting enough. Been working over time to try and take care of the kid. They both need some good food, the kind you know how to cook! If I could arrange it, would you be willing to help me out, Aunt Ettie? I kind of think it is something mother would have done."

There was silence for a minute at the other end of the wire and then Aunt Ettie's voice, very wary and suspicious:

"Oh! A g-u-r-l! You gotcha a g-u-r-r-r-l!"

Reuben laughed.

"No, Aunt Ettie, you don't get me right. This is not *my* girl! In fact I haven't any special girl, myself. And I didn't know this girl even by sight till day before yesterday, when she fainted away in the office, and my boss asked me to see that she got to the hospital. I found she was near crazy about the little brother who was in a day nursery, and no one to meet him when he was brought back to their room, so I promised to go and get him, and look out for him till she could come back. But now it turns out that she's not going to be allowed to come back to work right away. She's run herself down eating so little she can scarcely stand up, saving it all for the kid. So I thought if she could have a week or two of your mothering it would do wonders for them both. You see, Aunt Ettie, I have to go out west on a trip. At least that's what I planned to do, and I thought if you could look out for them while I have to be away, by that time the girl could likely take things in her own hands again. If you knew the kind of day nursery where I found that boy I'm sure you'd take pity on him. He's rare. And he's only five years old! But don't get any idea of romance about this, Aunt Ettie, or that's the end of it all. The girl wouldn't stir a step if she thought *I* was doing it. I don't know that she will even now. I don't know her very well. She's awfully proud and reticent, sort of independent, and her folks are all dead. I'd have to invent some tale about you wanting someone to stay with you for a little while because you are lonesome or something."

"Well—" said the old lady's voice, "that all sounds very interesting except the girl. I don't like the idea of the girl. Girls are so up-in-the-air these days, and they most of them don't act like ladies to me. I wouldn't be much at dealing with 'em."

"But you see, Aunt Ettie, this girl isn't that kind. She's shy and frightened and sad. I think even you would admit all that if you would once see her. I'm counting on you to do a lot for her, put her on her feet sort of, if she'll let you. Couldn't you see your way clear to trying it just for a few days?"

"Well, seeing it's you, I might *think* about it, but I'm not so sure. If it was just you an' the kid I'd jump at the chance. But a *girl* is a diffrunt proposition. I don't think I'd enjoy the idea of you having a girl, anyway. *Any* kind of a girl!"

"But I tell you she's *not my* girl, she just *a* girl. She's just plain girl, and she's taken an awful beating, too. But she's not *my* girl at all."

"Oh, *yeah?"* said Aunt Ettie incredulously. "Well Reubie, seeing it's you, I'll promise to *think* about it, but I ain't saying what I'll think."

Reuben was almost angry, yet very much amused withal. And it was so like Aunt Ettie! Strange he hadn't thought of this and guarded against this idea.

"All right, Aunt Ettie," he said wearily, "I guess I can trust your good heart to come out on top. I'll call you up again tomorrow to get your answer, and meantime I'll be looking around for a cottage. Which do you prefer, the mountains or the shore?"

"Shore!" said Aunt Ettie promptly. "I'm fed up on mountains right now."

"Well, don't be disappointed if the girl turns the idea down. She's determined to get back to work and support her brother."

Reuben turned away from the telephone booth with a grin. Aunt Ettie was all right. She hadn't changed a mite. She would take in even a dying dog and nurse it up, but she'd never let anybody know she was going to do it. She would be docile as a petunia when he called her up again, but she always had to have her say. She would probably have decided what kind of curtains she wanted at the cottage windows by this time.

But there was a stiffer proposition before him yet than ever Aunt Ettie represented, and that was the girl. She had a very firm little chin, and courageous eyes.

His girl! The very idea! He would certainly take great care that the girl knew he did not consider her *his* property.

He went to the room upstairs. It seemed to him that he had been gone a long time, but he felt a thrill to see the light of joy in the little boy's eyes. He was glad to see him. And he could see by both faces that they had been having a good time together.

"Well," he said as he stood at the foot of the bed and looked at the frail girl lying there, "it's just as I thought. That Evelyn-girl had your letters all finished and off. Those office girls, you'll find, are all pretty good scouts when it comes to a pinch. There isn't anything they won't do to help another. I've found that out before. They may look silly and frivolous sometimes, but they are right there when there is a necessity. And they are bright as they make them."

Then he turned to Noel.

"And now, young man, don't you think it is about time that we went away and allowed this sister of yours to take a rest? She's had a lively morning, and she needs to forget it all. How is that, nurse? Isn't that right?"

"Yes," said the nurse coming forward with a spoonful of medicine poised above a glass, "I was just going to suggest that you must take a nap before lunch, Miss Guthrie."

So Noel tiptoed very quietly over to the bed and stooping down kissed Gillian's finger tips softly. Then he looked up at Reuben and smiled.

"Awright, Reuben!" he said, sliding his small hand inside Reuben's. Reuben grasped it warmly and looked toward the sister with a glance that showed he really liked it. Gillian's eyes thanked the young man for his graciousness to the child.

So they went away and Gillian lay there thinking how wonderful it was that this young man had been so kind to them. It must be that God had sent him! And there was a look of more peace on her brow than had been there for a long time. Almost immediately she fell into a natural sleep, for once unhaunted by dreams of ugly uncles who kidnapped little boys.

Noel walked away quite happily with Reuben. His heart was set at rest about Gillian. He was not wise enough to realize how sick she had been, and that she was not yet on the safe side. He had faith to believe that God and the doctor and Reuben were going to cure her, so he was free to enjoy the other good things that had come to him so unexpectedly.

"Now, where do we go?" he asked with bright eager gaze.

"Why, I think we ought to go to your room and get those things your sister wanted. Did she tell you just what they were?"

The boy nodded.

"Yes, she put them on my fingers. The first is her kimono, the pretty blue one of our mother's. It hangs inside the curtain in the corner of the room. The next is a little box of clean clothes on the floor of the closet. There aren't many. Just in a pasteboard box. And I'm to put our mother's and father's pictures from the bureau in the box, and carry it very carefully. And then on my middle finger was her handkerchiefs and her little white collar, and then mother's pearl pin, because she was afraid someone might get in and steal it. It is the only nice thing she has left of mother's. I'm to pin it on a clean handkerchief that's in the middle bureau drawer, and get a clean pair of stockings. And then on my little finger is her hairbrush and tooth brush."

He was counting them out on his fingers most seriously, and Reuben watched him amusedly.

"And then," he went on, "we put my things all on the other hand. I've got some clean things, a pair of socks, and a necktie. She said I might bring that, only I don't know how to tie it very well."

"Well, I guess we can manage that," smiled Reuben indulgently.

"There's an old sweater, too. She thought I might need it if it got any colder, at night, but she said it wasn't very respectable. She said ask you what you better bring for me."

"All right," said Reuben. "We'll manage I guess. I have to get a new suitcase for myself and we can get it before we go there and carry the things in that."

"That will be nice!" said the child happily. "Can we take the things to her today?"

"Oh, yes, we'll run in about five minutes toward night. We mustn't tire her, you know."

"No, we won't tire her!" and the eager little boy gave a skip or two as he hurried along beside Reuben.

They got the suitcase and then took a taxi to the plain barn-like rooming house where Gillian and her small brother had made their home for some months past. Reuben's heart was wrung when he climbed the steep stairs, three flights of them, to think what that frail girl had gone through.

The little room was scrupulously clean when Noel unlocked the door with his key that hung around his neck, and they stepped within, but there was so very little in it that sudden tears came to the young man's eyes. How had these two existed?

The closet was a calico curtain hung from two nails to hide a row of nails driven into a board on the rough wall. There were two cots, just canvas stretchers. Poor children! What beds. Coarse sheets, cheap cotton blankets, an old thin wool blanket for Noel's bed. A pine bureau whose drawers opened crazily, a box with a tin basin and pitcher for a washstand, and on another box a rusty old hotplate with a tin teakettle and a saucepan for cooking. Reuben was appalled at the scarcity of what he had always considered necessities. And yet in the midst of all that poverty there were two handsome miniatures standing on the bureau, a man and a woman, both with fine faces; there was a worn Bible, and there was a pearl pin! It all told a sorrowful story, and revealed a lot of character in the girl who had dared to run away from her persecutor and take on herself the responsibility of a small child. It was heart-breaking.

Reuben helped Noel gather up his things and put them all in the new suitcase, and just as they were about to leave Noel said:

"Oh, yes there was one more thing. There is a little tin box in the bureau drawer with some papers in it. Gillian told me to be sure and bring it. She put a kiss on my chin to remember it before I left the room."

They found the tin box that was fastened with a tiny padlock.

"Are you sure your sister has the key for this box, Noel?" asked Reuben.

"Oh, yes, I'm sure!" said Noel. "She wears it around her neck on a ribbon."

What a child! And what a life theirs must have been!

"Now," said Reuben as they went down the long flights of stairs, "we are going to get some lunch, and then we'll spend a few minutes in the toy department of that store where we got the suitcase. Will you like that?"

"Oh, I will. Gillian always said that sometime, if she could ever afford a day off, she would take me. She did take me once to see a store window full of toys last Christmas, one evening. It was all lighted up pretty and had a Santa Claus in the window. It was very nice. Only Gillian had to hurry home to finish some envelopes she had to address, and we couldn't stay long enough to see everything."

"Well, we'll stay and see a lot of things, and then some other day, we'll go again and see some more, so you won't get too tired today. Remember we have to go to the hospital for a few minutes yet before dark."

The child was tired but happy, and after lunch he seemed to bloom right up again and be all eager for the toy department, so they went the rounds, and on the side Reuben purchased three or four games that he thought the boy could play, and took them with him. They would have a game tonight perhaps after they returned from the hospital. Really Reuben was enjoying all this as much as Noel.

All too soon for Noel it came time to get back to the hospital and even Noel was glad to climb into a taxi and rest his head back. It was hard work, this shopping, when you weren't accustomed to it!

The boy was jubilant when they got back to the hospital and Gillian saw that he hadn't forgotten anything. She seemed quite content to see the two lovely minatures on the little stand by her bed, the pretty blue kimono hanging on the wall ready for her when she might sit up, the clean clothes, the little tin box and the pearl pin. It all seemed to make her getting up more certain and more near.

But the sister looked sadly at the little pile of faded socks and underwear the child had brought for himself. There had been so little else for him.

"I was saving to buy him some new things," she said.

"Oh, he's all right," said Reuben. "We'll find plenty for his needs. And now I want to ask you a question. Would you mind very much if I took Noel with me tomorrow down to the shore for the day? We'd be back in time to come here in the evening and have a little chat with you before you go to sleep. You see I have an elderly friend, a sweet old lady, who used to look after me when I was a kid sometimes, and she's thinking of going to the shore for a while. I promised I would look up a place for her, and I thought I could do that tomorrow if it wouldn't worry you. I thought perhaps it might be a good thing for Noel, too, to get a sniff of salt air. Has he ever been to the shore?"

"No," said Gillian. "Oh, that would be wonderful for him, only I'm afraid he'll be a nuisance to you. I wonder if they wouldn't let him stay here while you are gone. He wouldn't be any trouble to anyone."

"No," said the nurse decidedly, "they don't allow children in the hospital. It's a special request of your doctor that he is allowed in a few minutes to see you. He wouldn't be allowed here without an older person to look after him."

"And I would be very much disappointed not to have him with me," said Reuben. "I have grown quite attached to him, and I'm anxious to see what he thinks of the ocean. Would it worry you to have him gone? I would take very special care of him and not let him out of my sight. But if it would make you nervous we'll put off the trip till you are stronger."

"Oh, no! I wouldn't worry!" said Gillian. "I only felt it would be a nuisance to you. I don't know how we ever are to repay you for all you've done for us already!"

"Please don't talk of repaying. You don't know what a pleasure it has been for me to have Noel all to myself. You know I haven't any family of my own, and I didn't know what I was missing till he came. But I'd be so glad if you don't mind his going. We could go down quite early in the morning, and return by the four o'clock train. Then we could come in just after you've finished your evening meal, and say good night to you. And the next day we'll tell you about the ocean. Will that be all right?"

"Oh, that will be wonderful for Noel, and of course I shan't worry. I'll just lie and rest and get ready to be up when you come back."

"Well, we'll see what the doctor has to say to that. Now, Noel, suppose you kiss your sister good night and we'll go over to the hotel and get to bed early. Because we have to get up early in the morning, you know."

Noel with bright face went briskly over to kiss his sister, and whispered in her ear:

"Don't you think my Reuben is awfully *awfully* nice, Gillian?"

"Yes, dear," she said softly and kissed his cheek. "Good night, dear, and be a good boy!"

"I will!" said Noel.

And they hurried away while the nurse bustled around getting her patient ready for her supper and sleep.

Reuben got his charge through a simple supper and into bed where in spite of his excitement he was soon asleep.

Then, shielding the light from his roommate, he went quietly at some important telephoning. But he saved Aunt Ettie until he should get to the shore the next morning and have something interesting to tell her about a cottage.

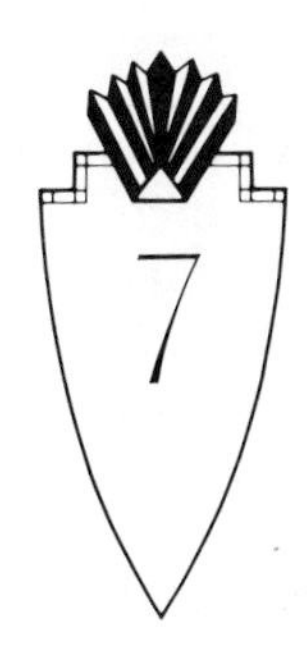

THE day was perfect. Dazzling blue sky, with little rosy scurrying clouds on the horizon. Even the city looked attractive in its early morning lighting, sun bright even on cheap window glass, and shining sharply from church spires and weather vanes. The air was deep and tangy, new washed by a storm in the night, not yet too warm for comfort. There seemed to be spice in every breath one took.

Noel's cheeks were almost rosy with excitement. He watched the way as if he were going through a world newborn just for him. All through the intricacies of the ferry trip, and the transfer to the train he seemed to have the details of the whole trip in charge, watching to be sure nothing went wrong. Reuben was much amused studying him.

When they reached the shore resort that Reuben had selected as a promising place to search for Aunt Ettie's cottage, Noel stared about him in a friendly way, as if all the buildings and streets must be expecting him, and welcoming him. He greeted the taxi man who was to drive them, with a smile as if it were to be a personally conducted tour.

Halfway down the broad avenue that led to the ocean, which lay like a blue line of mystery at the end of vision, he looked up to Reuben and remarked:

"The seashore is kind of a *white* place, isn't it? There is so much more light here than there is in the city. We will have to be very careful not to get it dirty."

Reuben smiled at the original ideas produced, meditating on the unusual type of the child's mind.

"Things don't seem to soil so easily at the shore," explained Reuben.

The child thought about that awhile and then he asked:

"Is that because there's so much water in the ocean that they get washed clean all the time?"

"No, I think it is because there are not so many things around here to soil. Things like factories with big chimneys pouring out dirty smoke all the time."

"Oh! Don't they have factories and big dirty chimneys at the shore?"

"Not usually."

The child pondered that.

"I didn't know," he said with a wise little pucker of his brows. "I'll have to think about that. That's what my Gillian always tells me I'll have to do about anything I don't understand. 'Think about it.' "

They drove to the beach first, and Reuben asked the driver to stop and let them look at the ocean for a moment. Noel was overwhelmed with the sight. Finally he drew a long breath and said wonderingly:

"And *God made* it *all!*" Then as they turned and drove along the shore road, he said, his eyes still turned toward the ocean:

"There's so much of it! He must have got very very tired making it all! And that's why He made the Sabbath, isn't it?"

Reuben looked puzzled.

"God got tired and He wanted to rest," explained the boy.

"I don't believe God gets tired," said Reuben, cautiously, because he felt he was getting almost beyond his own depth with this wise child. "He isn't like us, with a body that tires out, you know. He wouldn't exactly be a God if He got tired, would He?"

"Oh, that's so," said the child with a puzzled air. Then with a sudden bright smile: "But it feels good to rest sometimes, even when you're not tired. I guess God wanted to look over what He'd made and enjoy it awhile, and see that it was good. But what's that out there on the water? Oh, is that a *ship?* A *real* ship? I've seen pictures of ships. There is a nice one in that picture book you got me."

"Yes, that's a ship. I think they call that a three masted schooner. We'll probably see some more before the day is done. And now we are turning up this road away from the sea a little while, going to find a real estate man and see if he has any cottages to rent Aunt Ettie."

"Oh, yes! That will be fun! There's a nice big one, but that looks like a hospital or a hotel, it's so big!"

"Yes, that is a hotel. Don't you see the name up there in big letters? What's that first letter? Can you read it?"

"That's A," said Noel promptly. "And the next one is R. What does it spell? It's a long word."

"Why, that says Arlington House. That's a nice looking hotel. And now we come to private cottages. This big one on the right hand side is a fine one. I expect some rich man owns it. See, it's built of stone, and has big porches with comfortable chairs to sit on, and awnings over the windows, and flowers and evergreen trees outside."

"That's a nice one," said Noel, "but it's kind of too big. It doesn't look very at-homey, do you think it does? Is your Aunt Ettie a rich lady? Would she want a cottage as big as that?"

"No, she's not a rich lady. She's very plain and sweet and nice. She isn't really my aunt at all, you know. She used to be my nurse when I was a little boy, smaller than you are, but I liked her a lot and we all called her Aunt Ettie. No, I don't think she'd care for a big place like that. Just a neat little place would please her better. We'll find some 'at-homey' ones pretty soon."

So they drove about through many pretty streets, some of them shaded with beautiful trees, and back to the shore again for a block or two, then down other streets. Once they passed a white marble palace set in a lovely green yard by the sea, with no boardwalk in front of it, and just a far stretch of smooth hard beach. Noel looked long at it.

"That must be like one of the Heavenly mansions," he said slowly as he studied it. "When I get up to Heaven I think I would like to live in one as big as that if Jesus was there too, but it looks lonesome down here. It looks as if it might get blown into the sea sometime, and then where would you be? Is that where some very rich man lives?"

"Yes, it looks that way," smiled Reuben. "Now, here, see where we are turning. Here are some smaller cottages. Aren't they pretty, with flowers in their window boxes?"

"Yes, those look nice. When I get to be a man I'll buy my Gillian one like those. Won't that be nice?"

"Why, yes, I should think she would like that!" said Reuben heartily.

They came at last to a little white cottage among a small grove of maples, not far from the shore. A very plain little house painted white, with green blinds, and a porch overlooking the sea. There was moreover a lighthouse not far away which gave an added charm to the little house, in Noel's eyes at last.

It was just finished, with shining newness about it. There was no furniture in it, but Noel looked around, his face smiling.

"We could *make* some furniture for it!" he declared eagerly. "We could get some boxes at the grocery store. And some calico for closets to hang the clothes behind. My sister knows how to make a home out of a very bare room. We can ask her."

Reuben looked tenderly at the child.

"Yes," he said interestedly, "that would be nice if we had time. But if Aunt Ettie wants it she will want to use it right away, and so I think we'd have to buy furniture, unless the owner has other plans for it. We'll just go and see the agent and find out about it. This looks pretty nice. But let us go inside and see how many rooms it has. Aunt Ettie might want to have some company occasionally, so we'll have to have rooms enough. But some day I'd like to go to the shore or somewhere with you and furnish a little place just as you suggest. I'm sure it could be done."

"Sure it can!" said Noel. "Gillian and I did it. Don't you remember our washstand, and our 'rangements for the kitchen stove and the clothes closet?"

"Oh, yes, I noticed those," said Reuben. "We'll have to remember all those things and use them sometime, if we have a chance to work it out together."

They got out and went in, up the little flagged path to the porch. The front door was open and a workman was fitting the windows with shining copper screens.

There was a big living room all across the front of the house, with a fireplace at one side. There were three bedrooms, a bathroom and the cutest little kitchenette.

"Isn't it *grand!*" said Noel. "I shall certainly buy this for my Gillian when I grow old."

Reuben smiled.

"Yes, I think Aunt Ettie would enjoy this. Now suppose we go and see the agent, and find out whether it is for rent, and what the terms are."

So they went to see the agent who told them he had two other houses built practically on the same plan, that were furnished. They finally decided on one of those though their thoughts turned wistfully toward the first one they had seen. Aunt Ettie might be in a hurry to come right away, and not want to bother waiting for her furniture.

That settled they went to the beach, and Noel in a scrap of a bathing suit that Reuben found at a store near the agent's office advanced tremulously toward the great ocean, touching his bare feet timorously on the cool velvety wet sand, wondering at his first introduction to the seaside. It was all quite thrilling to the boy who had never since his memory had opportunity to go barefoot out of doors.

Reuben found a place along the boardwalk where they had tin pails and shovels for sale, and promptly provided him with all the paraphernalia of a summer child.

Reuben had hired a bathing suit and after a little he coaxed

Noel to venture in. A few minutes more and he was splashing and shouting with glee.

They did not stay in too long for a first dip, and as they came out Noel said:

"I wish my Gillian could go in here. I think she would love it. I shall take her sometime when I get grown up."

"Why of course you will," said Reuben, and wondered if the child would stay so dear and unspoiled when he grew up.

They had a delightful shore dinner, and Noel enjoyed every bite, and then they went back to the beach to build sand cities.

After he had inducted Noel into the ways of tunnels and sand mountains Reuben lay back against a sand pillow and thought out his intricate plans for the days ahead, wondering how it was all going to work out. He decided he wouldn't call Aunt Ettie till he got back to the city. That would give her more time to decide, and to get her a little excited about whether he had really meant his proposition after all. But he was sure she would love any of those little cottages they had seen.

At the last Noel had fairly to be dragged away from the sand and looked wistfully toward the ocean with its long smooth beach dotted here and there with dainty shells and seaweed. He pointed out a little group of sandpipers stepping daintily over the wet sand with their pink feet, and snapping up the tiny crabs. It was all most alluring and Noel could not bear to leave it.

Reuben watched him on the way home, falling asleep and resting his curly head against Reuben's arm. He loved it. He thought how grand it was going to be for this child as well as for his sister if the plan could be made to work out. What a wonderful thing for him to have even a week of seashore, if more could not be managed, to play in the sand and breathe the clean invigorating salt air. But there were several hindrances to overcome before it could be accomplished. In the first place there was Aunt Ettie, who was known to have a stubborn will of her own, or rather a stubborn "won't" of her own. There was no telling whether Aunt Ettie would give in or not, and if she didn't he would have to think out some other way to work this thing, for he was determined that if it was in his power that little white brave girl should have her chance to live, and that dear little loving boy should have a chance to laugh and eat and sleep and be happy, entirely away from that awful place where his sister had had to leave him.

But then, even if Aunt Ettie should be ready to serve the cause there was another will which he judged to be fully as "won'tish" as Aunt Ettie's, and that was Gillian's. He had not yet sounded the depths of her stubbornness and pride. There was only one person he could count on to help and that was the doctor. And perhaps the heads of the house where he worked, only he had resolved that he would never tell them about this. They were doing enough looking after the doctor and hospitalization. This was his own private venture, and he wasn't going to have anyone else butting in. He just *had* to get Aunt Ettie working for this, or he could never win over Gillian.

So he brooded over the matter, as the train rattled on over sandy scrub oak ground, back cityward, and the sun went lower and lower, until a ruby glow was almost in the sky when they got back to the city. A simple supper served at a counter, in a funny resturant away down by the ferry boats, where they sat on high stools and ate soup out of little round bowls, and little strawberry pies that Noel could take up in his hand. Then they hurried to the hospital to tell the waiting sister all about the shore.

The doctor came in while Noel was describing how wet sand felt to bare toes when you first stepped on it, and he was greatly intrigued by the account. He watched the child and listened and laughed, flicking away a vagrant tear that came unaware, and finally said:

"Well, Noel, you're the best medicine your sister has had all day. I think I shall have to get up a petition to have that rule ordering children not to come to the hospital revoked. If all children were like you I'm sure the rule would never have been made."

As they went down in the elevator together a few minutes

later he said in a low tone to Reuben, "Call me up around eleven o'clock. I'd like to know how you make out."

They went straight to their hotel room, and Noel lost no time in getting ready for bed, but when he was attired in his night clothes, he knelt bravely down as usual, and prayed characteristically:

"Dear Heavenly Father, I'm very sleepy, and I can't remember all the things to thank You for tonight, but in the morning I'll tell You all about it. And I thank You for letting me have such a nice time. Please get something nice for dear Gillian too, and make me a good boy. Please bless Reuben and the doctor and make my sister well, for Jesus' sake, Amen."

And Reuben on his knees beside the child, pressed the little hand and echoed the prayer in his own words.

Noel was asleep in five minutes, and then Reuben went to the telephone.

Aunt Ettie came first.

"Hello, Aunt Ettie. Is that you? How is crops?" It was an old childhood's greeting, and he knew she would respond to that if to anything. And she did.

"Fine and dandy, Reubie! But you've kept me in hot water all day not knowing whether you really meant this crazy scheme ur not. When you didn't call when you said you would I thought you were just kidding, and here I had all but hired a truck to take a van load of things down for me, and didn't know how to plan when to start. I've rented me house for the summer, with the right to buy if I sell to anybody, just as you said, and I've begun to get me things out to pack. And now if you didn't really mean it I'll have all that work to undo, now when I've really got me mind made up to smell the salt air once more before I go hence."

Reuben smiled grimly. Aunt Ettie was true to form. He had judged her rightly. He needn't have worried.

"Well that's great, Aunt Ettie! So you're really accepting my proposition, girl and all, are you?"

"Yes," said Aunt Ettie a trife grimly. "If you insist on the girl of course I'll have to do it."

"Okay then. Now, I've got the refusal of several houses.

They're all cute as the dickens. Do you want it to be furnished or unfurnished? Did I understand you to say you were going to get a van to take your things down? You planning to take furniture?"

"Sure," said Aunt Ettie firmly. "I don't wanta sleep on other folkses' old musty beds that have had just anybody on 'em. I want me own sweet smelling mattresses. And anyhow a lot of stuff I'm sending down is what the new tenant doesn't want and I wouldn't know what to do with it if I left it behind. I'd have to store it in the old barn, and it might get stole on me if I did, and besides, if I liked it down there I might want ta stay, and I'd like me own things with me. I'd feel less homesick. An' ef I was ta come back here, in case I didn't like it there, I cud likely sell the things down there as easy as I cud up here."

"Yes, I suppose you could," said Reuben. "You've got it all thought out, haven't you, just as you always used to do with everything. Well, Aunt Ettie, if that's the case I've got a little gem of a house for you, unfurnished. It was the one I liked best, only I didn't see how you could bother getting furniture. But I'm sure you'll like it. It's perfectly new, right in a little grove of trees so you'll feel at home, and it's not far from the ocean. You can see it from the porch and the windows. There's a nice fireplace in the living room. But there isn't any dining room. How will you like that? There's an alcove in the kitchen, or you can have a big table in one end of the living room, whichever you like."

"That's okay with me," responded Aunt Ettie glibly. "How many bedrooms?"

"Three, and one bathroom. There's a porch could be used for sleeping, too, in case you had a lot of company."

"Company!" sniffed Aunt Ettie contemptuously. "Besides if I did there's that big folding couch for the living room. That's as good a bed as anybody needs. We'll make out, don't you be afraid. When shall I tell Mr. Ames to arrange to come down? He said any day would do after the first of the week."

"All right, Aunt Ettie," said Reuben in a relieved voice. "You arrange the day that is best for you. If I can fix things to go down and meet you that day I will, but in case I can't get there till later I'd better give you the agent's name and address. You go straight to him and he'll take you to the house. It's number seven Grove Avenue, Sandy Haven. I'll phone him tonight that we're taking the unfurnished cottage and you are bringing furniture down early next week. Is there anything else you want?"

"No," said the old lady briskly. "You've spent enough money already. I'll send a telegram to your boarding house when I start, and you better send me a letter with that address again so I don't make any mistakes. Gubbye! I'll be seein' ye next week!"

Reuben turned away from the telephone laughing.

"Well, that's that!" he said. Then he called the real estate agent as agreed upon, and took the unfurnished house, arranging that it should be ready for occupancy when the tenant arrived early the next week.

It was late when he succeeded in tracing his New York detective friend on a person to person call, and got an answer.

"Yes, Remington, I've got a line on your case, and I've put a good man to work on it. We hope to have definite information for you in a couple of days, perhaps sooner. Shall I write to the office when I get it or where can I contact you at different hours of the day?"

When the matter was arranged Reuben went to bed, feeling that he had earned a good night's rest.

A telephone call to Reuben's boarding house early the next morning revealed the fact that there was quite a good deal of mail awaiting him there, and among the collection were two telegrams.

Reuben told them he would send a messenger boy for his mail as he might not be able to get there that day. The mail arrived by messenger just as they had finished breakfast.

The first telegram he opened was from his two college friends saying they would gladly stay over a few days at Grand Canyon if he felt he could arrange to join them early next week. He scribbled a regretful message to be wired to them, saying it was impossible at present, and they must go on as they had planned, letting him know from time to time where they were. If it turned out to be at all possible he might join them somewhere later.

The other telegram was from Ted the detective. "Got a line on your man. Call me up about two o'clock. Must ask a few questions."

That meant he would have to talk with Gillian that morning and get a little more information.

There were a couple of envelopes among the mail that looked like wedding invitations, and one of them had a faint violet perfume. He almost stuffed those in his pocket without opening them, and then thought better of it and tore them open impatiently. He had a great deal to do that morning.

The perfumed one was from Anise Glinden. An invitation, yes, to the first showing of *that play!* She had recovered from her animosity to want to have him see the play now that it was too late for him to be in it. Well, if things cleared up and he wasn't in the far west by that time he might run up for the evening just to be a little courteous after all her invitations. He didn't want to continue to keep up the battle between them, and of course since she was the daughter of his employer, it was right that he should show her some consideration. Since she was ready to ignore hostilities, surely he could afford to do as much.

He turned to the other thick square envelope and that *was* a wedding invitation in truth.

Mr. and Mrs. Stanford Delany
request the pleasure of your company
at the marriage of their daughter
Rose Elizabeth
to
Mr. Franklin Maynard Meredith, Jr.
on Saturday the fifteenth of July
at four o'clock in the afternoon,
at St. Paul's Episcopal Church,
Carrington, Illinois.

.He stared at the invitation in amazement. Rose Elizabeth was the younger sister of the girl he used to go around with so much, and she was marrying Frank Meredith, the son of the richest man in town. But what had become of *Agnes* Delany, the girl he used to go with? That was a wedding he felt would be almost obligatory for him to attend. Frank Meredith had been one of his closest friends in high school, and while Rose Elizabeth had been very young then, Agnes had been his girl in those days. It was true he had drifted from the knowledge of them all, but it was natural for them to send him an invitation. And here were other letters. A brief one from Frank, asking if he would come on and be best man at his wedding. And the last letter bore familiar handwriting. That was from Agnes, begging that he would come to the wedding.

"It is so long since we have seen you, and Frank is afraid that you won't come because you didn't get word sooner, but, you see, he had a cousin visiting him from England and his mother was determined that Frank should ask him to be best man. Then suddenly the cousin was called home on account of the war, and Frank of course turned back to you at once. He asked me if I wouldn't write and add my plea that you will come, even if you have to put aside something very important to be here. We *all* want to see you—"

And so, here was another girl, pleading for his presence! A girl he used to think he thought a lot of. Yet she had been practically out of his life and mind for the last seven years. He had supposed that by this time she was either married long ago or had at least forgotten him. Just a high school friendship.

But this was too much. Another complication for his vacation! Odd, wasn't it, all coming at once? And a big Duty standing in the way of all of them at present. Well, this wedding didn't come for nearly three weeks yet. The invitation had waited two days already at his boarding place. But there was plenty of time. He could surely manage to get there for the evening of the wedding, and probably the night before for rehearsal, and that would be all that would be required. He could leave on the midnight train after the wedding was over if necessary.

But in the meantime he had to manage the present duties. Of course by that time Gillian and her alluring young brother would be a story of the past, and he would be free to live his life as he would.

As he gathered up his letters, and prepared to go over to the hospital in time for the doctor's visit, he had a passing wonder as to what life had brought to his old friend Agnes.

She wasn't married, at least, for she still signed her name Agnes Delaney.

Then the day came along and gripped him with its duties and Reuben and the little boy started for the hospital once more.

The doctor was there already, and he opened the patient's door as they came by and called them in. His face was almost severe and when they came into the room it was obvious that Gillian was greatly disturbed. Noel sensed it instantly and went over to stand beside the bed and take his sister's hand protectingly in his own, looking up at the doctor with defiant eyes.

"I've just been telling this little girl that she positively *cannot* get up today and go to work," said the doctor looking at Reuben as if it were somehow his fault.

Reuben looked at the doctor and then turned to Gillian.

"Oh, you weren't thinking of doing that, were you, Miss Guthrie? I thought I made you understand that Mr. Glinden and Mr. Rand both want you to have all the rest possible, and get your strength entirely up to normal before you go back."

"But I *can't,* I simply can't be under obligation this way!" protested Gillian with tears swimming into her eyes, and a determined look about her chin and mouth.

"Now look here, little lady," said the doctor, "haven't you any sense at all? Don't you know you can repay people if they have to be repaid, a great deal quicker when you have your whole strength at its normal height? Your pulse is galloping as if it were running away, and you are as jumpy as can be. You can't properly take care of that child until you are well. I've done my best for you in the short time you've been here, but I can't work miracles. How many weeks or months have you been going on short rations, and bearing all sorts of worries into the bargain? And yet you expect me to put you in running order in a day and send you on your way, and it *can't be done!* You simply *must* have a rest, good nourishing food, and country or seashore air for at least three or four weeks, and even then I'm not sure you should go back to work if you are going to keep up this burden-bearing, and going around with the cares of the nation on your shoulders. It can't be done! I won't stand for it, I say!"

Suddenly Noel walked up to the doctor with the air of an older man and spoke in a clear little voice:

"Don't you scold my Gillian, *you doctor!* Can't you see you make her *cry?* I *won't let* you scold my Gillian!"

The room was very still for an instant as everybody looked at the daring little boy, and then quickly turned all eyes to Gillian and saw the tears on her face, the tears that her young brother had noticed first of them all. Suddenly a change came over the doctor's face and a kind of shamed look. Then he melted down into a real merry laugh.

"Well, you young man, I guess you're right, and I stand corrected. I shouldn't have spoken in a tone like that. Forgive me, Miss Guthrie. I was only speaking for your good, my child!"

"I know it," said Gillian, suddenly breaking down and sobbing softly in her outspread hands. "I know you're right, but doctor, I just *can't do it!"*

Then Reuben stepped up to the bedside:

"Wait a minute, Miss Guthrie. Don't get all upset that way. I've got something good to tell you that I feel sure will solve some of the problems. Suppose you quiet down, and let the nurse wash your face with nice cool water, and give you a swallow or two of water or orange juice, or whatever is right, and then when you are a bit rested we'll tell you all about it. You know, Miss Guthrie, you believe in God, and you've taught your little brother to believe in Him, and pray to Him. So couldn't you try trusting in Him for a little, and see what comes?"

It was a very strange thing for Reuben to say. He had never gone around preaching in his life, not even just plain philosophical platitudes, and he didn't know where he got the words, nor how he got the nerve, there before the doctor and the nurse! But it was very still in the room after that.

The frail young shoulders stopped quivering with sobs, and presently the girl lifted her tear-stained face and almost smiled at him.

"Thank you," she said. "I deserved that! I'll try to trust. I truly will. And I do want to do the right thing."

"Very well," said the doctor, "then we'll all try to be more reasonable, and make it as easy as we can for you. Now, nurse, where is that tonic? And just punch up those pillows a little and let her lie more comfortably. And boy," turning toward Noel, "you sit down and take it easy. Man! they needn't call you a *child* any more. You know how to take care of a sick sister already, don't you?"

The doctor spoke very tenderly, his voice almost hoarse with feeling.

"Now, Mr. Remington, if you'll step outside with me I'll tell you just how things are, and then we'll try to plan to get this little girl well in the shortest time possible."

So Reuben talked a few minutes with the doctor, told him the possibilities at the shore, and the doctor nodded in great relief.

"That's just what she needs, and if you can work it without a scene you're a better man than I am."

So after a little Reuben when back and found Noel telling his sister all about how the ocean looked, and how the sand was smooth and soft like velvet, and wet and cool; and he told her all that they had done that wonderful day at the shore. Told some of the incidents over twice. Then he told about the houses they saw for Aunt Ettie, and finally Reuben took up the story:

"That little cottage Noel is telling you about now, the white one with the green blinds, and the ocean just in sight from the porch, is the one I have taken for Aunt Ettie, my old nurse. I called her up this morning and told her about it, and she's just delighted with it. She's coming down early next week with a van load of furniture of her own, to fix it up for the summer. But there's one thing she wants, and that's some nice person to be with her, at least until she gets used to being in a strange place. And I thought of you. I don't know whether you'll think I was presuming or not, but the doctor had told me he wanted you to be in a place where you could rest for a little while before you went back to work, and I just dared to tell Aunt Ettie about you. Of course I told her you didn't know anything about it yet and I wasn't sure you would like the idea, but I promised her I would try you out and let her know as soon as possible."

"That would be very nice of course," said Gillian, with a gentle dignity, "and it was kind of you to think of me, but you know, Mr. Remington, I can't afford to pay what such board should cost, and I can't be dependent upon you or the firm either. You see I must save every cent to look after Noel. I don't think he should stay at that day nursery again."

"No indeed!" said Reuben. "I was going to speak about that, but we'll put that off a little till we have other things settled. You see this would be ideal for Noel, to have a few weeks by the sea. He needs to get some color in his cheeks. If you could have seen his delight yesterday I'm sure you would have felt good for him. And Aunt Ettie was just delighted at the idea of a little boy around again. But you misunderstood me. There wouldn't be anything to pay. Aunt Ettie wants a companion, just like a friend visiting her. As you got stronger you could help her a little about the house, dusting and getting the meals, you know, and there wouldn't be any obligation for even that until you really felt like it. So don't mention money again in connection with the arrangement. You'll simply be visitors, and be paying for your board just by being there and keeping Aunt Ettie from being lonesome."

"Oh, Mr. Remington, that sounds too good to be true!"

"It's perfectly true. Why don't you stop to reason it out that your Heavenly Father saw you needed some rest and good air, and He saw Aunt Ettie needed someone to keep her company, so He got you together? Don't you think God does things like that?"

Gillian was still for a minute.

"Perhaps He does," she said, "but if He did He certainly used you to bring it about. You see, Mr. Remington, I've got so used to expecting hard things to come to us that I almost forgot God sometimes looks after people who need Him. Thank you for reminding me. And thank you too about this. I'll think it over, and I'll pray about it, and if it seems right I'll be thankful to do it. Will it be time enough if I tell you tomorrow morning? I can sometimes think things out better in the night."

"Yes, that will be time enough. Saturday morning. Aunt Ettie expects to come down with her furniture early next week, probably by Tuesday, and I think she would be ready for you in a day or two. The mover will set up the beds for her, and there won't be much else that has to be done for the first night or two. You and Noel can help her get settled little by little, and lie down between times whenever you get tired. You'll find she'll mother you a lot. She used to mother me. So I'm sure she'll be ready for you as soon as the doctor wants you to get up."

"Oh, that sounds wonderful!"

"Well, I'm sure it's the right thing for now, so why not put it out of your mind till you get ready to decide it definitely. And now, Noel, I want to talk to your sister a minute about some business I'm looking after for her, and I know it wouldn't interest you. How about it if you were to run out to the reception room a few minutes? I brought a little book along in my pocket that I'm sure you'll enjoy. There are a lot of pictures in it, and some picture words I think you could read if you tried hard. See what you can do with it, and when we get back to the hotel you can read it to me perhaps."

"Okay!" said Noel reluctantly but taking the little package and looking at it interestedly. He would have liked to stay with his two idols, but he was ever ready to obey.

"I'm going out too, Noel," said the nurse, "just for a few minutes. I think they're going to let me have a cot over on the other side of the room, so I can drop down now and then, and I was thinking you might like to take a nap on it sometimes when Mr. Remington wants to leave you here a few minutes. How about it, Noel?"

"Okay!" said Noel politely. He had no special interest in

naps, but he reflected it might make it possible for him to stay near Gillian more. So they left Reuben and Gillian alone briefly.

"Now," said Reuben, "we'll talk fast while they are gone. I don't suppose you want the nurse to know all your affairs, so I'll be careful to stop when she comes back."

"Thank you," said Gillian.

"Well, I have a friend who is a detective. I don't know whether I told you that or not. He lives in New York, so this will give no clue to anybody for trying to find you. I telephoned him and gave that uncle's name, and asked him to see what he could find out, and to make it absolutely confidential. I know I can trust him because our firm often employs him when they want to look up somebody and see what kind of credit they have. This morning he telegraphed me that he had a line on my case, and that I was to call him up at two o'clock this afternoon, that he wanted to ask me some questions. I hadn't given him the hotel address, only told him I would call him again when he wanted me. He sent that telegram to my old rooming house. You see, we're being very discreet, so that nothing can be traced. But I thought I had better come over and ask a few more questions that he might want to know, so I won't hold up the investigation any longer than necessary. I think it would be very good for you and all concerned if you know just how things stand before you leave here, don't you?"

"Oh, yes, if that could be possible."

"Well, I think it can. That is, I hope it can. Now, I must have all possible names and addresses, and approximate dates of when he was with you, how often, how continuously. Also dates, if you know any, when you are sure he drew money for your mother. In fact anything you think would be of interest in trying to find him, or to find out just what your Trust Company said to him, and so on. Of course the Trust Company cannot be approached yet, not till we know whether he has been trying to work something through them. It is just possible, you know, that that may all have been a lie about the money being gone. If that's so there may be a chance there is some left for you. If it was to have been paid in installments, he would not have been able to get it all at once. Do you have any idea how much there was?"

"No," said Gillian, "mother always spoke of it as 'our money' and I never thought much about it while she was living. I don't suppose it was a lot. We always had things rather nice, but mother was careful not to spend on unnecessary things. I don't really think there is any left. The Trust Company would have let me know, wouldn't they, if there was any?"

"Not if he was managing it so that you wouldn't get letters from the bank. And of course after you went away they wouldn't know where to find you. Did he stay in your house?"

"Why, yes, some of the time. Most all the time after mother was so sick. He could easily have looked over the mail before we saw it. I was too worried about mother to pay attention to anything else at the time."

"Yes," said Reuben. "Well, we'll have to look into all those things. If there is any of your money left, even if it is very little, *you* should have it, and not a lazy bad old man! Now, if you'll give me those dates, and names."

So Gillian's thoughts were turned entirely away from the seashore idea for a time while she remembered dates and addresses, and told as much as she knew.

"I think there are some papers in that tin box you brought yesterday," she said.

"Well, perhaps you've done enough for the present," said Reuben as he heard the nurse coming back. "Suppose this afternoon you look up those papers if the nurse can hand the box to you, and see if there is any evidence that would help us now. And now, I'll call Noel back, and we should be getting out for some lunch for I'm sure it's almost time for yours, and you must get some rest."

So Noel came back with his face radiant about the new book. He showed it to his sister, and read a whole line about a little white dog who had a bone and a saucer of milk, for all the big words were in pictures, and he was greatly intrigued that he could read the story of "Where Was The Little White Dog?"

So they said good bye and went away to their lunch.

"NOW," said Reuben when they got back to their hotel room, "we'll get lunch, and after that I think it would be a good idea for you to lie down on your bed and take a nice long nap while I write some letters and do some important telephoning. Do you think you can do that?"

"Oh, yes, I think I can," said the boy thoughtfully. "I'll just be remembering the pretty little walkings of those sandpipers on the edge of the ocean, with their cunning pink feet, and their sharp little bills picking up crabs. And I'll be remembering the soft song of the waves as they came lapping in against the sand. And I'll be seeing the pretty ships gliding along. Oh, yes, I think that will put me to sleep."

"Very well," said Reuben trying to conceal his astonishment and admiration over the little mind that could make real poetry out of a nap and a few memories. "If you'll do that, when you wake up I'll show you how to play a game I bought yesterday. Okay?"

"Okay!" said the child emphatically.

So they ate a nice lunch of sea trout and bread and butter, with ripe tomatoes for a relish, finishing off with orange gelatine and cream. Noel was much intrigued that the fish had come from the sea, and ate with gusto.

"Nice little fish!" he remarked as he finished the last bite. "Nice little fish, swimming along in the big big ocean, and tasting so good in a nice lunch for Reuben and Noel!" It was almost like listening to a song to hear him talk away about everything. It was evident he was very happy.

They went up to their room, and Noel took off his shoes, and his scrap of a linen coat, and hung it neatly over the back of the chair the way he saw Reuben do, and then he climbed onto his bed, gave a smile at Reuben, and settled down for his nap, talking softly to himself, with his back to the window and his eyes softly closed.

Reuben sat down at the desk and wrote his letters; telling Anise Glinden he thanked her for the invitation and would do his best to attend the play; accepting the invitation to the wedding and telling his old friend he would be delighted to be best man. Then he wrote the dates down in his little notebook, and reflected on how his calendar seemed to be shaping up for his vacation in such a different way from what he had planned.

There were two or three business letters that had to be answered, and then it was two o'clock, and Reuben called up his detective friend in New York.

Noel was sound asleep by this time, looking like a young seraph, his lips parted, his long lashes lying steadily on his cheeks that were beginning now to take a slight flush of health over their whiteness. Reuben began to feel a thrill of pride in him as he stood watching him to be sure he was asleep, not wishing to waken him by his telephoning. And now as he began to talk he kept a watch on him to be sure the sound did not disturb him. Also he didn't care to have Noel hear this conversation about the old uncle if he could help it.

So he kept his voice low and steady and monotonous, and Noel slept on serenely while the worldly affairs of his family were being discussed freely over the telephone.

At first there were only monosyllables for Reuben to answer with, yes, and no. Then there were dates to be established, places of residences. Reuben answered them all from the notes Gillian had given him in his brief interview with her.

"Now," said Ted, "I've found your man beyond question! He's living in an insignificant little town, a suburb of the city where the Guthries used to live, and not over twenty miles from that Trust Company. I've also established the fact that the Trust Company still is carrying in trust the estate of the Guthrie family. They *seem* not to be aware that Mrs. Guthrie has died. We have a man who was able to examine the records, and we find that the last dividends were paid to this Mason Albee only two weeks ago, and have been delivered to him from time to time when they came due, since ever he got the first installment, allegedly for his sister. They claim that he brings a note from her every time he comes, and that he says his sister is a hopeless invalid, unable to move from her bed. Can you give me the exact dates when the mother authorized him to draw her money for her, and when she died, where buried etc.? Do you wish us to go at this matter in a legal manner with a lawyer for the family? We can use a lawyer from the vicinity of the Trust Company if you wish, to prevent the man finding out where the young daughter is. But to answer your question concerning the money, it is still in care of the Trust Company, and we are sure from what we have found out so far, that it has *not* deteriorated, either recently or at any time since the death of Mr. Guthrie."

It was quite a long conversation and sometimes there were questions that Reuben could not answer, and had to jot down in shorthand to refer to Gillian, but when it was over, and a suitable arrangement made for further contacts, Reuben turned away from the telephone and felt that good progress had been made in this the most difficult task of all that he had to perform for his wards.

Reuben looked at his watch and then at the child. He was still asleep! But it was getting late, and if he were to keep his promise about that game and then get to the hospital afterwards in time for the doctor and Gillian, Noel ought to wake up. So he got up and began to walk around the room, making no effort to be quiet, and then he began to talk in an even

tone that would not startle the sleeper.

"I wonder where that boy is that was going to play a game with me?" he said in a matter-of-fact-tone. "I wonder, wonder, *wonder,* whether that boy is still asleep, talking to those waves and birds and ships? Noel! N-O-el! *Hi,* Noel! Ready for a game?"

Noel began to stir and then his eyes came open dazedly and at last briskly, wide awake.

"I did have a nice nap!" he said in a pleased sleepy tone.

Suddenly he saw Reuben getting out the game, a board with colored corners in the shape of stars, and little stopping places for the men, red and green and blue and yellow. Noel came up like a jack-in-the-box, and was out on the floor, padding over to the second chair which Reuben had placed for him on the opposite side of the small table he had drawn out, and soon Noel was deep in the mysteries of Chinese Checkers, a highly de luxe edition of the game, and proved himself an apt pupil playing with small accurate precision, and fingers that handled the men delicately.

"Oh, but this is *fun!"* said the child. "Sometime I'll teach my Gillian to play this! I could paint a board like this on paper with my crayons, and I could use little pebbles from the sand pile on the vacant lot at our corner, couldn't I?"

"Why, now, that's an idea! That's quite original! But you see you won't have to do that this time because this is *your* game. I bought it as a present for you, if you like it."

Noel looked at him in astonishment, growing slowly into delight.

"I do! Oh, I *do!"* he cried eagerly. Then suddenly he got down from his chair and came around to Reuben, looking up into his face with a lovely look.

"I think I would like to kiss you once, if you don't mind!" he said shyly, and Reuben with a sudden thrill of wonder, reached out and putting both arms around the child drew him close and kissed the sweet lips.

It came to the young man as he did it, that he could not remember ever having kissed a little child before, and it was a sweet thing.

"I thank you!" said Noel, and climbing up on his lap put his arms around Reuben's neck and gave him a hard hug.

"And now," said Reuben, when they came up for air, "how would you like to go out and pick out a flower or two to take to your sister?"

It was partly to cover the quick embarrassment that had come to the young man that he said this. It seemed to him a new emotion that he had never realized existed, to have these loving arms around his neck, in honest admiration. He held the little boy very close, and their faces were quite near together for the instant, as he watched the effect of his words on Noel. The child's eyes got large with wonder, and a smile beamed out that an angel might have worn.

"A *real* flower?" he asked wonderingly. "One of God's dear flowers?" and his face was full of radiant joy.

Reuben suddenly knew that he loved that boy, and with a quick fierce movement he caught the boy close to him and kissed him again, and then quickly arose, setting the child down.

"Yes, a real flower!" he said huskily, trying to get rid of the smarting sensation that came where tears start. How could it be that a five-year-old could be so stirred by the thought of a flower? And strangely the thought of Anise Glinden came, with her gorgeous orchids pinned carelessly to her coat. With her heritage of hot houses, and gardens of rare and exotic flowers. Could that pampered girl ever have looked like this child, even when she was only five, at the mere thought of a real flower? It probably had never occurred to Anise that God had anything to do with flowers. If she had been asked she might have answered, "Why no, the gardener raises the flowers!" Strange thought to have come to him!

So they went out to a florist's shop and bought a rose, a single white rose, for that was what the child's heart seemed to think was most fitting. And when they got to the hospital they made a regular little ceremony of presenting it. Reuben felt as if he were having a part in a play, and he felt sure it was a play much worthier of attention than the one he might have a chance of viewing a little later at Glindenwold.

The nurse bustled in presently and made another ceremony of finding a fitting vase for the gorgeous rose, and exclaimed over it heartily enough to please even Noel.

"And see!" she said, turning to Reuben, "we have another cot now," and she pointed to the opposite corner of the room, "and permission for this little brother to take a nap on it sometimes when you need to leave him here while you go on some errand where it isn't convenient to take him along."

"Fine!" said Reuben. "And I can testify that when this young man takes a nap he really takes a nap. I thought he had been having some rather strenuous days lately so I promised to play a game with him if he would really go to sleep a little while. And he went! He slept so soundly I had to wake him up for the game when I got my letters written."

"Well, isn't that a grand little sleeper!" said the nurse. "All right, we'll try you out tomorrow afternoon and see how well you can do here. And by the way, Noel, there's a dear old lady across the hall who has a broken hip and she has to lie still in bed for a long long time till it gets well. But she heard your voice the other day, and she said she'd so much like to see you. She has a little grandson out in California and she's homesick for him. I asked our doctor if I might take you over to see her a minute. She wants to show you her grandson's picture. Will you come with me now just for a few minutes while your sister talks business with Mr. Remington?"

Noel was not a bit interested in old ladies with broken hips and he would far rather have stayed and heard what Reuben had to tell Gillian. But Gillian gave him the kind of smile that showed she thought it would be polite of him to go, so with a tiny suppressed sigh, and a forced smile, he went with the nurse. He never had enjoyed having old ladies purr over him, but he took up his cross and went, carrying with him the picture of his beloved Gillian with his great white rose beside her on the little bedside stand, and a lovely earnestness in her face. It seemed almost as if she was a little bit hopeful about something. Maybe she was going to ask Reuben to let her go back to work Monday. Oh dear! Then all these nice times would likely be over. Maybe he would have to go back to that awful woman at the day nursery again. Of course Reuben had said that he shouldn't, but Reuben couldn't do anything about it when Gillian got up and went back to work, not if Gillian thought it was the right thing for him to do. And of course he mustn't worry Gillian. He drew a deep sigh of worry as the door opened into the room where the old lady with the broken hip lay waiting for them to come visit her.

But over in Gillian's room there was a quick conference going on.

"Well, they've traced your uncle. He's still living in the neighborhood of your old home; at least he's only about twenty miles away in quite a secluded place in the country, an old farmhouse, the detective said. Now don't look worried. He hasn't the slightest idea anybody is looking for him. It has all been done in a most secret and professional way, and so far they have only got surface facts. One thing they want to know is, was he married when he was with your people, and had he any children?"

Gillian puckered her brows thoughtfully.

"Why, I think he had been married but his wife was either divorced from him, or else she was dead. That was it. I think she was dead. Anyhow he had been seperated from her for some time before she died. No, there weren't any children. He didn't like children. He called them brats."

"Well, he seems to be married again. At least that was the information that was given our man. And when I questioned if he was well off, they seemed to think he had enough. Can you tell me if he had private funds of his own?"

"I don't think so," said Gillian. "Mother was greatly distressed because he was always wanting to borrow money of her, and the more she loaned him the more he asked for. Mother felt he was a kind of parasite, and that it wasn't right to lend to him, and yet he would put up a pitiful story, and she was so sick that she was not fit to cope with him. He was dreadfully mean, and would call her stingy and selfish and things like that, and say she had no love nor loyalty for her own kith and kin. But you know he *wasn't* her own kith and kin really, and he was a perfectly well strong man and quite fit to work for his living. It was a terrible shock for mother when he told her that her dividends were dwindling. That he had been advised at the bank that these were hard times, and everybody was suffering. Mother couldn't understand it, because father had told her that he had fixed things so that couldn't happen. And mother would have gotten right up out of bed and gone to the Trust Company to see about it, sick as she was, but when she tried it she had a bad fall, and one side of her was paralyzed for a few days. So she tried to send a letter by Uncle Mason, asking the man from the Trust Company to come out and talk with her. But Uncle came back and said they said they couldn't be bothered to come to see people. They said the man who was her husband's old friend was in the hospital and couldn't do anything about it himself. Perhaps when he got well she could see him. But mother got rapidly worse after that and never rallied. And it was just the next month after her death that Uncle told me the money was all gone! I always felt that mother's worry about the money had hastened her death."

Gillian brushed away the tears as she reached under her pillow for the little tin box which she brought out now.

"I've found some papers in the box that may help," she said eagerly, "although I don't understand them very well. See, one is a letter from my father to my mother, and in it he says that he has arranged things so we shall always have a steady income. That even if things depreciated, there would always be enough to keep us from want. I never saw this letter before, and from what I remember of my father I feel sure he would not have written a letter like that if he hadn't been quite sure what he said was true. Here is the letter. You read it and see what you think. And here are the papers. I think he calls them securities."

Reuben took the papers and went rapidly through them, hurrying that he might have more time to talk business before the nurse returned with Noel. When he had examined them all he looked up.

"Would you trust me with these papers for a day or two next week, Miss Guthrie? I would like my man to see them before he goes ahead. He will certainly be able to tell us whether there is still anything remaining from what your father had put in trust for you, and even if it were very little, that is worth trying for."

"Yes, of course," said Gillian rather drearily, "but truly I have so little confidence in that uncle of mine that I feel sure if there was a possible way, and a cent for him to gain, he has by now got possession of it."

"Well," said Reuben ruefully, "I'm afraid he has been cashing in on what is left every quarter. My detective gained the general idea that this man he has been studying has drawn out dividends right along since the first time he went with an order from your mother. By the way, is this uncle a good writer? Do you think by any chance he could forge your mother's name? The young man, a friend of our detective, who works in that bank, seemed to have the impression that 'the old gentleman,' as he called him, had brought a written order from your mother every time he drew out money, and that the checks were always countersigned by her. He seemed to feel that the bank did not know that she was not living. Your uncle had told them she was bedridden."

"Oh!" said Gillian, a frightened look passing over her delicate features. "How dreadful! I ought to have done something about this before. But I was afraid for what he might do to Noel. He was capable of going before the court and claiming him as his own or something, and then disposing of him. I think it was his idea that I should work, and he would handle my money. He wanted me to get in the movies, or learn to dance in a show, hoping I could make a good deal of money! Oh, what could I do?"

Her head was down, and her hands up to her face, and when she raised her eyes to ask him that question there were tears in them.

"Nothing," said Reuben, "but what you did! I guess that was the sensible thing then, and you wonderfully cared for that dear brother of yours. You're not to worry, because now we are going to look into this thing carefully and bring that man to justice if he has been stealing the money you had a right to have."

"Oh, but I'm afraid—afraid! You don't know my uncle. I—think—I've no proof of course—but I *think* he served a term in prison once when he was quite young, and I don't think he would stop at *any*thing. I am afraid to have you find out anything more about this. If he ever found out about it he wouldn't stop at anything. He would have revenge on us. He is very vengeful!"

"Now, you mustn't get excited about this, my dear," said Reuben earnestly, putting a kindly hand on hers. "This man will have no idea where either you or Noel are. I'll look after that, and if our suspicions are true, when we get ready to act I'll have one of the best lawyers in the country act from the standpoint of the bank, not as if *you* had anything at all to do with it, and we'll act so promptly that there will be no chance for him to hang around and look you up further, even if he were free, which I hope he won't be after we get through with him, for I feel that a criminal of that sort is not safe to have around anywhere. But, my friend, you simply must control your anxieties, or the doctor will put a quietus on all our plans, and order you to stay in this hospital indefinitely, and you don't want that, do you?"

"Oh, no!" said Gillian looking up and trying to smile through her tears. "You have been very good to me, and I do appreciate what you have done." She gave a warm little pressure to his hand that was folded comfortably about hers. And just then they heard the door across the hall opening, and Noel's clear little voice saying politely:

"Thank you! I've been very glad to come. And I hope you'll get a letter from your little boy-grandson very soon."

Reuben shoved his chair back a little, and took away his hand that held the girl's, and Gillian like a flash gave a quick mop across her eyes with her handkerchief, and put on a pleasant smile.

"And now," said Reuben, just as the door knob turned to let in the other two, "have you thought about that other matter? And how soon can you be ready to go, always providing the doctor will let you?"

"Yes," said Gillian with downcast eyes, and cheeks that glowed delicately with excitement, "yes, I've thought a great deal about it, and I think it will be wonderful of course, if you are perfectly sure it is the right thing for me to do."

"Yes," said Reuben gravely, "I do indeed. What do you think, nurse? Wouldn't it be a good thing for this young lady to spend two or three weeks visiting with a nice old lady in a pretty little cottage down at the seashore with her little brother, before she attempts to go back to the office to work?"

"Well, I should say that would be wonderful! Why of course that would be the best thing she could do. I suggested something like that yesterday to her, but she seemed to think she couldn't afford it, and I know of course it wouldn't be good for her to get in debt and go to worrying again. But *visiting!* That's different. Why that's like being handed the earth on a gold platter! Of course you'll go, my dear! And think what a few days at the shore would do for that child! You wouldn't know him after a few days at the shore!"

And then, just at the crucial moment, the doctor walked in and looking at his flushed patient with her dewy eyes, and at the wondering excited little boy with stars in his eyes, and at the smiling nurse, he said, frowning at Reuben:

"What's all this about? What right have all this mob coming into this room, giving the jitters to my star patient, and upsetting all my plans? Don't you know I'm trying my best to keep this girl here in this bed for, say, six months at the least? And here you are making her look like a person who never dreamed of being sick. What have you been doing, young man, answer me that?"

Reuben grinned.

"Why I was just suggesting that I had a nice old lady friend who has taken a cottage down at the shore, and she's looking around for a young woman who would be company for her, with a small boy thrown in. I just sort of thought these two friends of mine might be interested in such a proposition, but Miss Gillian here is trying to tell me that she is going to get up and go back to the office to work tomorrow, and as for the boy, she thinks he's got to stay in the hot city all summer!"

Reuben was grinning, but Noel stood there with his eyes big as saucers, staring in troubled uncertainty first at Gillian and then at Reuben, as if his Heaven was suddenly crumbling to dust and ashes.

The doctor frowned and then winked at Reuben.

"Well, in that case, perhaps I would change my verdict. How soon will that old lady be ready for the angry mob?"

"About Tuesday or Wednesday, if all goes well!"

"Very well, then I'll allow Miss Guthrie to get out of bed and sit up for fifteen minutes tomorrow, just to celebrate Sunday, and see how that goes. If her temperature stays right and her pulse doesn't cut up any capers she may stay up a half hour the next day, Monday. And then if she is still all right, why, she can go as soon as they are ready. How is she going? By automobile?"

"Yes," said Reuben quickly, although he had as yet no automobile, but he resolved to purchase one at once. For a long time he had meant to get one.

"You going to drive her down?" asked the doctor.

"Yes," said Reuben with great satisfaction, and a smile of triumph on his face.

"Very well, if she behaves well from now on she may go as soon as the old lady has her bed ready for her, and a good meal in the getting."

Then the doctor went into his professional manner, and Reuben took Noel and departed.

"Reuben," said Noel as they went down in the elevator, "what will I do while you take my Gillian to the seashore?"

"Do?" said Reuben. "Why, you will go along with us."

"*Will* I? In a real automobile that isn't a taxi?"

"Yes," said Reuben. "Will you like that?"

"Oh, I will like that!" said the child. "And where are we going now, Reuben?"

"To find the automobile," said Reuben, and he almost looked like an excited child himself.

IT wasn't the first car that Reuben had owned, but since he had come to the east to live a car had not seemed a necessity. He had been working early and late, and had not many friends in this part of the country yet. He had been concentrating on getting a hold in the business world, and saving his money for a time when he should know just what he wanted to do most. He had reasoned that if he were going west for his vacation he certainly wouldn't want a car during his absence, as his plan had been to go by train, but now all was changed, and as he looked at the cars he wondered how he had got along so long without one.

They went out to try the car, and Noel was greatly intrigued to see him driving. When they got back to the hotel Noel sighed deeply that they were getting out.

"Won't the man let us have the car?" he asked anxiously.

"Oh, yes, he's going to bring it over Monday morning. There are one or two little things I wanted him to change, but he's bringing it in plenty of time for us to take your sister down to the shore. And you mustn't let Gillian think I bought the car just for this, you know. I have been meaning to get a new one soon, only I didn't have any time to see about it. So you'd better not tell her anything about it just now. It seems to make her worry if she thinks anybody takes any trouble for her, and we don't want her to get any such idea, you know."

"Of course not," said the wise child with a twinkly little confidential smile, that showed he understood.

They played several games that evening after supper, and when Noel finally got to bed he lay there thinking.

"My Gillian said this was Saturday night," he remarked thoughtfully. "Where do we go to church tomorrow? Is there a church over here somewhere?"

"Church?" said Reuben. "Oh, yes, *church!* Why of course! There are churches all over. Would you like to go to church?"

"Yes, I like to go to church, don't you? But I don't want to go if it isn't convenient for you. Do you have to do some work on Sunday?"

"Why no, of course not," said Reuben, rising quickly to what was expected of him. "Certainly we'll go to church. Is there some special church you know about that you would like to go to?"

"No," said Noel with a sigh. "We didn't have any regular church yet. Gillian and I tried a lot of them, but they all seemed kind of lonesome churches. Gillian said it was the same God-our-Father in them all, only some of the people didn't act as if they loved Him much. Once a nice man gave us a hymn book to sing out of, and smiled at me."

"Yes, I see," said Reuben, thinking back over the churches he knew. For Reuben had been brought up to go to church too, though he had rather got out of the habit since his mother died. It seemed that it always brought back thoughts of her, and how she used to be sitting there beside him in the old days at home. But he was instantly conscious that this child must go to church since it seemed to mean so much to him.

He tried to think over the churches he knew in the city, wondering where there would be one that wouldn't seem lonesome to the boy, and found he really knew so little about churches here that it would have to be an experiment, wherever they went. But they would go somewhere. He didn't want this child, nor his sister, to think him a heathen. In fact he had always meant to begin to go again somewhere when he got time and a few contacts that would make church a place congenial.

"That will be nice," said Noel. "Of course it isn't really lonesome where God is, even if we don't know the people. That's what Gillian says."

"No, of course not," affirmed Reuben heartily, feeling the inner rebuke. Here he had just been thinking about congenial contacts to make a church less lonely, and now as often since he had known this child he felt rebuked. The little boy had made Reuben feel that God wasn't really Reuben's friend, hard as his mother had prayed for him, and tried to teach him how to know God. He knew at once that here was something about himself that ought to be readjusted. It suddenly came to him like a vivid picture, those last hours by his mother's bedside, when she had made him promise to live a Christian life, and be ready to meet her in Heaven. She evidently believed firmly that he was "saved" as she used to call it. And he had promised eagerly and earnestly, fully intending to keep that promise, only life and its readjustments had come in and taken all his time and thoughts. Yes, here was something he must look after right away. It was curious how many things seemed to be brought to his attention since he had picked up this girl and her little brother!

"I like Sunday," mused the little boy. "Gillian doesn't have to go to the office, and I don't have to go to the day nursery, and we go out in the morning to church, and then in the afternoon we have Sunday School. After that if it's not too stormy we take a walk. Sometimes we take it anyway, with a raincoat and rubbers. I have a raincoat you know. Only my raincoat sort of leaks, and my rubbers are getting too tight. But they'll still go on. And perhaps by and by we can get some more. But I like Sunday. It's the best day there is."

He gave a bit of a sigh, and then he asked:

"Do you know how to make a Sunday School?"

"Why I used to go to Sunday School when I was a little

boy like you. I guess I could manage one if you would tell me when I make mistakes."

"That's nice!" said Noel with another little sigh of relief. "I was afraid you might not know, and I like Sunday School. Do you know any Bible verses?"

"Oh I think so. I used to know a lot of them."

The boy's eyes shone happily.

"You know about almost everything, don't you? Prayers and automobiles, and Bible verses, and the ocean. I guess you know a lot more than most men."

"Well, I don't know about that," said Reuben with a grin. "Now, how about your going to sleep? I've got to do some telephoning and letter writing."

So Noel went to sleep and Reuben went to work, but in the back of his mind he was trying to remember a Bible verse or two out of his Primary days, so that he wouldn't lose prestige with his young ward. And that night when the lights were out he spent some time on his knees on his own account.

The report from Ted the detective was that Mason Albee had taken a trip east, and was being shadowed from time to time to keep track of him. Reuben was a little uneasy over this. Suppose he should turn up somewhere and see Noel, or get on the track of Gillian? Although he couldn't see how that was possible, little as he must know of her movements, unless he had himself employed a detective. He resolved to be very careful and not let Noel out of his sight at all.

The report from the agent at the shore was that the cottage would be ready for occupancy Tuesday morning. The electricity was already in except for a few fixtures which would be set on Monday, the water would be turned on, and everything ready.

Then Reuben called up Aunt Ettie again.

"There! I thought that would be you, you spendthrift!" was her greeting. "Didn't I tell you to lay off that telephoning? Now, what's the matter? Has the girl backed out?"

"No, it's all right," said Reuben grinning at the familiar address of the old nurse. "I just want to know when you are likely to get started, so I can plan to bring down your two companions. The doctor seemed to think Miss Guthrie would be able to go early this week, and the agent says the house will be ready Tuesday morning. When will you be ready for your guests?"

"Well, we plan to get going right early Monday morning. If Ames gets the man he had track of to look after his cows. So, we'll likely stop over night at Ames' sister's house, and then go on early Tuesday morning. He thinks we ought to get to your seashore around noon on Tuesday. He wants ta unload, and get back ta his sister's fer the night so he can get home next day to his farm work, and a lot of trucking he has the balance of the week. Is that all right? I figure we can get the beds all up and make 'em, and fix a place ta eat that night, so you can bring your mob down Wednesday if you like. I'll be ready fer 'em. And I think you better stick around till I see if I can stomach that girl. I might havta make you take her back, if she's one of these up-in-the-air kind."

"Oh, but she's not!" said Reuben firmly.

"You wouldn't know!" said Aunt Ettie promptly. "I'll havta see her meself."

Then he got to thinking of Agnes. He had accepted the invitation to the wedding, and written the groom, but he hadn't answered Agnes' letter yet. How was he going to write Agnes? Like the old friend he used to be? Did he want to go back on that same footing? Of course he was only a kid then, just out of high school, and Agnes and he had been awfully good friends. Why, Agnes had asked him to kiss her good bye when he left the old home place. She had said she would never think as much of any boy again as she did of him, and he, poor fool, had told her he didn't think he would ever find another girl that he liked as well as he did her. She was pretty and vivacious. She had sparkling black eyes and black curly hair that was always done in the most tricky way. And her eyes could speak volumes, which her assumed shyness would not allow voice. At least that was how it seemed to him now as he went back over his former friendship with her.

His mother had never quite liked Agnes. She had told him

that Agnes was too sophisticated and she wished he would find a girl who was not so forward, and always ready to take the front of the stage. But he hadn't ever seen that in her. She had seemed a sweet shy girl to him, very real and genuine, very ready to do anything to please and have a good time. He wondered, had his mother merely been over-anxious that he should have the best in friends as well as in all other things. Or would she have been jealous of any girl upon whom his fancy rested? Perhaps that was it. His mother hadn't really known Agnes. Agnes belonged to an ultra-fashionable set, and his little quiet mother had never been intimate with that sort. She did not play bridge, and was never a club woman. She loved her home, and her painting, and her sewing. She delighted in literature, in reading good books and magazines, she longed for her son to be a scholar, like his father, to have fine standards, and a wide outlook on life, to admire genuine things, and not be deceived by glamour and glitter.

And in the long run Reuben felt that he agreed with his mother on what he wanted to become. But he was just a little uncertain whether his mother, if she had really known Agnes, would not have counted her real.

He remembered the look in Agnes' eyes when she had said good bye, the feel of her face against his when he had shyly kissed her, the soft lips, the yielded pressure in his arms. He hadn't been in love with her then, he was sure, but he had been intrigued by her. He had felt as if this might be merely the beginning of something that in the far future might materialize. Yet he had been content to leave her, when he went away to college, and later to study abroad for a while, and he had not cared to go back to the old home town on his return. In fact he rather shrank from going because both father and mother were gone, and the thought of Agnes had not been enough to draw him back. At least not just then. And so he had taken this most promising position in the Glinden firm, and dreamily sometimes thought of how the day would perhaps come when he would go back, a successful business man, and see Agnes again, maybe to find her all the more charming.

But now as he thought over her pleasant letter with its flattering persuasion to come to the wedding, his heart quickened a little at thought of her.

He was in a position now to go to her and renew the old acquaintance. He would have something to offer her now, if he still found her desirable. And it would be good to see her again, and catch up the broken threads of life. To go again with the girl he had fancied as a school boy.

So Reuben wrote to Agnes, but in spite of him as he wrote formality crept into the penned words:

> Dear Agnes:
>
> How pleasant of you to add your word and your urgency to the wedding invitation. And I am going to do my best to come, although I had made other plans for my vacation, and this comes right in the middle of it. I had intended going to the far west for a few weeks, but now this invitation has come I cannot forbear accepting it and meeting all my old friends once more.
>
> It doesn't seem so long, does it, since we all separated at commencement and went our different ways? I can scarcely believe that your little sister Rose Elizabeth has grown old enough to be married. It is certainly going to be exciting meeting you all again, and finding out what has happened to each one of us.
>
> So I thank you for adding your voice of persuasion to the invitation Frank sent and I shall surely plan to be present.
>
> I am greatly anticipating seeing you once more, and renewing our old acquaintance.

His pen paused and he was about to finish with "Yours as ever," and then he changed his mind. Was he really "as ever" to her? He didn't know. He tried to think of her sanely and coolly, and recall her vivacious face, but every time he did there came the sweet little quiet face of Gillian, framed in soft brown hair that rippled away from her delicate features, and Agnes' face wasn't at all like Gillian's. No, he had been away from Agnes too long to sign himself "Yours as ever," he decided. Then hastily he finished, "Sincerely," signed his name and let it go at that. What he had written was certainly sincere, and yet committed him to nothing, and that was the best way to have it. Why, Agnes might have changed greatly. She might be engaged to someone else. It didn't matter. He was "Sincerely," and he could take whatever relationship he chose when he saw her. At least he could do this much for the memory of his mother's anxiety.

And the more he thought about it the more he was convinced that he had taken the right attitude after such a long absence. And besides, there was Anise Glinden! And then he laughed aloud. Anise might be interested to make him perform a part in her play, to flirt with him for a little while, and throw her wiles about him, but he had no desire to have any permanent attachment to Anise, and he was quite sure she herself would try to look far higher in the social world, than to a junior employee of her father's.

But then he wasn't considering marriage with either of these girls. He had definitely decided long ago that he must reach a certain point in his worldly climb before he wanted to be tied up by marriage. Well, it would be time enough to decide when he got to the old home town, had a chance to talk with Agnes, and see if she had the same power over him that he used to think she had.

So he turned his thoughts to business in the immediate present, wrote a few more letters, jotted down notes of things he wanted to do, and finally went to bed. But there was a distinct anticipation in his mind as he thought of that wedding invitation. As he drifted off to sleep he tried again to think how Agnes would look and how they would meet. And yet before he knew it he was planning about taking Gillian to the shore, trying to arrange the minutest details so that the journey would not tire her. He was thinking out how he ought to do his own packing, and how to get wedding things ready in time. He must decide whether to take Noel with him to his rooming house when he went to get his own wardrobe, and what garments he would leave in a packed suitcase ready to pick up before he went to the wedding. He felt he must plan to stay a few days at the shore to be sure that Gillian and Noel were safe and happy with Aunt Ettie, and be sure that Aunt Ettie was happy and satisfied with the two he was leaving in her charge, before he went away. Those matters must be adjusted or he was certain he would have no enjoyment out of his vacation no matter how he spent it. He didn't want to be thinking of Gillian taking Noel and running away again. He didn't want to have to get a detective to hunt her up when he returned. He was determined that the lives of these two whom he had been trying to help must run along smoothly from now on.

So at last he fell asleep, and awoke to hear distant early bells chiming from far steeples, and to realize that this was Sunday and he was expected to "make" a Sunday School today. It seemed an appalling obligation, but he found there was a new eagerness in his heart over it.

Then, there came the memory of Ted's word about that Uncle Mason who had gone east. Would that old reprobate turn up and make trouble? Was it possible that he might come while he was away at that wedding? Because if he thought that possible he wouldn't go at all. It would be terrible for Gillian to be frightened again in that way. He must try to get this business hurried up and the old criminal in jail safely before he left his charges.

But Noel awoke joyously. He awoke singing. At least he was so still that Reuben thought him still asleep until he heard that sweet little voice singing old long-forgotten words:

Safely through another week,
God has brought us on our way!
Let us now a blessing seek
Waiting in His courts today!
Day of all the week the best,
Emblem of eternal rest!

Reuben looked over at the little smiling face:

"That's what my Gillian and I sing every Sunday morning!" said Noel. "Do you know that song?"

"Why, yes," said Reuben, strangely stirred by sweet memories. "My mother and I used to sing that together when I was a little boy."

"Oh, that's nice! Let's you and me sing it together now," and Noel's clear soprano piped up again, Reuben trailing along with a low growl quite creditably.

That was a strangely happy day for the young man, almost as if he were put back a number of years into his own childhood days. Perhaps the angels guided them to the right church, where the gospel was preached simply and clearly. His heart was stirred to realize how long he had wandered from the way his mother had brought him up. Condemned he sat and listened, with the small boy's hand nestled in his, and felt as if God were there looking into his heart. It wasn't that he had done great wrong. He knew that outwardly he kept the law, and stood for that which was right. But in this sweet quiet atmosphere where he could feel the presence of God, he realized that he had walked far away from God. It wasn't as if he hadn't known the way of life since babyhood. But he hadn't realized till now how far he had gotten from the things that make for joy and peace in this world.

So he didn't merely sit there and let his mind wander all over next week making plans. He really listened, and there was a sweet seriousness upon him as the service closed and they went out. The young minister grasped his hand and said, "Let me welcome you. I wish you would come again." And Reuben responded heartily, "Thank you, I will. Your sermon helped me."

Noel was content, feeling that a real Sunday had begun in the right way.

They went to the hospital as soon as they had finished the delightful chicken dinner and ice cream that their hotel served, and found Gillian eager for their coming. She was sitting up in a big chair, with a blue kimono about her, and her eyes so very blue that Reuben was startled. It seemed they had caught the color from the garment she wore. Reuben thought to himself, "Why, she's beautiful! She's like her little brother!" and he looked in wonder from one of them to the other.

When the nurse went out of the room for a moment Gillian handed over an envelope. Quite casually, so that Noel who was examining the pictures in a magazine belonging to the nurse did not notice.

"I found this envelope in the box," she said. "It has some papers, and a photograph of that uncle I was telling you about, though he is only in the background. The picture was taken of mother and Noel, but he stood there. I thought it might help in identification. There is also a copy of my mother's signature."

"God!" said Reuben. "That will all help of course. I'll take good care of these."

And then Noel came over to stand beside Gillian, and they spoke of other things. Of the cottage by the sea, and the kindly Aunt Ettie whom he hoped they would both like. Reuben told some little incidents of his remembered childhood when Aunt Ettie was a part of his home life.

Then the nurse came in asking Noel to go across the hall and see the old lady again who had a little basket she wanted to give him, so Noel with a shy smile followed her, and then Reuben and Gillian were able to talk again about the business in hand without fear of worrying the sensitive child.

Soon after Noel and the nurse returned the doctor arrived, looked critically at the invalid, touched her pulse, smiled.

"So, little lady, you're sitting up! How long have you been sitting up?"

"The time is almost up, doctor," said the nurse, "five minutes yet."

"Well, well, you're standing it pretty well? How do you feel?"

After the doctor was gone, the nurse said it was time to get her patient back into bed.

"And if you want to leave the boy here awhile he can take a nap over on the cot."

Noel looked up at Reuben with a smile of hesitation.

"But we have to have Sunday School yet," he said in a low tone to his sister.

"That will be all right, Noel," said Reuben reassuringly. "I'll be back in plenty of time for that."

"But really, Mr. Remington, you mustn't feel yourself burdened with everything Noel asks you to do," said Gillian quickly. "Mr. Remington has other things to do, darling," she added, turning to the child.

"He said he would like to," explained the little boy with disappointment in his eyes.

"Why, certainly I would like to," said Reuben. "I'll be back in an hour and a half at the longest. Will that be too long, nurse? All right, Noel. Here! Can you tell time by the clock?"

"Oh yes," said Noel.

"Very well, then, when the hands on that clock over there on the bureau point to half past three, you can watch for the sound of my footsteps. Will that be in time for your Sunday School? It may be later than some Sunday Schools of course, but since it's *our* school we can have it when we like, can't we?"

"Oh yes! That will be nice. And then I can stay with my sister all that time?" asked Noel.

"Yes, if the nurse says so. She will tell you if she wants you to go into the little reception room for a few minutes, but you'll be all right."

"Yes, I will be all right!" and he waved his small hand in parting.

So Reuben went out to his rooming house to get a few things that he needed, and Noel retired to the cot in the corner and obediently closed his eyes.

And about that time in a distant city, an elderly man with a gay-Lothario air about him, and an uncanny eye, boarded a through train for the east. He gave a quick keen look about him as he swung up the steps, to make sure no one was especially watching him.

The reason for this hasty journey was that when he had gone to the Trust Company where he had been for several years cashing coupons for a supposedly "invalid" sister, they had mentioned that the sister had a daughter who would come of age in a few weeks now, and that it would be well for her to appear in person and go through certain formalities before she could be entitled to receive funds to which she would fall heir. They had asked the uncle to bring her in at once and get the matter over, but he had told them that she was away on a long visit in the far west. He had looked in vain for her in regions round about and to the west, and now the time was getting short. The date of her coming of age was near at hand. He must do something about it.

They had tried to find out her address, and had said they would write her themselves, but he had narrowed his sly eyes, and given his disarming smile and said she was traveling, and he didn't know just where she was going next. He had promised to try and get in touch with her at once, and perhaps bring her with him when he came again, and then he had gone his nonchalant way with the booty he had acquired again so easily. If that girl didn't turn up pretty soon he wouldn't dare to go back, not unless he could think of another good story to tell. Was there some way he could work it to say that she had been killed in an automobile smash up? Or he might say that she had gone abroad as a Red Cross nurse in the war, and was reported missing. Oh, there would surely be a way if he got busy and really thought about it. But of course the best way was to find her and extract from her somehow a letter to the Trust Company, or maybe force her to go with him and get the first payment on her own money. Then he could forge a note from her perhaps, ordering them to pay her money to him. Somehow he could work it, he was sure. But he must know where she was. Just last night a boy who used to bring milk to the house when he was living with the Guthries, before Mrs. Guthrie died, had told him in answer to his questioning, that he had seen Gillian and the boy boarding a midnight train for the east soon after Mrs. Guthrie had died. Careful enquiry at the railroad station had given him an idea about how far that fifty dollars would have carried the two. So he decided to go east and hunt her. He really didn't want to get in with the police again, and have them enquiring into his affairs. He didn't care to go to jail again. He was getting on well now, had a nice home and a smart wife. No use in risking any trouble. He'd better find the girl and scare her so badly she wouldn't ever dare to bother him again. And if he could work it to get her share of the money her father had left, so much the better. She was young and strong and could work, and he was getting on now in years and it was fair that he should have a little comfort in life.

So he crawled into his comfortable berth in the sleeper, lay down to his crooked plans, and was carried on toward the two young things who were haunted day and night by his memory.

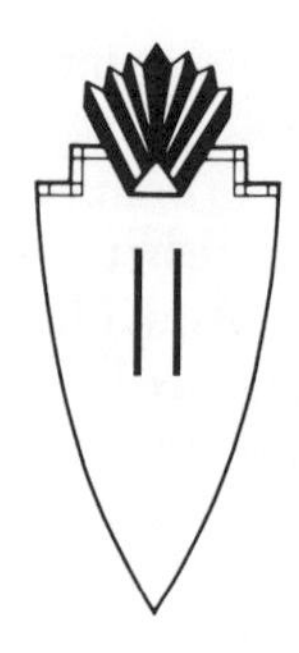

REUBEN made a quick trip to his room, got a suitcase full of the things he would need for the trip down to the shore with the Guthries, packed another bag with things he would likely need if he went to Glindenwold for that play, and got still a third group of necessities he would want to have ready to be picked up when he came through the city on his way to that wedding.

After all it didn't take long, and his mind could be at rest that he could easily prepare in a few minutes for any of the trips he contemplated.

He felt strangely averse to bringing Noel into the picture here at his rooming house for the present, to set gossips' tongues wagging. All sorts of stories could grow up in a place like this from a very small nucleus, and he didn't want Gillian the subject of any such surmises, nor did he care to be talked about himself. Gillian would hate to have it bandied about in the office that she had been under the special supervision of one high in the graces of the firm. So he went in a taxi, and saw no one but his landlady, who handed him some mail, and asked if he was having a pleasant vacation. He assured her that he was, and said he would probably be back in a few days and stop to leave laundry and to get another suitcase.

He arrived back at the hospital a little before the hour he had set for Noel to watch for him, and was rewarded by a radiant smile.

"He did come back, Gillian!" he said jubilantly. "He always does what he says he will!"

"That's a pretty big contract for me to live up to, young man!" said Reuben with a grin. "How about yourself? Did you take a nap?"

"Yes sir, I did!" said the little boy. *"Didn't* I been, Gillian?"

"Yes, he had a good nap, and so did I," responded the sister. "It was so good to have him back, and know just where he was!"

"Poor child!" said Reuben sympathetically. "This must all have been very hard for you. But I hope things are going to be better now. I'm sorry I have to take him away from you tonight. But you'll have to remember that your loss is my gain. I'm really getting a great deal from the companionship of your small brother and I shall always be thankful that it fell to my lot to take you to the hospital."

"Well, so shall I," said Gillian shyly. "I don't believe there are many young men who would have been good enough to take over a small boy and do for him as you have done. It's been wonderful!"

"Now don't start throwing bouquets, or I shall have to say a lot of things about what I think you've been, to do what you have done, for a good deal longer than I have served."

"Yes, but he was my own. All I had left in the world, and he was just nothing to you but a little stranger who hadn't a claim in the world on you!"

"Oh, you're mistaken there!" said Reuben suddenly serious. "You forget that he is one of God's children. I'll own I had very nearly forgotten God's claim on me, but he promptly made the presence of God in my life very much more real to me than it ever was before."

His tone was very solemn as he said it, and brought tears to the eyes of the sister.

"Oh, I'm glad you told me that!" she said shyly, "because

I know from my own experience that that is the only worth-while thing there is in life, when the ordinary joys are taken away."

"Yes, I guess you're right," said Reuben diffidently. This kind of talk was entirely new to him, and he felt very shy about it.

"Come, come, come!" said the nurse breezing in suddenly. "It's high time this little lady was tucked up in her beddy-bye. Time for you two good people to be going home. And don't come too early in the morning, either. She needs to have a longer rest after all this excitement."

So they went back to the hotel and had Sunday School.

Noel's knowledge of music was a strange combination of sweet old hymns, and stirring choruses, and many of them were out of Reuben's knowledge. He had heard the old hymns in his childhood and could remember several verses of some of them while the tunes seemed inwrought in his early life. But the modern choruses he had scarcely heard, and Noel had the pleasure of teaching some of them to him. It was remarkable how truly interesting it was to hear the sweet boy-soprano piping out solemn words joyously, as if he meant them.

There is a song in my heart today,
Something I never had:
Jesus has taken my sins away,
O say but I'm glad.
O say, but I'm glad, I'm glad,
O say, but I'm glad;
Jesus has come and my cup's overrun,
O say, but I'm glad.

"Now you sing it," said Noel.

So Reuben tried to several times, and at last they succeeded in singing it together to Noel's satisfaction.

"Don't you like that song?" asked the boy with a bright look.

"Yes, it's a nice song," said Reuben, "but I was wondering if you understand what it all means?"

"Oh, yes, I understand it. My Gillian always tells me all about a new song before we learn it. Don't you know what it means?"

"Why, yes, I think I do, but I'd like to hear you explain it. What do you think that means, 'something I never had'?"

"Oh, why that means you've just found out that Jesus loves you and is your Saviour and you're glad because Jesus has forgiven your sins. He took all our sins on Himself you know, just as if He had sinned them, only He never did sin, you know. And He took them just as if they were His, and then He bore the punishment that ought to have been mine because I'd done the sinning."

Reuben smiled amusedly.

"But what do you know about sinning?" he said. "A child like you! You have no sin in you."

"Oh yes, I have," said the child earnestly. "Don't you know the Bible says 'All have sinned and come short of the glory of God'? That's one of the first verses I ever learned, and Gillian told me all about Adam and Eve in the garden, and how they broke the only command God had given them, and He had told them if they did, that death would come into the world, to them and to their children, and everybody has had sin in them since then because their fathers and mothers were sinners, so *everybody* had to be punished."

"But what do you call sin? I don't believe you've ever stolen or killed anybody, or even told lies."

"Oh, those things aren't all He meant by sin. The very worst thing of all, the thing that makes people sin, is that they do not believe God."

"Believe God?" queried Reuben perplexed. These great truths from the mouth of a mere babe were perplexing!

"Why yes, believe that Jesus is God, and that He died in your place, and believe that He's your own Saviour. Because it wouldn't make any difference how much Jesus died for us, if we didn't *take* Him. It wouldn't do us any good, you know.

Like as if when you bought that picture book for me and gave it to me, then I had laid it down on the counter as if I didn't care anything about it and went off and left it. It wouldn't do me any good."

"I see," said Reuben, his eyes suddenly sober, startled that even a child could teach a great truth like that.

Then Noel suddenly looked at him with a troubled gaze.

"Don't you believe that?" he asked in a worried voice. "Aren't you saved? Didn't you take Him for your Saviour the way Gillian and I did?"

Reuben was suddenly embarrassed.

"Oh, why, yes, I *think* I did, I'm sure I did when I was a little boy, only I haven't been walking very close to Him lately. But yes, I *believe."*

Noel gave a sigh of relief.

"That's nice," he said happily, "I'm glad you're saved. I wouldn't like to think that perhaps you wouldn't be in Heaven when we get there. Now, let's sing another song. Let's sing 'Step by Step.' "

So Noel said over the words, and Reuben jotted them down in shorthand, and then together they sang, Noel's voice leading.

Step by step I'll follow Jesus,
Hour by hour I'm in His care,
Day by day He walks beside me,
Through the years I'll know He's there.
He can still the mighty tempest,
He can calm the troubled sea,
He the waters trod, He's the Son of God,
He's the One who always walks with me.

They had a brief closing prayer time, and then the session was declared over for the day. Reuben lifted up his head and found a mistiness in his eyes. He felt God had been there in the room, and stood close beside that little boy who was leading him in a new-old way that his mother had taught him years ago, and his heart went out to the child with a thrill of real love. He felt like thanking God that He had sent this little child to abide with him for a few days and call his thoughts back to a way that had been his in the past. Surely it must be that God had arranged things this way, that his vacation which had been planned in such a different way had gone all awry, just that he might get into close with God once more. Was that it?

And when later the boy lay in the bed beside him, his young sweet breath wafting softly, regularly, Reuben began to think about what the child had said, and to wonder if he himself was really "saved," or had he only accepted a form as a child, and nothing more? And suddenly he found his heart going out in longing to be sure it was real. "Oh Lord," he cried in his heart, "if it didn't mean anything before, You know it does now! I take Jesus Christ as my Saviour *now!*"

He knew better than to expect any great feeling of exaltation. His mother had taught him better than that. But he did feel that God had really spoken to him through that little boy, and he was conscious of an inner quietness and rest.

Then he got to thinking about that girl Agnes. She used to be active in Sunday School and church affairs. He could remember her serving at the table one night when there was a young people's banquet in the church. He remembered how pretty she looked, wearing a bright scarlet dress, with a trifling scrap of a white apron, and her cheeks scarlet like her dress. Yes, hadn't she taken some part in a meeting they had once? It seemed to him he could remember her standing up before a crowd reading a little item of missionary news. He couldn't remember what the item had been, but he did remember Agnes had a new hat with a wreath of tiny rosebuds around it and a broad floppy brim, and how charming her face looked beneath it. Yes, she had definitely been identified with the church's religious activities, though somehow he couldn't remember that he and she had ever talked about such things, as this small boy had been discussing with him, as if he loved it.

This sister, Gillian, must be quite unusual to have taught a mere baby what sounded to him like theological doctrines.

Then suddenly the problems of the sister took possession of his mind, and he began to plan what he would do in the morning to get in touch with that detective and find out just what had been done, and whether there was any danger that that old reprobate of an uncle might possibly appear on the scene and make trouble. It might be a good thing to get Dewitt, the company lawyer, in readiness to take over the matter if it should suddenly require expert service. Perhaps he would call him on the telephone, or still better, perhaps he might be coming down from New York on Company business, and he could get a few minutes with him.

And so, planning a campaign for the next day, Reuben soon fell asleep.

The next two days were filled with business. Twice he had to leave Noel with the patient and nurse while he went hither and yon to interview men who could advise him what to do about Gillian's inheritance, and just what would be the best and most lawful way to go about it for her.

Meantime Gillian was having perplexities of her own. The problem of her wardrobe suddenly appeared to her as something important when the nurse remarked Tuesday morning that she was going out shopping for a couple of hours that afternoon, was there anything that her patient would like her to get?

Then the paucity of her meagre outfit came sharply to mind.

"You know you're going to the shore, and you can't get along very well on just one dress and a kimono and a handful of underwear."

She might have called it a "handful of *badly-worn* underwear," but she stopped just short of that. Still the idea got across to Gillian's distraught thoughts.

"Oh, I oughtn't to go!" said Gillian in despair. "I knew from the first that it was a crazy idea. I really shouldn't have said I'd go. But of course, they've been so kind, perhaps I could get along for a couple of days with one dress, and I really didn't mean to stay longer than that!"

"Nonsense!" said the nurse quite vexed at herself for having brought up the subject. "You'll get along nicely all right on one good dress. Don't get that notion. When you think what wonders the sea air is going to do for you both! You don't need to think of clothes. But if it'll make you feel any more comfortable I could go to your rooming house and get some of your other things for you."

A scared flush came to Gillian's face, that died away quickly and left her very white.

"No, thank you," she said with a sigh. "There isn't much there either. I was running rather low because I was paying off debts after our mother died. But I've a little bit of money now and I can buy what I really need when I get out again. I think I'll make out. I think perhaps Mr. Remington may be going near my rooming house tomorrow, and he can take Noel. I'll tell Noel a few things to get for me. I've my coat and dress and that will be all I need for just a short time. There's a little cotton house dress too, that will help out if it gets hot. It will do to work in."

"Work!" sniffed the nurse. "If that woman you're supposed to be going to visit lets you work much she'll not be worth visiting! I'd like to go along and just tell her a few things about you, but I suppose I'd not be allowed to."

Gillian laughed.

"You're very kind, but I think I'll make out, and you know it's going to be wonderful just to get a glimpse of the sea."

"Yes, of course," agreed the nurse, pursing her lips. "I just asked in case there might be something you were worrying about and wouldn't know how to get. But I'm sure you'd get by anywhere. You're good-looking and that makes a big difference."

"Good-looking!" exclaimed Gillain, and burst into laughter. "I'm certainly not good-looking. I'm too thin and too dark under my eyes. I used to be a cute little girl I guess, but that's long ago. I've had too many things to worry about to be good-looking, even if I was in the beginning."

"Well, you've got the makings of good looks all right," said the nurse, firmly. "Give you good food and good fresh air for a while, and a nice long rest, you could stand up with anybody for good looks. Well, you think about it and if you think of anything you'd like me to get for you I'll be glad to do my best, and of course anything you get nowadays you can always return if you decide you don't like it."

"Thank you," said Gillian quietly, "I don't think I'll need anything more just now."

The nurse went on her way while Gillian was eating her lunch, having taken careful note of the general size of her patient's garments, and when she returned Gillian was asleep. Reuben and Noel had gone on errands, and she was storing up strength for the journey on the morrow, trying to forget such unhappy things as scant wardrobes.

But the nurse was a bit noisy stirring around the room, and presently Gillian opened her eyes and smiled.

"You all right?" asked the nurse.

"Oh yes," said Gillian. "Fine! I think I slept most of the time you were gone. Did you have a pleasant time?"

"Yes, I did!" said the nurse. "I found some lovely bargains. Would you like to see what I got?"

"Why yes, that would be lovely!" said Gillian politely. "I haven't been shopping in so long that I haven't any idea what is being worn now. It will be fine to see a fashion show."

"Oh, this isn't much of a fashion show," laughed the nurse, "just plain little things. You know this time of year there are lots of summer things going for a song, and I came on some lovely things. At least I thought they were. You see I have a young niece who rather depends on me to get her some bargains now and then, so I was real glad to find these. Why some of these little frocks were only a dollar and thirty-nine cents! What do you think of that?"

"A dollar and thirty-nine cents!" gasped Gillian. "Why, that's almost cheap enough for me, if I weren't saving every cent to get Noel a new suit. But I don't suppose dresses as cheap as that are really worth buying, are they?"

"Oh yes, they're really neat and pretty, and well cut too. They've been much more expensive of course. You know when there's a sale there's always one or two real bargains, and if you have an eye for that sort of thing you can tell which are worth buying. I was salesgirl in a department store for a year and a half before I took up nursing, so I generally can spot a bargain. Here, what do you think of this one? Isn't that neat?"

She broke the string, cast the wrapping aside and spread out a cute little percale with tiny blue flowers over a white ground. It had a bit of really attractive white lacy edging at neck and sleeves, and was as pretty as could be.

"Why, that is lovely!" said Gillian interestedly. "But you never got that for a dollar thirty-nine."

"Yes, I did! Isn't it wonderful? There were only three at that price that were attractive. Here's one in pink and white, pink ground with white collar and cuffs, and white buttons. Isn't that nifty? And this green one. I think that's the prettiest of all."

"They are all lovely," said Gillian. "I had no idea you could get anything as good as this at that price. If I had known that I might have got one. I've a little bit of money, not much."

"Help yourself," said the nurse. "I only brought these out to look over and decide what I thought Maysie would like best. But wait till you see the others. Here's a brown linen for $4.95, real bargains I call them, and a dark blue linen. That's only $3.98 because the belt is gone, but you could easy wear a leather belt, either white or black. Aren't they pretty!"

"Oh!" said Gillian wistfully. "I'm so glad you let me see them. Perhaps if I get well enough by next week to take a few minutes off for shopping there will be some of them left yet. You know dresses like those last two could be worn in the office every day. They would be just the thing. Of course I have to look neat and nice there!"

"Of course!" said the nurse. "Well, look them over! I shan't try to decide tonight. Of course they are all returnable. And even if you want one that I had thought of I can likely get another by just calling up. I got the saleswoman's number."

And then suddenly right into the midst of this fashion show walked Reuben and Noel, and the child was all eagerness.

"Oh, Gillian! I have a present!" he said in a little radiant breathless voice.

"A present!" said Gillian watching the joy in his dear little face. "Where did you get a present?"

"From my Reuben!" he said exultantly.

Gillian gave one startled look at her little brother, and at the sizable suit box he held out, its cover removed showing an array of small garments. Then her eyes sought Reuben's.

"Oh, Mr. Remington!" she said reproachfully. "You have done so much already for Noel. Please don't make us utterly ashamed!"

"Oh!" said Reuben gently. "I hoped you wouldn't take it that way. Sometime pretty soon, perhaps on the way to the shore, I shall hope to have opportunity to tell you all that your brother has done for me, and then I think you will not grudge me the joy of getting a few things for him. It has been a great pleasure, truly! Of course they may not be what your choice would have bought, but can't you let him wear them a little while for me? You can throw them away or give them away when the summer is over and get more of the kind you would choose yourself, you know, and I would have great pleasure in having him wear these for me."

Gillian looked at him and saw that he genuinely meant it, and her eyes were wide with sudden tears flowing down her cheeks.

"Oh! I thank you!" she blurted out through her tears. "I can't refuse you if you ask that way. If it really has been a pleasure. But it's too wonderful! I can't think it has really happened to us!"

"Of course it's been a pleasure," said Reuben most earnestly. "I wonder if you ever thought how it must be to have nobody left in your family to care for or to buy things for? A little brother has been a wonderful blessing to me for these few days, and I'm going to miss him terribly after this time is over. So I hoped you would take this in the same spirit in which it is given, and not think of it as anything great at all. Just a little gift to my little brother! They really are very simple inexpensive things, and they will soon be outgrown, you know, and all too soon will be too thin for cooler weather. Couldn't you just take them and think no more of it?"

"Oh yes," said Gillian, "but—Mr. Remington, please by and by when I am able to save a little money and things are going better with me wil you promise to let me repay you for these things?"

He looked at her sadly a moment and then he said, with just a shade of disappointment in his voice:

"Why, of course if that is the only way you will take them, I'll have to say yes, but it will really be a lot more joy to me to give these things outright to the boy whom I have come to love as if he were my own."

And then Gillian looking into his eyes saw that it was true as he said, and she dashed away her tears and put out her slender hand to his.

"Well, all right," she said sweetly, humbly, "if you really feel that way, then thank you more than words can tell!"

And Reuben stood there for a moment and held that frail young hand in his warmly, and thought that suddenly, surprisingly, this girl seemed somehow to belong too to the whole scheme of things that was weaving a web about him, and undoing his vacation.

Noel, during these few minutes of their conversation had stood doubtfully, anxiously watching the two dear faces, fearful lest his new present was not to be really his after all. For of course he would not accept them if Gillian did not approve. But there was one thing that was gradually coming sharply to his consciousness as he listened, and that was that Gillian didn't really know his beloved Reuben the way he did, and it seemed a great pity to him. He wondered how he could remedy that.

And then he saw Gillian's tears. Why would his sister cry because he had had a present, and such a nice present?

And then he saw their hands together in that strong clasp and radiance grew in his beautiful young face.

"You do like my present, don't you, Gillian?" he said and his voice was like a cherub's voice straight from the source of joy.

And suddenly Gillian turned an endearing smile toward him.

"Yes, dearest," she said, and leaning over kissed him tenderly on his forehead. "Yes, oh, yes! It was wonderful of Mr. Remington to give you all this."

"But you haven't seen them yet, Gillian. Take them out and look at them, sister. They are just *splendicious!*"

Then amid the laughter that his newly coined word brought she reached for the box and took out the garments, one by one, and admired them even enough to satisfy Noel, and certainly enough to more than warm the heart of the happy giver, who had really been having the time of his life selecting them.

The nurse, meantime, had discreetly taken herself out of the room, after staying long enough to find out what was going on. Being deep in sympathy with them all she kept her distance, now and again returning at brief intervals to be sure she got all the facts and be perfectly certain there was nothing more she ought to do to be ready for the morrow.

"And now," said Reuben at last, "I telephoned Aunt Ettie just before I came. She has arrived safely, and moved in. At least she says the beds are up and made. The electricity is on, the gas stove is in working order, and she'll be ready for her guests any time tomorrow. How soon would it be convenient for you to start? Nurse, you ought to be able to answer that question."

The nurse stepped up importantly.

"The doctor ought to be here around half past ten. I should think she ought to be able to leave soon after that. He knows she is expecting to go, and he will want to see if she is all right before she starts."

"Very well," said Reuben. "We'll start around eleven, then, unless the doctor has other plans. And oh, by the way, Miss Guthrie, I met Mr. Rand about an hour ago and he gave me this to give to you. He said it was from your fellow workers in the office. They sent you their best regards and hoped you would have a lovely vacation."

With trembling astonished hands Gillian took the envelope he handed out and opened it, and out of it fell a check for fifty dollars, and a little card with good wishes signed by all the people in the office.

"Well now, isn't that just perfectly lovely?" said the nurse wiping pleased tears from her eyes with her apron, as she took the card Gillian held out for her to see.

"I don't think I shall be able to sleep at all tonight," said Gillian.

"Oh, yes, my dear, you'll sleep like a top," said the nurse.

Then Noel went close and said in a small jubilant voice:

"Oh, isn't everything just wonderful, Gillian? Isn't it just like our God to make all things so nice for us?" And Gillian pressed a warm kiss on the small happy lips.

Then Reuben led the boy away, with a good night and a promise to be there in the morning for her, and Gillian and the nurse were left alone.

The nurse had the patient all quietly prepared for the night, and was about to turn out the light when Gillian spoke:

"I wonder, nurse, if you would mind if I changed my mind about those dresses you brought home? Would it really be all right if I took one or two of them? Now that I've got all this wonderful money I think I ought to get enough things to look all right. Mr. Remington says that there's a possibility some of the girls may run down for a day to see me while I'm at the shore, and I don't want to look too shabby, you know."

"Of course not," said the nurse briskly with a kind of satisfaction in her voice. "I was really hoping you'd take some of them."

"And you are sure your niece won't be disappointed?"

"Oh, no, how can she be disappointed about something she's never seen? Besides, I've been thinking. There's a yellow one I'm most sure she would rather have. And there's plenty of those sprigged ones. I can get more like them. So it will be all right. I'll go right down tomorrow after you leave and get them."

So with her heart at rest about her scarcity of suitable garments Gillian fell into a deep refreshing sleep.

12

BEFORE Reuben left the hotel the next morning he had a lengthy and disturbing talk with the New York detective, and then with the lawyer in whose hands he had placed the matter for the Guthries. It was definite that the uncle was determined to find his niece and nephew.

The lawyer had been in consultation with the Trust Company who had verified the facts that had been reported to them concerning Mrs. Guthrie's death two years before. They were ready to cooperate in finding the man and bringing him to justice. They had a warrant for his arrest ready, if it should be needed. But it was all too evident that the old reprobate was in this immediate neighborhood somewhere, and there was no telling how he got his information of Gillian's whereabouts, nor where he would turn up next.

Reuben was much distressed about it all. He felt that he should get the girl out of the city as soon as possible. It would be a shock to her if the man came to the hospital before she got away. Though how he would find out she was there was a puzzle. But sometimes crooked people had crooked ways of finding out things, and Reuben was taking no chances for his wards. He would get them away as soon as possible.

Also it would be most unpleasant for Gillian at the office

if that old uncle turned up there and told any lies about her. She wouldn't feel that she could go back to the only job she was sure of. And he must take great care that Gillian did not find out any of this before their journey. She must be as calm and rested as possible. But about all this Noel of course knew nothing, and he was engrossed in a couple of tricky puzzles Reuben had got for him, waiting patiently in a new little brown linen suit for the ride that he and Reuben were going to take Gillian. It was a great day and he was very happy.

Reuben felt a tug of joy at his heart as he came after Noel and found him curled into the big chair by the window working away at the two keys that somehow would not come apart.

"I've got the pigs all in the clover pen," cried the boy holding up a little metal box, "but I can't get the keys apart. Show me again, Reuben."

Reuben took the keys, gave a twist and a turn to them and held them up one in each hand.

"Now," cried Noel, "I'll try again!"

"Not now," said Reuben. "We're going after your sister now and take the nice long ride to the shore. Put the puzzle in your pocket for another time when you have nothing to do!"

So joyously Noel obeyed and they went together down to the car, to find the porter had already stowed away their bags.

Gillian had just finished a bowl of soup when they got to the hospital, and was all dressed up in the new dark blue dress, her eyes like two stars. Reuben stopped a moment to stare at her. Could this be the colorless girl who had slumped before him that day in the office? Did she really look like this? The soft flush on her cheeks was not painted. The light in her eyes was genuine and from within. And how different she seemed now, dressed and sitting up.

"Oh, Gillian! You've got a new dress!" said the little boy jumping up and down gaily. "A new dress, Reuben! Doesn't she look pretty in it?"

Gillian's cheeks suddenly grew pinker and she said:

"Noel! Hush! What an idea! It's just a dress, a simple little linen dress, and cost almost nothing. You make me feel embarrassed, darling!"

"Oh!" said Noel, somewhat abashed. "But she does look pretty in it, doesn't she, Reuben?"

Reuben grinned.

"Why certainly. Of course. Doesn't she always look pretty?"

"Y-e-es," said Noel thoughtfully, "but sometimes she looks prettier than other times. Isn't that right, Reuben?"

"Why yes, I suppose it must be since you say so," said Reuben gravely, and then with a twinkle he turned to Gillian. "The chariot awaits, lady. Has the doctor been here?"

"He's just coming," said the nurse from the doorway. And then they could hear his footsteps coming down the hall.

"All set?" said the doctor's cheery voice. "Now, lady, are you going to be a good little girl so you can keep away from the hospital and not come back to see me any more?"

A bit of laughter and banter, and then they were on their way to the elevator, Gillian in a wheeled chair, although she insisted she was able to walk.

"Not till you have to, little girl!" said the doctor. "And now here are a few rules I'm giving you to keep well by. Look out for them every day, and some day perhaps you will thank me."

"I'll thank you now, doctor," said Gillian with a shy smile. "You've been wonderful to me."

A few minutes more and they were in the car, with good byes to nurse and doctor, and the kind interne who had brought her to the hospital, and then they started off.

Reuben threaded his way into the street and through the city traffic, out into a broad highway, rolling smoothly along in the bright day.

"Well, are you comfortable?" he said, looking over at the girl as she sat in the back seat against the soft cushions.

"I should say!" she smiled. "This is a wonderful car."

"You like it? I hoped you'd find it easy. Are you sorry to leave the hospital?"

"Oh, no I'm glad, so glad! Athough they were very nice

and kind to me, and I did get a good rest of course. I guess I was rather tired, although I didn't realize it until just the last few days."

"Yes?" said Reuben. "Well, I'm glad you realize it now, and I hope it will be a good lesson to you always to eat plenty and sleep plenty and rest a lot. Now, are you sitting comfortably? Would you rather have Noel back there beside you? I thought perhaps this way you could put your feet up after a little and sort of lie down."

"Oh, I'm very comfortable. Let Noel stay in the front seat if he doesn't bother you. I know it's just the delight of his heart to be sitting in front with you."

Reuben glanced down at the happy child knowingly.

"We're pals, aren't we, kid?" he said with a grin.

Noel sat there seraphically happy, watching everything on the way, and Gillian lay back quietly with peace in her eyes and on her brow.

And about that time, back in the city, an elderly man with sly eyes and a debonair air, walked pompously up the steps of the hospital and demanded at the desk to know where he could find Miss Gillian Guthrie's room.

The girl at the desk was a substitute for the regular desk nurse, and didn't know. She looked in the regular list, but couldn't find the name, and then she called to another nurse who was passing through the hall.

"Who? Guthrie? Oh, that's the girl that was on the second floor, private. Why, she's checked out! Yes, they went this morning. A swell car came for her. No, I don't know where she went. You'd hafta ask her nurse, Miss Hepburn. But she's off for the day. No, I don't know where you'd find her. Seems ta me I heard her say she was going on an outside case. She's a special, you know." Then the elevator came down with a clang and the nurse went on her way upstairs, and though the persistent gentleman kept on trying, for he was not one to give up easily, he finally had to go away with the assurance that the regular office girl would be back tomorrow, and she would likely know all about the patient he was searching for.

But out in the beautiful day, secure in Reuben's handsome new car, Gillian was rolling away into a sunlit world, with her beloved little brother within reach, and nothing to do but rest and be thankful. For the morning at least there was nothing to worry about.

She glanced down at the neat lines of her pretty blue dress, and marveled that it was herself so arrayed, marveled that there had been a way for her to get such a nice looking dress so very cheap. That was such a nice kind nurse. Sometime she must write her a letter and thank her for all her kindness. But just now she didn't even have to think about it, just be still and enjoy everything.

They were going over the big bridge across the river now and Noel was asking a lot of questions. She was sitting so she could see the eager light in the boy's eyes, and she wondered if he was annoying the driver. Somehow this morning, being dressed herself like a human being again, and not just a kimonoed patient, she began to see this young man who had been such a strong helper in her time of need, as a man of the business world again, a younger but still an important member of the staff of heads who constituted the firm for which she worked. A sudden shyness had come upon her. While she was lying there in bed, helpless, and he the only contact with a world in which she had been sadly inadequate, he had seemed more like an old friend, but now as she looked at his fine profile, noted the kindliness about the firm lips, the genuine interest in his pleasant eyes as they looked at Noel, she felt a startled wonder that such a man had taken time and trouble to help her and Noel in their time of distress. Of course it was likely just the firm doing it for the sake of the old man, her father's friend, who had written them a letter before he went from the world forever. But they had known the kind young man into whose hands they had put her case, and known he would do all in his power to make things right for her. She must certainly write the firm a letter too, when she felt stronger and knew just what to say.

And now this blessed rest by the sea that was before her!

How wonderful it was going to be! Of course it might not turn out to be so perfect as it was in anticipation, but at least she would believe in it until it proved itself otherwise. That was the only way she could possibly hope to get well and carry on for Noel, just take things as they came and believe in them as long as she could, and not carry that awful burden of fearfulness that she had been carrying for the last two years. It was wonderful to relax, and just be happy for even a little while.

Then she began to watch the young man again, covertly, because she wouldn't presume to be staring at him. He represented to her the firm for whom she worked, and she must give him all quiet respect, and not for an instant presume upon his kindness to her in her stress.

Then suddenly as she thought about what pleasant lines there were in his face, he turned and flashed a smile at her, as if she were an old friend he had known all his life.

And perhaps he caught the wistfulness in her eyes, for he turned again and smiled, that smile of genuine interest and concern about her welfare.

"Feeling perfectly comfortable?" he said. "Not too much air from this window? Of course it's a warm day, but you mustn't get chilled, and you know it is easy to get chilled when one has been in bed for several days. I don't want this experiment to end in your having to go back to the hospital again."

"Oh, no, I'm perfectly all right," Gillian assured him. "I feel as if I was on my way to Heaven," she said with a look of childish happiness that made her resemblance to Noel plainer that ever.

"Oh, not Heaven just yet, I trust!" laughed Reuben. "I'm glad it seems delightful to you, but we don't want you to leave even for Heaven at present, do we, Noel?"

Noel turned startled eyes to his.

"Oh, no! Not my Gillian! Not for a long long time!" and then he looked fearfully back toward his sister as if to assure himself that she was all right.

But Gillian and Reuben suddenly laughed, a sweet clear laugh which somehow seemed to bring them both together, and make them feel more intimate.

"That's all right, son, don't worry!" said Reuben as he saw that the anxiety was still in the child's young eyes. "Can't you see how pink her cheeks are? She's all right. She only meant she was having a nice time!"

A slow smile began to dawn on Noel's face, and he turned to Gillian again.

"Is that right, Gillian? Are you only having a nice time?"

"Yes, dear, I'm having a wonderful time," she reassured him. "And so are you, aren't you?"

"Oh, yes!" said the child with emphasis, a great sigh of satisfaction. "I wish—I wish—it could be—like this, always!"

"Why yes," said Reuben heartily, "that would be nice, wouldn't it?" And then suddenly in his heart he felt that was the truth. This was a very happy occasion for him also, a combination that gave rest and peace in the heart, and a kind of rare anticipation of what was to come the rest of the day. He didn't stop to analyze that feeling and wonder why it was there. It was enough to take this day and enjoy it, and feel that in no way would he have it different. This sweet girl, and her dear young brother there in his care, wholly dependent upon him, just out to have a good time together. Yes, he wouldn't at all mind if this were to go on forever. Even if he never saw Agnes again, nor went to that wedding at all. He had gotten along for several pleasant years without Agnes, and though she might be a very fine girl, and have developed wonderfully, why should he worry about her? He was just happy today. And as for that Glinden girl, well, he had always been doubtful about her. She might be all right in her own environment, but it was a far cry between her environment and his and why bother about her? Not today anyway!

They passed the airport and stopped to see a plane take off and another one come in, and enjoyed Noel's wonder over them. They passed a field of flowers bright colored and lush. They went into a thick grove of trees, and then came out to a quiet miniature lake where water-lilies lay on its mirror surface, their chins resting on wide still green leaves. Noel wished he could go out and pick one, and wanted to know if he could wade out there and get just one.

"No, that lake would be too deep to wade in, but perhaps sometime during this summer we'll find a chance to go water-lilying where there is a boat. They sometimes have such ponds at the shore. Maybe there is one not too far away from the shore where you are going and when I come down to see you I'll try to see if there is a boat we could get to have a try at some lilies!"

The bright little face was full of joy at the thought.

"And perhaps there'll be some swans. Did you ever see swans?"

"Did I, Gillian? I don't remember."

"No, I don't think you have ever seen swans except in picture books."

"Oh yes, once in a picture book!" said Noel. "They have long curly necks like white snakes, don't they?"

"Something," said Reuben with a grin. "Well, I think we'll have to make it our business to hunt up some swans sometime, and let you get acquainted with them."

And then as they went on under clear skies, and into the sunshine, there came a tang in the air.

"I smell the ocean, Reuben," said the little boy. "I do, don't you? Gillian, did you know the ocean had a smell? You smell it, don't you, Reuben?"

"Oh yes," said Reuben. "It smells of salt, and fishes having a nice time swimming in the waves, and sand, and little branches of seaweed."

"Yes," said Noel. "I thought that too only I had no words to make, you know. But you always have words. And then there would be little white sandpipers, too, and lovely big gulls. Wait till you see them, Gillian. You'll like it, oh how much!"

"Yes, I shall like it!" said Gillian gaily, twinkling her eyes in response, and Reuben looking back caught her lovely expression, and was stirred to sudden wonder over her unexpected beauty. She was really a beautiful girl, with that little pink in her cheeks, and her eyes so bright, and her hair blowing in soft tendrils of curl about her face. She looked so different from the girl he had brought away from the office that it almost seemed she could not be the same.

And now they were coming into the region of summer holidays. Long stretches without trees, tall thin grasses by the way, coming separately out of the white white sand, and a far line of thin blue against the sky line.

"There's the ocean!" said Reuben in an eager voice. "See it, Noel? Over there. And there's a couple of ships! Can you see them sailing along?"

"Yes! Yes! I see them! Look, Gillian! Look quick! Those are ships! Real ships!" called the excited child.

And then they drove into the little seashore town and down the street where they first had entered, straight down to the ocean that Gillian might get a whiff of real sea air, and see the ships before they sailed away out of sight.

Gillian sat up and drew in long breaths of the good air.

"Oh, this is enough to make anybody well if they were very sick!" she said, as she put back her shoulders and drew in another deep breath. "Oh, it is so long, so long since I can remember smelling salt air!"

"Well, now," said Reuben at last, "I think we had better go and find our cottage and Aunt Ettie. You are getting too tired, I am afraid, and you need to lie down and shut your eyes, and forget everything but just breathing."

Smiling, he turned the car up the beach and drove till they could see the white cottage standing on its bluff, looking out to sea, its green blinds folded neatly back, like a lady waiting for guests.

"There it is! There's the cottage, Gillian! Look!" cried Noel. "Isn't it pretty? See the porch and the little evergreen trees, and the window boxes in the windows with real flowers in them!"

And so they drew up in front of the little white dream cottage that Gillian had been trying to vision all the way down. She saw that it was real, and just as pretty as they had said.

And there came Aunt Ettie bustling out the screen door, shutting it carefully behind her, and then hurrying down the little front path, rolling her sleeves down from her elbows to receive her guests properly. And she looked just as Reuben had said she would.

For the first few sentences Aunt Ettie was entirely occupied with Reuben, scolding him for being a half hour behind the time he had said he would be. And then she turned to Noel and sized him up.

"You're for all the world like this man useta be when I first went to live with his mother a great many years ago," she said, and Noel looked up and smiled as if she had just crowned him king. That won her entirely, and she said:

"Well, hop out and let's begin to live. There's a plate of cookies in on the dining room table—oh, I forgot, there isn't any dining room—but you run in and you'll find them—and I'll warrant you'll be hungry by now, no matter how late you had your breakfast. Good healthy boys are always hungry!"

Then she turned her attention to Gillian, and Gillian looked into her true kindly eyes, and smiled. Not a smile that claimed anything for herself, just a smile of thanks for the kindness toward her little brother, and Aunt Ettie was won at once.

So Reuben helped Gillian from the car, and up the walk to the pleasant doorway. Gillian exclaimed with pleasure over the sight of the sea from the porch, and then they went in and Aunt Ettie bustled about getting Gillian settled, much against her will, in bed. Gillian lay there and looked around on the still clean little room with the white curtains blowing out into the air, and the salt smell heartening her, and then Aunt Ettie came bustling in with a cup of hot tea for her to drink. She made Reuben come and lift Gillian high on the pillow so she could drink it. It was all so homelike and pleasant that tears of joy came to Gillian's eyes.

"Oh," she said, through her tears, "this is all so good, just like the way mother would have had it!" And that went straight to Aunt Ettie's heart.

"Bless your dear little soul!" she said lovingly. "I'm glad

you've come to keep me company. It's going to be wonderful to have a little girl like you to mother, and that blessed little boy too. I might have known my boy Reuben would have just the right person to send to me, and I needn't have worried a mite. Now ain't that something. How one does worry over things that never happen. I worried a lot over you, and here I am pleased as Cuffey. Now, you lie down and shut your eyes and take a real nap while I go and look after things. You know we just moved in last night and aren't half in order yet, so there's plenty to do."

"Oh!" laughed Gillian, "but I should get up and help you! I can work. I really can."

"I haven't a bit of doubt of it," said Aunt Ettie severely, "but I've got orders from your doctor. Reuben just gave them to me, and I'm not to let you do a lick of work for a least a whole week. So, you just lie still. I don't want to lose my reputation of being a good nurse and a good manager."

Then Aunt Ettie went out and shut the door, but the great salt breeze continued to go through from one window to another, and sweep the air clean with every breath, so that the nice soft old blanket of homespun real wool that Aunt Ettie had drawn up around her shoulders felt so good to her, and she sank into a most restful sleep.

But Noel was down on the beach with Reuben picking up a delightful collection of delicate shells which he meant to offer his sister as a gift when she woke up. His cheeks were pink, his curls blowing wildly in the fine seabreeze, and his eyes like stars.

"Now, Noel, isn't that enough shells for this time? Suppose you put them in this big handkerchief of mine, and let's go back to the cottage and see if Aunt Ettie doesn't need us to help in some way. You know she has to get supper, and this is the first night and it will likely be hard work. She's hardly got things unpacked yet."

"Oh, I would like to unpack for her!" said Noel, ready to go at once.

"Well, we'll go and see what she wants. Perhaps she would like to send us to the store for something she needs."

"Yes? I will go to the store for Aunt Ettie. Where is the store?"

"Well, suppose we go first and find out if Aunt Ettie wants anything tonight, and then if she does, I'll go with you and show you where it is so that you can go by yourself sometimes if she should happen to need something when I'm not here."

"Oh, yes, that will be nice!" And Noel went happily with Reuben.

Yes, Aunt Ettie wanted some sugar. She seemed to have brought almost everything else she needed at present from the farm back home. She had brought eggs, and newmade butter, and several bottles of milk and cottage cheese, two roasted chickens, a slice of home cured ham, a loaf of homemade bread, another of gingerbread, and an apple pie. She had kept them all fresh by packing them in a tub of cracked ice on the way, and putting them at once into the refrigerator when she arrived. But she hadn't a scratch of sugar. Not a grain, she said.

So Noel and Reuben went to the store, and Reuben gave Noel careful directions about care in crossing streets, and waiting till traffic was clear. Not that there was any great amount of traffic, but he wanted to make sure that Gillian had no more worries than was necessary.

"You must feel that you are to guard your sister, any time I am away," he said earnestly.

"Are you going to be away, Reuben?" asked the anxious little voice.

"Well, occasionally, now and then," said Reuben.

"Then it won't be much fun, after all, will it?" He sighed.

"Oh yes," said Reuben, with a sudden regret that he had to go. "You'll be taking your dear Gillian to walk on the sand pretty soon, and you have to be the man of the house and take care of Aunt Ettie and the yellow cat. You haven't seen the yellow cat yet, but Aunt Ettie loves her very much and takes her everywhere she goes."

"Yes, I like cats very much," said Noel politely, and then after quite a pause, "When do you have to go away, Reuben?"

Now Reuben's first plan had been to go to the city the next day, and attend to one or two matters, and perhaps the next day run down to Glindenwold for the week end. But since he had arrived at the shore with these two dependent upon him, and Aunt Ettie so wholesome and like old times, he had a strange urge to stay here a little longer. After all, why should he hurry away? He could just as well put off his going a few days.

"Well I was thinking of going day after tomorrow," he said cheerfully.

"Oh!" said Noel sadly.

Then after a long pause:

"Do you *want* to go away, Reuben?"

"Well, no, I don't know that I do. But—there are things that I sort of *have* to do," he finished lamely.

"Yes," said Noel sadly, "I suppose there will always be things like that! My sister has 'em too. But I'm just afraid that after you are gone, she will think she has to go back to work. I think you would be the only one who would be able to make her understand that she ought to stay here."

"Well, now, Buddie, don't you worry about that. We'll see if we can't make her understand that it is positively necessary for her to stay here. And besides, I'll be coming back again, you know, perhaps several times."

"Oh, will you?" the smiles beamed out again. "Well, then, that's all right!"

And when they got back with the sugar his sadness had all disappeared.

THEY had a wonderful evening. Gillian got up for dinner. Stuffed roasted chicken, little new green peas out of Aunt Ettie's home garden, little new potatoes also out of the home garden, coleslaw made from new cabbage out of the same garden, and juicy fat tomatoes, ripe and red from the same place.

It hadn't been much work to get that meal. To warm the chickens, and cook the peas and potatoes, and slice the tomatoes. The coleslaw had traveled in a glass jar from New England, and the old sprigged china had belonged to Aunt Ettie's mother. It seemed a charmed meal; the apple pie and cheese made just the right ending.

"Like old times, Aunt Ettie," said Reuben with a tender light in his eyes.

After the meal was ended Reuben and Noel went out and helped wash the dishes and put them away in the little new corner cupboards, and they let Gillian wipe the silver which they brought her on a tray with a clean towel. Then Noel put it away in the small sideboard drawer. Oh, it was just like a real little family, as Noel announced joyously. And then after supper Reuben brought out his games, and they played Chinese Checkers for a game or two, till Reuben thought it was time for the invalid to get to bed. So he suddenly gathered her up in his arms and carried her into her pretty little bedroom just off the living room, and laid her down on her bed as if she had been delicate glass and might break. Gillian gasped, and laughed, and then lay still in wonder to think she was being taken care of this way. And for a long time after they had said good night and she had crept into her sweet comfortable bed, she lay thinking it all over and reading a lecture to herself to the end that she was not to allow herself to presume upon all this, not even in her thoughts. For Mr. Remington was a very important man in the firm, and going to be still more important. Moreover, Miss Glinden herself was interested in him, and probably he in her, and she must not get notions in her head, or get to thinking too much of him, for he was a very attractive man, and she was a little nobody to whom he was merely being kind. But try as she would she couldn't get away from the memory of how gently he had carried her, as if she were really something precious. Perhaps as her mother must have carried her when she was little. How grand it was that Noel had such a friend! For, leaving herself entirely out of the matter, he was the kind of man who would likely always be a kindly friend to Noel.

So when morning came there was Johnnycake, and new laid eggs, poached like little golden disks, and strawberries, also from the home garden. Oh, Aunt Ettie had done a great deal in those few days before she had left her New England home, and she was just reveling in taking care of this new delightful family.

So by morning Reuben hadn't any idea left of going away that day. He was much more interested in staying. He proposed that they take a ride, and get lunch on the beach somewhere, or take it with them.

So Aunt Ettie put up chicken sandwiches, and pie and gingerbread and pickles and cheese, and went along, and such a day as they had! Noel and Reuben put on their bathing suits and took a good dip in the ocean, and Gillian and Aunt Ettie sat on the shore in sand chairs that had been scooped out for them, and watched. And when the two bathers came out, refreshed and happy looking, Gillian was like a new creature, with all the worry and wrinkles blown away and the look of a sweet happy child in her face.

When they were ready to start back Reuben stooped and picked her up again and carried her across the sand to the car, Aunt Ettie watching with entire satisfaction. This girl was different, just as her boy had claimed. Well, that was nice. Only why was he going away so soon? With a nice girl like that why wasn't he staying and having a good time? Could it be that there was another girl somewhere that he had to go and see?

So Aunt Ettie began to worry about that.

"Your vacation isn't over yet, is it, Reuben?" she asked at supper that night after she had dealt out the excellent fried fish that lay in a fragrant brown heap on the big platter.

"Oh, no, Aunt Ettie," said Reuben. "It's only just begun."

"Then what do you have to go away for? I don't see why this place isn't as good as you can find for a vacation."

"Yes, I guess it is," said Reuben, "but you see I got into some things before I found this place, and I have to fulfill them. I promised several people, and they wouldn't understand why I couldn't come."

"I should think it was your vacation," said Aunt Ettie discontentedly. "I should think you had a right to spend it as you please."

"Yes, you would think that, wouldn't you? But there are reasons, and one can't exactly be rude about such things, you know. Besides, one is a wedding of one of my old college friends, and I've promised to be best man."

"Oh, well, a wedding of course, but that only takes a few minutes, or at least it couldn't take but one day."

"Well, you may be sure I'll get back as soon as I decently can, from that and all the other things. You know I like it down here, and you all seem to be fairly good playmates. I think I could have a rare good time. However, I guess I've got to do the proper thing, especially as some of it involves the people for whom I work."

Gillian looked up thoughtfully, and remembered a golden

haired girl who had passed through the office, toward her father's inner sanctum, and returned a little later in company with young Mr. Remington. She had caught a sentence as they passed the desk where she sat.

"I certainly shall be terribly disappointed if you're not there on time!" and her little trilling ripple of a laugh that followed, wafting back through the swing door into the hallway.

"Well," said Reuben smiling indulgently, "I think I'll take another day at least. I shall not go until day after tomorrow."

"Oh, goody, goody, goody!" shouted Noel, putting down his fork and clapping his hands exultantly.

And all this tended to make Reuben feel that he really belonged in this little cottage, and was happier than he had been since his mother died.

The next day they concentrated on the house, getting it in full running order, unpacking the rest of Aunt Ettie's goods and marveling on how much she had been able to cram into that one van load. Also, how many things she had thought of and known that they would need. Reuben entered into the life there as if he were back in the old days when his father and mother would go away for a little trip and leave him in the care of faithful Aunt Ettie. The other two forlorn children, after the first few hours, entered into the friendly atmosphere, too, and seemed to feel as much at home as the rest. And then they drove to the next little town where was a florist, and came back with more flowers for the window boxes, and more flowers for the little garden beds that Reuben with the earnest assistance of Noel, dug for them. Aunt Ettie sttod around and gave directions, beaming delightedly on them all. She hadn't had such a good time in years.

They took a ride in the early sunset glow, drove to a point that jutted far out into the ocean, where both sunset and sunrise could be seen, and they parked the car and sat to watch the sunset, Noel nestling between Reuben and Gillian. As they drove back along the beach they watched the pearly tints of rainbow beauty begin to ripple over the sea.

"I used to know a poem something about that," said Reuben. "I can't remember who wrote it. It began, 'Where the quiet colored end of evening smiles, miles and miles.' "

"Oh yes," said Gillian. "I love that," and she went on with it reciting it exquisitely. " 'On our many colored pastures, where our sheep, half asleep, twinkle homeward through the twilight, Stay or stop, as they crop, Was the site once of a city, Grave and gay, so they say.' That is Robert Browning. I learned that when I was a little girl. I could always see a picture of it, with the sheep coming homeward through the colored twilight. It almost seems as if I had really had a great oil painting of that once, it was so thoroughly fixed in my memory."

"Oh, did you?" said Reuben, watching the expression of the sweet face. "I think I must have had such a vision myself, for the picture seems very real to me too. I think they used to pay more attention to such exquisite poetry in the days when I was a boy then they seem to now, for I can't remember that my young cousins had anything to do with poetry, during the year I lived with my uncle, except to avoid it whenever it was mentioned. They were in high school but they seemed to regard poetry as sissified and to be held in utter contempt. It may be that their teachers didn't intend that reaction to their English course, but that's the way it seemed to turn out. But—you are a little younger than I am. I'm curious to know how you came to know and love poetry."

"Oh—I had a mother," said Gillian, her face kindling with fervor. "She loved poetry, and she read it to me, and made me memorize a great deal, and often recite it. It was like lovely books and pictures stored away in our minds. It was my mother who taught me to love poetry."

"Yes, I know you had a wonderful mother," said Reuben with a significant look toward Noel, whose sweet eyes were lifted watching the evening sky. "I had one myself, but perhaps I haven't stayed true to what she taught me as you have. I did have a lot of poetry in my head, however, and sometimes it comes out."

"My mother began with the Bible," said Gillian, her face sweetly reminiscent of other days. "And that is poetry, so much of it, you know, although it doesn't rhyme. It was through the Bible that mother taught me to love poetry."

"There's a song about the twenty-third psalm," remarked Noel suddenly. "Sing it, Gillian. 'The Lord's my shepherd, I'll not want.' " So they sang the old psalm, and Reuben remembered enough of it himself, to limp along with tenor accompaniment.

Suddenly Reuben laid his hand across on Gillian's hand that lay in her lap.

"See!" he said, pointing to the sea with his other hand, "over there to your right! The new moon, so very slender it is, scarcely more than pencil line in a lovely curve."

"Oh, yes," said Noel. "See, Gillian. It is like the blade of a sickle that the man cuts the grass with at the edge of the sidewalk. And there's a little star, just one, coming out to walk behind the moon, like the little page boy in my story book, that always attended the young prince when he went out to ride in his little gold chariot. Look, sister! Look up there! The sky is so clear. Don't you think if we had some very strong glasses we could see all the way through it, and see some angels going by? Maybe we could see our mother and Jesus if we had the right kind of glasses."

"Not yet, Noel dear! Not till we go up there. We have only our earthly eyes yet and we can only see them by faith. Now see, there comes a lovely ship and it's sailing right across the front of the moon. Isn't that a lovely sight. Oh, this night is marvelous!"

"Yes," said Reuben reverently. "It's a night to remember always, in such company as I have with me now. I dread to go away tomorrow!"

"But you'll come back?" asked Noel anxiously.

"Oh yes, I'll come back!"

"How lovely and smooth that beach looks, with the tide so far out; it seems like a marble pavement, with a path of silver just beyond. How I would love to walk out there toward the water, just a few steps. Don't you think I could?" Gillian asked Reuben.

"Why yes," said Reuben, "if you feel like it. This beach is marvelously smooth and hard when the tide is out. It is the finest beach on this coast. Here, let me help you. You mustn't walk far, for I don't want you to be all tired out while I am away."

He helped her out and slipped his arm under hers, supporting her wrist comfortably, and making her feel that walking was one of the easiest things she ever did.

Noel went around to his other side, and took his hand, nestling it against his arm, and Reuben felt a great tenderness come into his heart for these two who were for the time being under his care, and also a great reluctance to leave them. Yet he must go to Glindenwold. Tomorrow night was the last night of the play, and he didn't want to be actually rude to his employer's daughter.

So at last they went quietly back to the cottage, where they found that Aunt Ettie had been setting bread because she knew Reuben loved homemade bread, and baking a batch of caraway cookies—also because he liked them.

Reuben had meant to go early in the morning, but he was lured into going in bathing just once more before he left, and then afterwards sat on the porch reciting poetry with Gillian until a delightful lunch was forthcoming unexpectedly, served out on the terrace looking toward the sea.

Aunt Ettie was the siren who lured him to stay on.

"Reuben, I wonder if you could help me set up that other bed in my room," she said, coming out to the porch after she had finished putting away the lunch dishes. "I thought I didn't want it because it takes so much room, but the cot isn't very comfortable, and I believe I'd sleep better on my own bed."

"Of course!" said Reuben readily. And when the bed was up there was Aunt Ettie up on a step ladder hanging some curtains, so Reuben stayed to hang the curtains. So, with Noel and Gillian going back and forth putting little dainty touches to Aunt Ettie's room, and then to some of the other rooms, the afternoon sped away incredibly fast, till Reuben suddenly found he had missed the four o'clock train, and would have to go in his car.

"Well, that's all right," he said. "Perhaps it would be more convenient to have my car with me anyway, then I am freer.

Besides I have one or two errands that I really ought to do before I go out to Glindenwold."

Gillian caught her breath as Glindenwold was mentioned. It suddenly seemed to bring down a curtain between them and their new friend who had been so wonderful to them. After he had been to Glindenwold he probably would forget all about the simple pleasures in the little white cottage by the sea.

Then she chided herself. Why shouldn't he forget? She hadn't expected the pleasant easy day or two would last forever. And she simply must not get to depending on this young man who had many other more important interests than looking after two orphans who in a few days must get back and hustle for theselves as they had been doing. Only now that she had had a little breathing space, and kindness, and someone to sympathize she surely ought to be able to do better than before. As soon as he was gone she must sit down and think out a way to put Noel in a place where he would be happy and comfortable as well as safe.

So she kept her face bright during those last minutes when Noel and Aunt Ettie were officiously trying to help him pack, and she gave him a bright smile when he said a hurried good bye. And that smile stayed with him all the time he was gone, persistently coming in between other things, and dividing his attention between what he had been doing and what he was about to do.

"I wish you were all going with me," he said with a radiant farewell smile as he was about to drive away from the cottage. His eyes lingered a moment on Gillian's slim figure, in her neat pink print.

Gillian caught her breath softly, with a faint flush in her cheeks, which she instantly subdued to its normal pallor, and gave an impersonal smile.

"Oh, that would be pleasant," she said, "but I'm afraid I wouldn't fit into the environment where you are going."

But Reuben answered quickly, fervently:

"Oh, yes, you would fit in *any*where!" And then he drove away, smiling. But those unconsidered words of his stayed with her all the evening, though she did her best to banish them, and tell herself they were only polite nothings, a kind of patter that all people of the world used for pleasant conversation. But at least it served to lift her out of the inferiority complex into which she had been slipping. Then she sat down with the evening paper in front of her as if she were reading, and tried to think out a plan for living in such a way that Noel could have the right kind of environment while she was away at the office. Next week of course she should go back to the office and begin to earn money again. These few dollars that had been given her from various sources would not last very long when she got back to the city and was on her own. Of course, beyond buying those cheap dresses she hadn't had to spend any of it yet so far, and when she did return to the city she wouldn't have to worry lest they wouldn't have a square meal the first night. But she must guard every cent now, and save them to care for Noel.

Of course if any of the money her father thought he left for them should materialize, as Reuben seemed very sure it would sometime, then they could be comfortable. But she simply must not count on that, nor even let herself think about it, until it did come, if it came at all.

She played a game with Noel, with her thoughts on ways and means more than on the game, and Noel finally wearied of it and decided to go to bed.

"Do you think Reuben will come back tomorrow morning, Gillian?" he asked wistfully as she kissed him good night.

"Oh no," said Gillian decidedly. "I think he intended to stay several days. And Noel, you must get over the idea that Reuben belongs to you. He has only been nice and kind to help us when we were in trouble. And he has a great many interests of his own that will occupy him most of the time. We'll have to learn to take care of ourselves and have a good time without him. Come now, shut your eyes and go to sleep and in the morning you and I will take a nice long walk on the beach, and pick up some lovely shells to take back to the city for you to play with."

So Noel smiled again and went to sleep, secretly hoping

that somehow Reuben would overcome this depression that seemed to have befallen them and come back to make a nice time again. He couldn't believe that Reuben was going to slough them off the way Gillian seemed to think he would.

Meantime Reuben rode into another world, his mind gradually turning from the pleasures of the past few days, into the duties of the moment. He had to plan just how quickly and how many of his plans for his shopping could be performed when he reached the city, before the stores were closed and it was time for him to speed toward Glindenwold.

GLINDENWOLD was approached by a long road, almost like a bridge, stretching to a far island like a mirage against the horizon.

The road of the approach was as perfect as a road could be. A heavy white fence that looked like marble guarded either side above the blueness of the water, bay on one side, sea on the other. And in the distance the dark green of pines and other decorative shrubbery grew, continuing the illusion of an island of palms in the tropics.

The sunset light came from behind Reuben's car, and dyed the water all about with rainbow shimmers of evening, and suddenly Reuben found himself wishing that Gillian was there to see it. How she would appreciate the beauty of the scene! And even Noel would bring some of his choice beauty-loving phrases to describe it.

Then came the rememberance of how Gillian had said with that quick recoil that she wouldn't fit where he was going. He wondered if she had come in sharp contact sometime, somewhere, with the young daughter of her employer. His soul resented any possible discourtesy on her part toward Gillian. She wouldn't be able to understand how rare Gillian was, he felt quite sure.

As he approached nearer to the island, a shadowy form of a palace began to rear its head. White marble, with all the traditional beauty of a palace. And it grew upon the vision, the nearer he drew.

Then he thought of Noel's remark about wishing for some very strong glasses so they could see some angels going by. If Noel were here now he would say this island home looked like the Heavenly City. But Reuben was very sure that when he got there it would fall very short of his ideal of the Heavenly City.

There was a wide imposing entrance arch, with great iron gates that were standing wide when Reuben reached his destination, and within there were many trees and lovely foliage, much of it with a foreign look, as if it were handtrained and ought to be under glass.

Reuben drove slowly in the winding drive, glimpsing tennis courts, swimming pools, even the first tee of a private golf links, and nearer the house two large conservatories, as if the outside grounds were not enough for the needs of the house.

The drive led about through lovely vistas, where one could glimpse the sea now and then, dashing and spreading high foam above great rocks beyond. At length he came to the great white palace itself.

Almost in awe Reuben got out of his car and surrendered it to the liveried servant who advanced to meet him.

He went slowly up the steps, followed by another liveried man who was carrying his modest luggage. He suddenly felt as Gillian had expressed it, that he didn't belong here, and he wished he hadn't come! If he had been back in his car at that instant he would have turned around and driven back to the city. But he wasn't in the car, and a train of servants were about him, ready to announce his arrival. He had never supposed himself to be a coward, so he went on up the marble steps.

Just at the top he turned and looked across behind him through a wide vista that showed the sea in its majesty, and something in that vision gave him strength. For suddenly there came to him the memory of a sweet poem set to an old English melody that he and Gillian had sung together the night before, each so surprised and pleased that the other knew it.

This is my Father's world, and to my listening ears
All nature sings, and round me rings the music of the spheres.
This is my Father's world: I rest me in the thought
Of rocks and trees, of skies and seas, His hand the wonders wrought.

He stood there an instant steadying himself with the thought, and the echo of another line rang in his heart:

Oh, let me ne'er forget
That though the wrong seems oft so strong, God is the ruler yet.

And then he turned and followed the servant into the wide reception hall, presently arriving in a gorgeously appointed chamber, with the information that dinner would be served in a short time.

A man arrived and took possession of his suitcase, unpacking his things and putting them in closets and drawers, laying out on the bed things suitable for the evening.

Reuben had never been accustomed to a man servant, presuming to dictate his movements. He knew enough to smile and take it all as if it were his habit, but he didn't like it. Still it was what he had let himself in for in coming to a place like this, and he smiled in derision at himself for being in such a position. "Posing as a man of the world," he murmured to himself. Well, it didn't matter. One could profit by all sorts of experiences of course, and it would be amusing to look back upon. Why would one want all this affectation?

So presently he thanked the man and dismissed him, and went about his dressing rapidly enough, spending most of his time looking about the apartment, gazing out the windows, taking in the thought of living in a place like this. Supposing he were rich and had no conscience to hinder him, would he like all this ostentation?

Well perhaps he might get used to it, but it wouldn't be his choice. He liked better the thought of the little white cottage. Then he went on humming the words of the song:

This is my Father's world: He shines in all that's fair;
In rustling grass I hear Him pass, He speaks to me everywhere.

Was that true? Would there be anyone who would be aware of God tonight, in this beautiful place? Were there people here who knew God at all? If he was sure there were none then why was he here? What was making him have these strange serious thoughts? Questions such as his mother used to ask? Such thoughts as the little boy Noel had voiced? Well, evidently he didn't belong here any more than Gillian.

Then came the announcement of dinner, and he knew he must go downstairs. He brushed his hands over his forehead and eyes to put such thoughts away for the present. He was here, he must go through with this thing, and he must do it with honor, not dishonor, and not by yielding any of his principles!

Down in the wide splendid rooms, among a throng of gay people, milling about in garments that were the last word of fashion, he was met by cocktails on every hand. Everybody was drinking cocktails. He didn't drink and didn't intend to, but he found it was a continuous process to try to convince the waiters that he didn't.

And then came Anise, dawning on him in a golden dress that emphasized her golden hair. It was set off by golden jewels and touches of black velvet in straps on her white, white flesh, a great deal of which was in evidence. Anise in the full regalia of her world. She was lovely, yes! He forced himself to consider her and found that indeed she was beautiful, more beautiful than he had ever found her before in daytime fashionable attire. There was a glamour about her now that she did not ordinarily wear.

She had beside her a young man to whom he had been introduced just before they came out to dinner, and who apparently was the young actor who had taken the place she had wanted Reuben to take. He gathered that they had been seen a good deal together of late, and were supposed to be very much attached. At least Anise was allowing that impression to get abroad. He watched her furtively and felt almost relieved that it seemed to be so. And yet, he rather wondered at himself. Here was he, indifferent toward a friendship that had been offered him, almost forced upon him indeed. All this wealth and beauty did not tempt him to wish he had accepted it when he could have had it. Was she purposely giving such notable attention to the actor, he wondered. He saw her glance his way now and then, but most casually. Well, it was all right with him.

He wondered what she would say if she could know that several times he had thought of Gillian in comparison, and always with a sense of rest and peace. Gillian was lovely. She wasn't just a painted glamour girl like Anise. Anise was exotic as a flower, but not one really to love.

He was startled at the thought. It hadn't occured to him before, that thought about loving in connection with Gillian. He put it away peremptorily, as not to be even considered in this atmosphere. It seemed a desecration of Gillian.

And then, of course, back in his mind there was always the thought of Agnes. She had been there through several years. For he had always meant, since high school days, that some day he would go back to Agnes. The bright high spots of his boyhood still hovered on the edges of his memory. He had stayed away from her at first because his mother felt he was too young yet for such close ties. She thought he needed more maturity for such momentous decisions as the selection of a life partner. And he, because he adored his mother, and felt her judgment to be wise, had yielded. And then when his mother was gone, he had been interested in his own career to the extent of devoting his entire thought to being a successful business man. Being out of the habit of Agnes, and in the habit of waiting till wisdom dictated it was time to move, he had not suffered disappointment in waiting a little longer before going to see Agnes again. In fact he had almost forgotten that he was keeping that as a sort of goal for the future in the back of his mind. He just hadn't been thinking about girls. Yet he still felt that he owed a kind of fealty in his very thoughts, to Agnes. At least until he was sure she was *not* the girl he wanted for his life companion.

When dinner was over the company drifted toward the theater, and Reuben with the rest found a pleasant seat, with the girl who had been sitting on his right at dinner. She was doing her best to be entertaining, although Reuben wasn't entertained. He was wondering at that moment whether Noel had remembered to put the crumbs on the plate at the back door for the birds. But he would of course, dear little fellow who loved the birds so much that he would gladly have gone without his own supper rather than have the birds miss theirs!

And as he sat there idly talking with a girl who was desolate because the man she wanted was with another girl, he wondered why after all he had come to this affair. It was not out of curiosity, just to see this famous costly establishment. Not just because he feared his employer might be offended and he might lose his job. No! He wanted no job that was dependent upon an employer's whims! Was it because his employer's daughter had been so attractive? He studied her from afar as she drifted about among her guests. She was attractive of course, graceful, and willowy, lithe and with pretty regular features, though her expression was one of habitual discontent. Had he been intrigued by this girl? Was that the reason why he was here, to test her out and be sure he did not want a closer friendship? Well, if that was it he would likely know before this evening was over whether he wanted to waste any more time in an atmosphere like this or not. It seemed to him now that just the atmosphere, all these people, their way of thinking and doing, were so alien to his own way of living that the answer was plain enough. Could he ever win a girl like Anise to live a simpler life? Was it worthwhile to try, even if he cared for her? After all this prodigality of luxury could she be content to keep a little home like other young women, and be happy just in their life together? Probably not.

Then she appeared just behind him and stooping, whispered in his ear.

"Would you like to come up on stage with me, and get the play from that angle, as if you were a part of it?"

There was condescension in her tone, as if she were offering him a great favor, and Reuben's independence instantly recoiled from it.

"No thank you," he said decidedly. Here she was at it again trying to get him into that play. He closed his lips firmly with an impersonal smile. "I think I can get the effect from here better."

With a haughty shrug Anise sailed away and disappeared from the room. And just a few minutes later the curtain rose, disclosing Anise sitting in her boudoir before her mirror in very lovely but very scanty array.

Reuben looked at her startled. What was the idea? And why had she asked him to come up on the platform with her? Had she some wild idea of forcing him into a scene like this? Or had she only thought to put him behind the scenes where she could talk with him between acts? Well, let it go at that. He had the definite feeling that she meant to trap him somehow. The more he watched her the more he felt that she was not to be trusted.

But while he was trying to think it all out the girl at her dressing table arose and began to pirouette about the stage, lifting delicate bare arms with sinuous enchantment, bringing her hands almost together with a rhythmic motion—like candy-pulling, the watcher thought amusedly, or as if she bore a skein of yarn on her extended wrists. Then more steps on dainty feet, a whirl about as if she were a thistledown. Ah! She was a dancer now, moving in exquisite harmony with low music that seemed to grow from some invisible distance, not far away. The dancing grew wilder and wilder, and suddenly from behind the scenes the young actor who had sat beside her at the table, moved in from the side, resplendent in costume of crimson velvet, most brief in its proportions. He seemed to blend into her movements, taking her in his arms, until the two were like one figure. And Reuben could scarcely restrain the merriment that suddenly danced into his eyes. Had Anise actually expected him to take this part when she first asked him to be in the play with her? Had she visioned him beside her doing this?

Well, perhaps this was merely an opening scene to introduce this actor man, and the real play would be in the next act.

But the play went on, through hectic days of the lives of two professional dancers, with more or less questionable situations and impassioned love scenes. Reuben was filled with amusement. Could it be possible that this girl had thought she could force him to play a role like that? Oh, probably not. Probably the young actor had put his own construction on the scenes and changed the lines to please himself. Surely she would not think that he could have lent himself to such a part. Well, what difference did it make? It just wasn't his world and what could he expect? This was a place where he didn't belong. All his birth and traditions, and breeding and experience were against it.

As the play worked its way on to its sordid end Reuben grew bored. He wished he could get away. But of course he couldn't, not until this play was over, and perhaps not then right away. Having come he must be courteous.

He stole a furtive glance at the time, and sighed involuntarily, wishing he were back in the shore cottage playing Chinese Checkers with Noel and Gillian. Only they would both be asleep by this time, and he wished he were also. All these alien thoughts and scenes wearied him inexpressibly.

When the play was over at last, and everybody was milling about and saying how gorgeous and glorious and heavenly and perfectly divine it had been, Reuben worked his way to find his hostess, intending to make excuse and get away that night. He shrank inexpressibly from spending another day in this company.

When he found her at last she received him rather eagerly as if this was what she had been waiting for all her life.

"Oh," she said prettily, "I'm so glad you've come! I'm worn to death! Come, let's go and take a walk and get rested. I'll show you the walk by the sea. You haven't been down there yet, and it's marvelous! There's a cushiony seat down there and we can see the moonlight on the sea. The breeze is something wonderful down there."

This seemed about the easiest thing to do, so Reuben courteously assented, and they slipped away from the throng and out into the coolness of the night.

"I suppose it's very selfish of me to take you away from the dancing," said Anise affectedly. "They're all going to dance now. But I'm really worn out. I've danced so much this evening, you know. And perhaps when we come back we can have a dance or two before they break up. They don't usually stop much before dawn when we are out here. Do you mind my taking you away?"

"Oh no," said Reuben with almost a sigh of relief. "I'm not a dancer, you know, and it's much pleasanter out here in this wonderful night."

"Yes, I like it," said Anise with that weary drawl she affected. "I think you'll love it down here. It's the darlingest spot, so hidden from everything else. It's only very specials I bring down here. I haven't told many how to find it. It's quite secluded, and I just felt I must get away from the crowd and have a real quiet time. I knew you would be the very one to help me at that sort of thing."

Reuben looked at her curiously. This was a new role for her to play.

She was leading him down through the garden, out beyond it through a young grove. The way led among the trees, and over gnarled roots here and there and once or twice she almost stumbled, and then reaching for his arm snuggled up to him. She handed him a small flashlight like a little pencil and so walking, leaning against him, they went through the darkness, Anise's lissome body pressed close to his side.

Reuben didn't like the situation at all. He had no desire to have her forced almost into his arms. When he found a girl to love he wanted to win her fairly. He was getting more and more sure that he couldn't love this one. And yet she seemed rather sweet now with the moonlight through occasional breaks in the foliage, shimmering on her ashblond hair, and on the pearly whiteness of her face turned up so close to his shoulder.

"This seems a hard walk for you to take in those little gold sandals," he remarked. "They weren't built for this kind of hiking."

"Oh, well, it isn't very much farther," she said, suddenly slipping a little and clasping her other arm about his arm, forcing him to put out his other arm to keep her from falling.

Willingly she yielded herself to his assistance, and he was relieved as he turned the tiny torch ahead, to see the seat she had spoken of, luxurious with deep cushions, nestled in a bower of greenness. He led her over and seated her comfortably among the cushions, taking the trouble to put a couple of them behind her, and make it seem restful to her.

"Oh, thank you!" she said putting her head back and closing her eyes for an instant, just where a ray of moonlight touched the cushions and made a picture of her. "You are so helpful, and you know just how to make one comfortable. But now, sit down here beside me and tell me honestly just what you thought of the play. I know you will be honest whatever you say, and I really want to know the truth."

Reuben stood looking down at her. He didn't want to sit down beside her. In the first place there wasn't room at either side of her to sit in comfort. Even now as he stood before her he could smell the perfume of her hair, and it was alluring. It stirred his senses. He resented it. He did not want to take her in his arms.

So he continued to stand and look down at her.

"Why, I thought it was very well done, didn't you? I can't say that I cared much for the play. There didn't seem to be much plot to it, or any point to the outcome, but I suppose it was as good as a play like that is expected to be, wasn't it? You certainly did your part without a flaw so far as I could see. But of course I'm not much of a judge of such things.

I don't have time to go to plays, and never care much for them any way."

The girl sat still staring out of the darkness straight at him, frozen in a kind of angry disappointment.

"Oh!" she said petulantly. "Why do you stand there? Why don't you sit down close beside me? Don't you see I'm tired and need comfort, not just contemptuous criticism. Sit down here and kiss me! Can't you see I'm in love with you? Take me in your arms and kiss me."

Reuben stood there in shock of horror! She must be drunk of course or she would not so far forget herself as to talk this way. She must have had a stiff drink just after the play. He had caught a whiff of it on her breath as they came along through the darkness. But, what was he to do with her? He stood there for an instant looking down at her in perplexity and then she suddenly burst into tears. That in her experience had been the ultimate card to play. It always brought her what she wanted.

But suddenly Reuben's heart grew steely hard, and his nice voice was cold as he answered.

"I'm sorry," he said, "But you see I'm not in love with you! And it takes love to make a kiss of any value."

"Oh, if you would just sit down and put your arms around me, and let me kiss you I would show you that you do love me!" She reached out white arms and tried to draw him down, but Reuben drew back away from her.

"Love," said he, "is not made up of touching lips. It comes from the heart. You don't know what you are saying. You have been drinking too much. The best thing we can do is to forget all this. Shall I help you to the house, or would you like me to call your maid for you?"

And then before the angry girl could answer, they heard footsteps coming down the path, and voices.

"I'm sure Anise went down this way," Reuben heard a girl's voice say, and then the unmistakable voice of the actor. "Yes, I'm sure she did!" A flashlight blazed in on them, Reuben standing back, aloof, and Anise huddled on the cushions.

"Oh! Here you are," said the soothing voice of the actor. "I've been looking everywhere for you. They want us to dance again together. Come on, or the whole company will be down here after you."

"We were just coming in," said Reuben calmly. "I'm afraid Miss Glinden is not feeling well."

"Nonsense!" said Anise sharply. "I'm quite all right, darling. Yes, of course I'll dance. I just came down to get a bit of rest for a minute before we went up to the ballroom. You were wonderful, Crispin, all through the play. You were just adorable. Come on, let's get back!" and she took hold of the young actor's hand, and led the way through the darkness. They were out of sight almost instantly, their voices dying away in the distance.

And then Reuben discovered that the colorless little individual whom Crispin the actor had left on his hands was the same girl who had sat beside him at the table. He would have to pilot her back to the house and he couldn't quite remember where he had left off in the uninteresting table conversation they had tried to carry on. But she all too evidently was preparing to sit down among the cushions, and expecting him to do the same.

So he plunged immediately into a discussion of the surroundings.

"Isn't this the most marvelous place?" he said. "By the way, have you seen this view of the ocean just beyond here? Come out this way." He guided her lightly over to the path and out to the point of land where they could look over the moonlit sea.

The girl was charmed with the view, and would gladly have lingered, sitting down on rustic benches that were placed to get the loveliest views. They stood for a moment looking off to the pathway of moonlight, and Reuben said rather sadly:

"It is hard to realize that off there a few thousand miles bombs are falling, men are killing one another, and terror reigns."

The girl shivered.

"Oh, don't" she cried. "That horrid war! We've got an English woman in our apartment house, and every time we meet her she is telling such terrible tales of how her home was destroyed, and she and her children haven't any idea whether they'll ever see any of their family again. I'm just fed up with it. Don't let's stand here any longer. You've just spoiled this wonderful view for me. Let's go back to the house where there's music and dancing, and we won't have to think about gruesome things. I don't see why we have to be bothered with their troubles over across the ocean. It's their war not ours."

He looked at her wonderingly.

"No," he said sadly, "it isn't ours *yet.*"

"Mercy!" said the girl. "You aren't one of those tiresome people who are always harping on the possibility of war over here, are you? Because if you are I positively won't listen! You give me the jitters."

"Sorry," said Reuben. "Come, if you want to get back to the dancing this is the shortest way, and I think you'll find it the easiest, by the beach, because it is lighter here, and I don't happen to have a flashlight. Miss Glinden has taken hers with her."

So they hurried along the beach, the girl avoiding looking out to the water, puffing along quite out of breath.

"Why yes," she admitted. "It's a lot cheerfuller in the house at this time of night, don't you think? And I do hate that war. I don't see why they allow war in the world. Don't you think it ought to be stopped?"

"Undoubtedly," said Reuben with a twinkle in his eyes, "but how would you go about it?"

"Why, it ought to be against the law!" said the girl firmly.

"Yes?" said Reuben.

He drew a breath of relief when he took her into the house and landed her in the ballroom with some intimate friends of hers. Then before he could be seen by Anise, or assigned to any other function, he made his way hastily up the stairs to the room he had been given. His idea was to pack his things and slide out the back way, if there was such a thing in this elegant mansion, and drive back to his own environment.

But he found it wasn't as simple as that. The functionary who had assumed the right to unpack for him and lay out his evening clothes, had made way with his two suitcases, and search for them as he might he couldn't find hide nor hair of them. There probably was some proper place to park such things as luggage during the stay of a guest, but it was all a mystery to him. He searched in the closet and under the bed, he even walked down the hall and peered around for a possible trunk room, but saw no sign of his luggage. So finally he resorted to the bell which he discovered in a remote position and was rewarded by the appearance of a man who in due time produced the desired suitcases.

Reuben explained to him that he found he had to leave at once, and the man showed himself deft in the art of packing, and also of calling for Reuben's car to be brought around to the side door, as Reuben had told him he did not wish to disturb the guests, and would just leave a note for Miss Glinden.

He wrote the brief note at the desk in his room.

> My dear Miss Glinden:
>
> I am sure you will pardon me for not disturbing you for farewells. I find that I shall have to hurry to get back to the city in time to meet an engagement tomorrow morning, and then go to another appointment.
>
> Thank you so much for giving me the opportunity to see the play of which I had heard so much. I am sure you must feel rewarded with your success.
>
> Regretting that I could not have thanked you face to face, and looking forward to meeting you when we all get back to the city in the fall,
>
> Very sincerely,
> Reuben Remington

He handed the note to the man with a generous tip and followed him down the back way to his car, and as he drove out the ornate gateway, and sped down the great white drive across the sea, he gave thanks that he was away.

Once he turned and looked back at the splendor of the great white palace, lit from ground to turret and marveled at its beauty.

"So that's that!" he said with a grim smile. "Imagine it! I think that will be about all of that number! And I'm glad it is over! If by this I lose my job, and the prestige that I have gained by hard work, well, it can't be helped. It's done, and I'm definitely *not* in love with that girl. I hope that's the end of her as far as I'm concerned." Then he put it out of his mind, and went whirling happily along the moonlight way back to the real things of the life he had grown to enjoy.

He glanced at his watch. It would be too late by the time he had got back to town to go to the shore tonight. It would just waken them all, spoil their night's rest. Too late to go to his rooming house, as his landlady would not be expecting him, and would likely waken and come up to see if all was right. He would just go back to the hotel where he and Noel had stayed. It would arouse no comment and he could leave as early as he pleased in the morning.

So he sped on to the old hotel, and felt lonely for the child who had been with him there, and pleasantly thrilled that he was going back to him in the morning. Perhaps there was a church there and he could take them all to church. That would be nice. He must waken early in the morning and get down there in time. That would please Noel.

So he fell asleep at once, forgetting all about the unpleasant termination of the evening. What would Anise Glinden have thought if she had known that she had made no more impression than that?

WHEN Reuben reached the shore and drew up in front of the cottage a joyous shout heralded his arrival, as Noel came tearing down the steps and flew out to greet him.

"You did come back this morning!" he shouted. "I said you would, but Gillian said you couldn't. She said you had gone to visit somebody and you would have to go to church with them, even if you didn't want to stay. But you came! You did come back. Didn't they want you to stay and go to church with them?"

Reuben smiled amusedly at the idea of anybody at Glindenwold wanting him to go to church with them.

"No," said Reuben. "They are not churchgoing people. So I came back."

"Oh," said Noel, "what do they do on Sunday? Just read and take walks?"

"Well, I didn't stay to see," he said smiling, "but I heard them talk about playing tennis and going swimming and seeing a moving picture."

"Oh," said Noel gravely, "then they don't know what Sunday is for, do they?"

"Is for?" queried Reuben puzzled.

"Yes, they don't know it is like the Lord Jesus' birthday—it's

His resurrection day, you know—and we can just spend it with Him and be happy, like Gillian does on my birthday, whenever she doesn't have to work."

"No," said Reuben, "I don't suppose they do."

"What did they say when you told them about it?" he asked innocently, almost sadly.

"Why," said Reuben in startled astonishment, "I didn't say anything about it. I didn't have any opportunity. I think they would have laughed. They wouldn't have known what I meant."

"Oh!" said Noel thoughtfully. "I guess there were people like that in the Bible, weren't there? I'll have to think about that. But I'm glad you are back. Now we can go to church, can't we?"

"We sure can," said Reuben. "I had that in mind in coming back this morning."

"Oh, that is nice! I'm glad you are like that! Gillian will be glad too. Mrs. Aunt Ettie told her she ought not to try to walk to church."

"Of course not!" said Reuben firmly as if that decided it.

But he thought it all over afterward. The preposterous idea of expecting the Glindens and their guests to go to church. They were so obviously not churchgoing people. The absolute faith the child had that he, Reuben, would have reasoned with his hosts about the matter and tried to induce them to go in the right way! Poor baby! He had a lot to learn about the utter indifference of the world to things that made for righteousness.

And yet, as he thought about it, he realized that the child had only taken literally many things that Reuben's own dear mother had tried to teach him when he was a child, and he had so far gotten away from the memory of her teaching that it even seemed to him a matter of little moment.

Well, at least he was glad to be back, and he came with zest to the rather late, and most elaborate breakfast that Aunt Ettie had delightedly prepared.

Gillian was dressed in her new dark blue dress, and looked as pretty as a picture in spite of the big apron of Aunt Ettie's in which she was smothered. Already the good food and the rest and the wonderful salt air had made a difference in Gillian. Perhaps also the relief from constant anxiety had much to do with it. But Reuben looked at her with interest. Who knew that the colorless girl he had helped down to the ambulance could bloom into delicate beauty like this?

Questioned about whether he had had a good time the night before he didn't seem especially enthusiastic.

"It's a wonderful place of course," he said, reaching for a second hot biscuit, to the great satisfaction of Aunt Ettie. "Have you ever seen it, Gillian?"

Gillian's cheeks flushed as she shook her head.

"Oh, no. I never had time nor money to go and see things, and of course I wouldn't have been invited."

"Well, I kept wishing I had you all along. I know you would have enjoyed it. It's an island, you know, with a long approach apparently slung across from shore to shore. It must be more than a mile long, a sort of bridge, fenced with a great white wall."

He went on with the description, telling of the grounds and the sea and the marble palace gleaming in the setting sun until both Noel and his sister almost stopped eating so interested they were.

Aunt Ettie too was interested as the story progressed and she asked questions that would have convulsed the Glinden household if they could have heard it.

"What would they wantta live on a niland for?" she asked suddenly in the midst of his description. "Seems like that's sort of tempting Providence, with all them hurricanes, and storms they're havin' nowadays. I'd wantta get on land if 'twas me. And sakes alive, what would they wantta waste money cartin' trees and dirt out ta sea? 'Twould be a gradeal easier ta hev a place like that on land where everybody could drive around and see it."

Reuben flashed a smile of appreciation at her.

"There might be something in that, Aunt Ettie, but I have a hunch you'd enjoy being out there in good weather."

He went on describing the beauties and the wonders of

the place, not forgetting the opal tints of sea and sky, and then the midnight blue pricked with stars above the looming beauty of the palace, and her response was:

"H'm! That's all very well, but what I'd like ta know is, what did they give ya ta eat? Was it any better'n my cookin'?"

Reuben grinned again.

"Not nearly as good, Aunt Ettie. But it was different. They had a lot of dishes you would have called queer, I think. Stylish things they have in French restaurants. They were good of course. But I like your good home cooking better."

"But what were they, Reuben? Was there fish of any kind?"

'Why, yes, I think there were combinations of fish. They had lobster salad for one thing."

"Lobsters!" exclaimed Aunt Ettie in disgust. "Those ugly big red crawly critturs that make faces at ya with their claws, an' you kill 'em an' eat 'em when they're alive? I call that a crime, scalding poor red devils like that even ef they are good ta eat. Fer me, I shouldn't care ta visit people like that."

"Well, Aunt Ettie, I didn't stay very long, did I?" he laughed.

"No," she admitted reluctantly, "but you haven't finished. What did ya hev fer dessert? Some kind of pie, ur ice cream? And what did ya hev ta drink? Coffee? Ur lemonade?"

Reuben smiled amusedly at Gillian, who was taking no part in this phase of the conversation.

"No pie, Aunt Ettie," he said indulgently, "and no lemonade that I saw. Ices and cakes, and fancy things. Coffee, yes, and wines."

"Now, Reuben Remington! Ef I ain't ashamed of you! The way your mamma brought you up not to drink wine. And you goin' to a place like that! I never'da thought it of ya!"

"I didn't *drink* the wine, Aunt Ettie," he answered in a gentle tone, "and I didn't eat a lot of the things they had. But I don't think you need to worry about me that way. I feel just as my mother taught me to feel about things like that. Now, can we wash the dishes and then get our best bibs and tuckers on and try to find a church?"

He looked at Gillian pleasantly and she smiled assent and hurried to the kitchen with a handful of silver to be washed.

But before the dishes were done there came a telegram for Reuben from the detective in New York. It was a code that had been agreed upon, and there were some things about it that kept Reuben's mind occupied and a little worried all during service, so that he did not get the good from the message that he had from the one the week before.

That afternoon they went down on the beach and had their Sunday School, and even Aunt Ettie came at Noel's earnest solicitation. She listened interestedly to the verses and songs and even to the simple practical lesson that Gillian tried to give.

Reuben was much impressed. He tried to imagine Anise Glinden in such a position, and knew she wouldn't be able to qualify. The thought came to him, would Agnes be able to do it? Undoubtedly Agnes could do almost anything that anybody else could do if she once got the idea, and wanted to do it. But would she want to? Would she have the knowledge and the spirit to do it? Well, that would be one of the things he would be finding out perhaps when he went to that wedding. Until then he would try not to think about it.

The next day he had a long telephone conversation with the detective, and later in the afternoon he had another talk with Gillian, going over the papers in that tin box, and asking her questions that might help in the matter of her inheritance.

The thing that made him uneasy was that the detectives, having traced Uncle Mason Albee to the vicinity of their shore cottage, had suddenly lost track of him, and no amount of expert work seemed to be able to bring him to light. Of course they hoped that he would be found within the next few days. There was a possibility that he had returned to his home and given up the search for the niece who had money in her own right; that of course could be verified in a few days at most.

So the days went by and Gillian and Reuben and Noel played together like three children, going bathing, going fishing, going boating on a little lake full of lily pads and great white blossoms, taking rides around the vicinity, playing at collecting houses they would like to buy if they were rich, building sand cities, and comparing reminiscences of their earlier lives. It was all very fascinating, and the days passed swiftly and joyously, so happily that they were tired enough at night to fall asleep at once on retiring, instead of staying awake to think of the burdens and perplexities that would come when all this good time was over and they went back to the world.

Then one evening, after a particularly wonderful day in which they had found much enjoyment, Noel looked up to Reuben with that lovely trustful smile and said confidently:

"Oh, Reuben, you won't ever go away from us again, will you?"

Aunt Ettie watched all their faces sharply. How would Reuben take this? Did he realize how he was involving them all with his charm, so that separation was going to be very hard?

Gillian gave a quick look toward Reuben and then dropped her glance to her almost empty plate, and made as if to go on eating. Reuben looked at Noel with a kind of dismay in his glance.

"Well," he said half apologetically, "of course I have to go to that wedding, and it's almost time for that. I hadn't realized. It's only four more days before I have to start."

Noel gave a soft little sound like a hurt rabbit, and sat there looking at him sorrowfully.

"Then will you come back?" he said with a sigh of resignation.

Reuben's swift glance around saw the sudden dismay in all their faces. In his own mind there was the same question as to what that journey to the wedding was going to bring about; a sudden memory of Agnes, and what she might do to this pleasant atmosphere that had been enjoyed by them all. Would she be the old Agnes who had charmed him so much in his early years? And would she fit in with these who had come to mean so much to him? Would this delightful comradeship ever be renewed in the same easy harmony? Quickly he put aside the question and answered cheerily, "Of course I'll come back." But it was there all the same in the back of his mind all day, and all the succeeding days, growing like a cool little unobtrusive barrier between them all, especially between himself and Gillian.

Or did he just fancy that there was a coolness about her smile, an aloofness, that had not been there before?

The morning he left, Noel asked, after looking at him with a long mournful wistfulness:

"Do you *hafta* go to this wedding?"

"Yes," said Reuben. "I promised, you know, and I'm not just a guest. I'm the best man, and it's altogether too late now to back out and tell them they must get another best man. It would be very rude."

"Oh!" said Noel mournfully. "I didn't know."

But the mournfulness stayed with them all day, until Reuben was ready to start. And Gillian withdrew behind the distant smile she used to use when she first came to the shore. Reuben was going away. Would he ever come back? He was going among his old friends who had the claim of years upon him. He had been good and kind, but she must let him see that she did not expect this great friendliness to be the same always. It was just a lovely interval and now she was well, and did not need close attention any more.

They went through the forms of having a good time. But the coolness and stiffness were there in spite of them.

And when Reuben was about to drive away, Gillian stood on the porch beside Aunt Ettie and smiled a demure good bye. Somehow Reuben didn't know what was the matter, nor why he felt so reluctant to go.

"I wish," he said, pausing with his hand on the wheel, and leaning from the window to speak to her, "I wish that I had taught you to drive. I could just as well have left the car with you and gone on the train. Only I would have worried lest you might get hurt in a smash-up or something."

"Me? Drive?" said Gillian with sudden pink in her cheeks. "Oh, I wouldn't dare take the responsibility of your lovely car even if I could drive!" she said aghast. "But thank you just the same."

"Some day I will be old enough, and then I will drive your car for you, Reuben," announced Noel.

"Yes," said Reuben with a tender light in his eyes. "Of course you will, Noel."

And then amid the gay laughter of them all Reuben drove away wishing with all his heart that he hadn't promised to go to this nuisance of a wedding.

THE home town looked much the same as ever when Reuben arrived there early the next afternoon. He had had a pleasant uneventful trip, during which he had been doing a lot of thinking, more particularly about Gillian and the winter that was before her. He had arrived at the conclusion that she ought to have a longer rest than just another few days before she went back to the office. Yet he was morally certain it would be difficult to convince her of that. He tried to work out some plan by which Aunt Ettie could be made to help in a scheme of things, to combine a home for Gillian and the boy, and provide someone for Noel to stay with while his sister was working, but somehow the whole thing was perplexing. If only that inheritance of hers would materialize, even if it were only a few hundred dollars, perhaps she could be reasoned into seeing that it would be real economy to use some of the money right away. But the more he thought about it the more he was sure she would not do it. He had had the utmost difficulty in convincing her that she must stay with Aunt Ettie to the end of the month, anyway. But of course he couldn't hope to do anything more till he got back. Why think about it? It only served to make him restless. Why hadn't he come out in the open and talked to her about it before he left? Was it just that he was lazy and didn't want to spoil the good times they were having?

He drove down the old street where he used to live as a boy. The house looked much the same as always, only it had been newly painted, and looked nice and fresh. Some children were playing in the yard, and he found himself resenting their presence. It seemed as if he should see his mother sitting in the baywindow with her sewing and keeping a watch out for him. It made his heart beat faster, and the tears stung in his eyes. He drove on by and took his way toward the Meredith home. That had been another familiar place to him in the old days, but there was nothing about it to bring tears. He had lived through happy days at the Merediths', and he was eager to see his old friend.

And there, suddenly, at the corner before he reached Meredith's house, he saw Agnes hurrying down the street in the opposite direction. She hadn't seen him, for he had but just turned into the street, and he couldn't see her face, she was too far away. But he was glad to have this glimpse of her before having to talk with her, just to get himself adjusted to the thought of her. Of course he ought to have been doing that exclusively for the last two days, but his thoughts had been so occupied with Gillian's troubles that Agnes had hardly been in his mind at all.

But this was Agnes, she was unmistakable. He would know her anywhere. Her walk, her carriage, the little tripping motion of her twinkling feet, as if she were just about to dance, the way she held her head.

He studied her in the distance before she turned another corner toward her home. He distinctly remembered how the sight of her in the distance this way used to stir him. How he used to quicken his step and catch up with her. And now he was decidedly slowing his car. He didn't want to see her yet. It had not quickened his pulse at all to see her. But then of course he was older now. And so would she be when he saw her face to face. Yet the witchery of her smile would likely be the same, the glances in her big dark eyes. He turned into the Meredith drive, and swung around to the garage, as though it had been yesterday that he had been accustomed to drive in there and burst into the house by the kitchen door, along with Frank.

Then a voice from an upper window called:

"Rube! Old man! Hi there! Good work, got here on time all right! Come on up, the same old place!"

That was Frank. Good old Frank. Didn't sound a day older. He swung from his car, slammed the door, and went up the back steps eagerly. He didn't dread to meet Frank. They had been through high school together, roomed together in college. Fellows were different. But you couldn't tell how a girl would turn out after a long time of separation.

And so he hurried up the stairs, meeting none of the family yet, and glad that it was so.

It was good getting back. They had a great talk, while Frank went on packing his suitcase over and over because he got so interested in talking that he put the wrong things in the wrong places.

All the news of all the crowd he heard, and yet Agnes hadn't been mentioned. And then just as they were dashing about getting ready to answer the dinner summons Frank remarked quite casually:

"Seen Agnes yet? She promised to write you seconding my invitation. I didn't know whether she would or not. You never can tell just what she'll do since she broke her last engagement."

"Oh, was she engaged? I hadn't heard that," said Reuben with studied indifference.

"Yes, engaged to Shaft Howard for almost a year, and then they had a falling out, and in a month she was engaged to Ned Stewart. I guess she was pretty daffy about him for a while, but when Nellie Darnell came to town he went with her too often to please my lady, and she broke that off so hard it snapped. Now she seems gayer than ever. Who knows but she'll take you on the rebound?"

"Oh, no," said Reuben. "I'm not interested. Don't worry."

"But I thought you used to be pretty well gone on her," said his friend.

"Well, it may have seemed that way. We were children in school then. But I imagine Rose Elizabeth must be a beauty now. I congratulate you."

"Thanks. She is. Wait till you see her. But you'll find that Agnes isn't far behind. Maybe you'll change your mind when you see her. It would be awfully interesting to me to have you for a brother-in-law."

"That would be a consideration of course," laughed Reuben. "I'll bear that in mind if I ever get interested." And laughing they went down to dinner together.

Reuben had always been fond of Mr. and Mrs. Meredith, and they of him, and they had a pleasant time at dinner. Then the young men went out together to the wedding rehearsal, and on the way to the church they talked more.

"But really, Rube, I'm interested to know about your affairs, you know, you close-mouthed fish, you! You're not married yet, are you? I assume you would at least have let us know that."

Reuben grinned in the dark.

"No, I'm not married yet," he said, after consideration.

"Well, are you engaged yet, you old sly fox?"

"No, not to the best of my knowledge. I really haven't had time yet, if you must know."

"Time, you idiot. You've had all the time there is. What's the matter? Haven't there been any girls?"

"Oh, yes, there've been girls. Too many girls sometimes."

"Heavens! Man! Have you got more than one?"

"Yes," said Reuben solemnly, "there have been three I've been considering."

There came a resounding slap on Reuben's broad shoulder.

"Quit your kidding, man! You always were too close-mouthed. And this is no time to shut your mouth. A wedding is a joyous time, and if you've got any joy of your own you should announce it!"

"Well, that's a thought. I'll do that little thing if I can find anything to announce before I leave."

"That's the talk! I'll hold you to that, fella!" and then they went up the church steps together, and there was Agnes right inside the door! Her face was turned vivaciously up with a saucy answer for one of the ushers, for all the world as if she were just standing at the door of the high school telling some young man of the senior class what she thought of him.

She was becomingly dressed. Agnes was always becomingly dressed, in rather dashing noticeable clothes, but they were suited to her rather impudent prettiness.

She flashed a quick smile at Reuben and grasped his hand in both of hers. She had little hands. He had always admired her hands. But when he looked for the seashell tips that had always been little pearls to his eyes he was startled to see instead elongated pointed objects of a deep bright crimson color, and as they touched each other, or anything in fact, they gave forth a metal sound. Oh, he had seen the nails of fashionable women, girls like Anise Glinden who followed the very latest of fashion's dictates, but he had not expected it of Agnes. He had been looking for those pale pink petal-like nails, and was shocked to see these others instead. For an instant it went through him unpleasantly. As a boy he had held those hands in his own, shyly, with almost a reverence, but he would not like to hold these. It gave him a sense of shivering to think of it.

He lifted his eyes to her laughing lips as she greeted him, and found they were bright and too red, and almost thick in their contour, like other fashionable women. He had not expected to find her so. Her cheeks were bright with rouge, well applied, he supposed women would say. She was a brilliant picture of a woman, but somehow all the outward adornments seemed to have erased her heart. Or was it that there could be no heart where lips were as bright as that? Only flesh, and raw flesh at that.

He was not a fool, nor blind. He had seen such highly painted women every day for years, and never looked sharply at them, nor even paused to dislike. But to see it on Agnes, whom he had always idealized, ah, that was a different thing! It was a distinct shock.

A few minutes later while they were waiting for a member of the wedding party who was to come in on a train presently, Agnes put her hand possessively on his arm, and the little bits of crimson shells clattered softly as they brushed his sleeve.

"Come, Reuben, let's walk outside around the church for a few minutes and start knitting up the raveled fabric of our friendship, as it were."

She laughed gaily, yet kept that enameled little hand in place upon his arm, and he had no choice but to obey, feeling almost a reluctance lest he would meet with other shocks. Yet this was what he had come to find out. He must know what she was. Had he or his mother been right?

They stepped down to the paving stones that led around the beautiful edifice. Grass and shrubs were cut trimly around the paving. A step brought them around the corner into the soft darkness of the summer evening.

She put her other hand across and touched his hand.

"For the love of Heaven," she implored, "give me a cigarette, Reuben. I'm simply dying for a smoke, and I must have forgotten to put my case in my hand bag. I came away in such a hurry."

He looked down at her astonished, thinking at first she was joking, for there had been no cigarette smoking among the girls he knew in the old days. Surely Agnes had not taken that up too. But he saw by the earnestness of her face that she meant it, and he felt a cold disappointment. Other girls smoked, yes, he saw it constantly, but Agnes never had. It wouldn't have been considered refined when he went to high school for a girl to smoke.

A second it took to adjust himself to this change.

"Sorry I can't help you out," he said almost coldly. "I still don't smoke."

"Reuben!" she said, perhaps almost as much shocked as he. "Surely you haven't kept that up in these days! You are not tied to your mother's apron strings yet, are you?"

"Apron strings?" he said a bit haughtily. "I don't remember that she wore apron strings. My mother has been in Heaven a number of years. Perhaps you didn't know. But I don't smoke."

"Aren't you a model, Reuben? But of course I know your mother is gone. Sorry and all that, darling, but I had supposed you would have grown up by this time."

Then Reuben remembered suddenly that their final quarrel had been about whether a young man need follow his mother's advice. He hadn't liked the sneer on her pretty lips when she had said, "We young people owe nothing to our parents. When we are old enough to be in high school we have a right to use our own judgment about what we should do." Somehow Agnes' voice brought back some of the things she had said that had made him feel his mother must be right about her.

On the whole he was rather glad when one of the ushers came running after them to say that the absent one had arrived and the rehearsal was about to begin. Just how Agnes was going to get on through the rehearsal without a smoke he didn't stop to think. He was disturbed enough about her already, just to have his ideal fade. She had said she was dying for a smoke. Would she fall by the way up the aisle?

With lips set, and almost a prayer in his heart he followed her into the church again.

"So absurd that they won't allow one to smoke inside the church," she murmured. "I could easily borrow a cigarette from Bobby and get a whiff or two before we start! It isn't a sacred service tonight, just a wedding rehearsal. They have an awful fanatic of a rector here. Well, so long, Reuben. See you at the altar." She slid away to whisper to the said Bobby, whispered to him, and presently disappeared for a few seconds. Then she reappeared with a look upon her of having had her life saved.

Reuben took his place at the head of the aisle and watched the gay procession come hippity-hopping up the aisle in slow and measured tread. But his eyes were upon Agnes, studying the changes that the years had made in her. Changes that he had not been able to discern in the dimness of twilight outside the church, and he was shocked again. Not so much because she was like a hundred other fashionable girls, but that she who had been set upon a pedestal for his young worship should be discovered on a level with girls to whom he was either utterly indifferent, or else heartily despised.

Well, he had not come to fall in love with her and marry her. He could exist if all his idols fell. There was still a girl now and then like Gillian Guthrie, or—well, at least there was Gillian.

Up to this present moment he had not thought of Gillian as someone to love, to marry perhaps, only as someone very frail entrusted to his care. But now he remembered her with a kind of relief. Not everybody had to be a fashion plate, nor ape men's vices. He thought of Anise huddled among those pillows in the leafy shadows, drunk. And then his eyes sought the sparkling loveliness of little Rose Elizabeth, the bride, as she came demurely up the aisle. Well, she made a lovely bride. Perhaps she was painted too, and had crimson finger tips, but it did not shine out so glaringly to him because he had only known her as a child. Agnes he had thought almost an angel and she didn't look in the least like an angel now. A very pretty sparkling girl, full of pep and gaiety, smart and bright and hard, but not the kind of girl you fell in love with.

Strange that he had to go to Glindenwold, and then come away out here to this wedding to find out that it was really Gillian he loved. And then his heart gave a wild sweet throb so in tune with the wedding march that joy came right out and stood in his eyes for anybody to see who had time to notice. Only they weren't noticing, for Agnes was taking her steps up the aisle in the eyes of the world, and she thought Reuben was watching her so she was being very careful about them.

But never a step did Reuben see, for he was thinking about Gillian, and wondering if he could ever persuade her to love him.

So far Reuben was concerned he had finished the work he came to Carrington, Illinois, for. Though there was the rest of the evening, standing around and talking to them all, saying a lot of nothings that everybody expected him to say. There would be a lot more talking to do with Agnes; he would probably get it rubbed into him thoroughly that his mother had been right and he had been wrong. And there would be tomorrow in which he would likely be asked to go on various errands, probably in Agnes' company, more talk, more covert sneers and laughter, in spite of which he somehow felt that Agnes still liked him as much as she used to. The trouble was she wanted to make him over according to her own pattern. And there would be the wedding itself, and the wedding supper, and the afterwards, seeing the bride and groom off, tying ribbons and old shoes on a car they were not going to use, and flinging rice and confetti. Oh, it was all to go through, but thanks be, that was the end. Agnes wouldn't want it to be the end, but he knew now definitely that he did. That never, never would he want to see more of Agnes, nor fall in love with her, nor marry her, not even if he stayed till doomsday to find out. He had found out now. He loved Gillian Guthrie, and he meant to marry her if he could get her.

EARLY on the morning after the wedding day, a policeman of Sandy Haven district walked down the street to the little white cottage were Aunt Ettie presided, and knocked at the door.

Gillian was in her room making her bed with her door open a crack to hear when Noel would call that he had his small spelling lesson learned. He was sitting on a little chair that Aunt Ettie had salvaged from the days when Reuben was a little boy and she was his nurse. She had brought it along with Noel in mind, and he loved it. Gillian heard Aunt Ettie hurry in from the kitchen to open the door so she went on making her bed, but she could quite well hear all that the policeman said.

"Mornin', ma'am," he said, "I represent the police in this district an' I wantta ask you a few questions. You the one they call Aunt Ettie?" He eyed her severely.

"I am!" said Aunt Ettie. "But what's that ta you?"

"Not a thing, my good wumman, not a thing. I'm merely identifying ya. Listen, did a party come here ta call this mornin' ur last evenin', name of Albee? Mason Albee? Sort of elderly, wearin' a wide brimmed soft felt hat and fairly longish hair?"

Aunt Ettie pricked up her ears but her eyes remained steady. Even a policeman couldn't tell what was going on behind her firm shut lips, and her steady glance.

"Never seed the party!" she declared.

"Well, he's likely ta cum, so they tell me, and when he does, ef I don't ketch him on his way, give me a call, won'tcha? Ask fer Sam, an' ef the old party can hear ya then don't say nothing only 'Okay.' Understand?"

"Sure I understand. I begun ta learn English as soon as I was born," said Aunt Ettie competently, "and I ben studyin' it mostly ever since."

They faced each other for one grim instant, these old warhorses, with maybe a twitching of the lips and eyelids, but never a smile did they crack. Just measured each other, and turned away content.

"Well, s'long!" said the policeman. "I'll be seein' ya." He opened the screen door.

"What—" said Aunt Ettie with her expression timed just right, "is the little old idea, anyways, comin' here? What's me and my household got ta do with the old bird's business? I guess I rate that much knowledge ef I'm ta be ordered ta call you up on the telephone."

The policeman turned back with a grim smile, showing he could appreciate a joke if it was pressed upon him.

"Well, ya see, lady, I'm not supposed ta tell all the outs an' ins of the law, but bein' as you've enquired, an' showed yerself fairly willin' ta cooperate in the round up I can jest give ya a hint, that this here old party is wanted by the law fer somethin' on the order of crooked, I infer, an' bein' as they found out where he was a-goin'ta be around this time, they give me the high sign ta watch out fer him."

"That's all well enough fer you o' course, but what I wantta know is how they picked me house ta search fer the old rascal, in place of some other cottages. I never heard tell of him."

"Well, that's as it may be!" said the policeman. "I'm jest tellin' ya what I'm supposed ta give out. You see this here information was sent down from the N'Yark office, in a kinda code

I guess you'd call it, an' it implied the old party was searchin' fer some relative ur other who was livin' with you."

"Well, I ain't got a relative by thet name, not on neither side, an' that's the truth."

"Well, now you jest keep yer shir—beg pardon, ma'am—that is, jest keep nice an' cool an' don't get het up about it. Likely the old party'll find out he's made a mistake, ur they didn't ask the right address, ur else he's just kiddin' 'em. You see he's wanted fer questionin' and he's likely stallin' fer time. So, jest you call me up when an' *if* he comes, an' I'll see you don't get inta no trouble personally. Good mornin'! I'll see you later!"

The policeman passed out of the door and walked slowly down to the street, pausing every step or two to jot down something in his very important looking little notebook. Aunt Ettie watched him out of sight, and then went outside and removed a dead leaf or two from her rose geranium, paused to look up and down the street, gave a quick searching of the ocean as if perchance the vagabond might come tripping over the waves. At last she went into the house.

"Gillian," she called, but there came no answer.

She opened Gillian's door which was standing ajar but Gillian was not there. She went outside and called again, but still no answer. Then she called louder:

"N-o-o-el!" and then listened, but there came no quick answering young voice. Several times she called, and called again from different points. She went to the door and looked down the street. Then she went to the back door and looked off down the sand dunes, but there wasn't even a speck there to show where they were sitting. Usually Gillian went down to the beach with Noel in the morning, but not till after they had been to the store for the marketing. Well, perhaps they had gone while the policeman was there. Gillian would know pretty well what if anything was needed for that special day. Gillian was all for saving when Reuben was not at home, showing her economical training during her hard days. But surely—well, she would wait a little. If they had gone down town they would be back in a few minutes and come to tell her what they had done.

So she went back to the pudding she was making for dinner that night, hoping against hope that Reuben would be home for dinner. Yet he couldn't of course, because the wedding was not till seven o'clock and he couldn't get away before that when he was best man.

How she wished that Reuben was back! If that uncle of Gillian's really came, what was she going to do? Gillian had told her just a few words about the trouble they had had with the uncle, and she had an uncanny insight into things that nobody exactly *told* her. She was shrewd enough to guess most of what went on about her. This that the policeman had said fitted together with what the girl had told her. Gillian's uncle was coming to find her. He had done something crooked about Gillian's money. That was plain enough from the few facts she had gathered. Well, she certainly wished that Reuben was here now. He would know what to do. He had given her a telephone number to call if anything happened, and she could call him up, but likely Gillian would come back pretty soon, and she could talk it over with her. True, Gillian hadn't said much about this uncle, only that he was unkind and wanted to put Noel in an orphanage. That likely would be enough to make her afraid of him. Enough to make her run away from him. And likely he had got to a place were he couldn't be crooked with the money unless he got hold of the girl again. Aunt Ettie hadn't lived in this world so long for nothing. If she came on a situation that she didn't understand she could always "shut her mouth and saw wood" as Reubie used to say she did. So Aunt Ettie proceeded to shut her mouth and saw wood. That was what she would do when that old uncle arrived, if he ever really did. Likely it was only a false alarm, and there was no point in worrying Reuben while he was away having a good time at a wedding. Better wait until something real to tell him, *if* she ever did.

So although she had been hovering near the telephone, and looking up that Long Distance number that Reuben had given her she decided to wait awhile. She had gained much of her reputation of being able to handle difficult situations by that very means.

Meanwhile she kept a weather eye out both beachward and townward for Gillian and the boy, but neither of them came. Also for a second visit from the policeman. But the street was empty save for the folks who had taken the next cottage and were now getting settled and going back and forth to the village for this and that. Of course, if she needed anybody in a hurry, and couldn't get the policeman right away, there were always those people. She could easily scream loud enough to make them hear her. Although Aunt Ettie had never yet descended to the undignified situation of having to scream for help.

The thing that worried her the most was a thought that had been suggested by her highly excitable imagination. Suppose those two had gone to the beach and been caught by the unprincipled uncle, or had been met in the street and he had found a way to spirit them out of town without anybody suspecting. And she, Aunt Ettie, not knowing anything about it wouldn't know whether to report such a thing to the police, or to let things drift until Reuben came home. And then suppose Reuben should blame her. He never did blame her yet for anything she'd ever done, but in a case like this he would have a perfect right to blame her. And yet, what could she do?

So she went to work to make an extra fine lunch, cold tongue, rice fritters, and lemon soufflé. And she watched the clock anxiously as she watched the road from the village, and both ways up and down the beach. But still they did not come.

She even went out down the dune a little way to look toward the beach at their favorite place, but no one was there. Rare, old-fashioned tears came streaming down her cheeks, and what to do about it she did not know. Should she call up Reuben and tell him about it? But Reuben was nearly two days' journey away, and what help could he bring?

'Twas then she heard a knocking at the door, and in fair fright she flew back in at her kitchen door, ran the water to let on she had not heard the knock and give herself more time to get her breath and her habitual "snap," or poise as others would have called it.

The knock came again, imperiously, importantly, and Aunt Ettie came and stood in the kitchen doorway where she could look through the living room, the mistress of her mansion.

"Well?" she demanded, her chin held high, one hand firmly gripping the door frame, the other clenched beneath her apron.

"Good morning, ma'am," said the debonair stranger. "I am wondering if you could tell me where to find my niece, Gillie?"

"Gillie?" said the canny Aunt Ettie. "No, I don't know anybody called by that name."

"But I was told by the neighbors that you had a young woman here helping you. Wouldn't that be my niece? Won't you call her? I have come a long way in search of her."

"Oh! That girl!" said Aunt Ettie loftily. "Yes, I did have a girl, but she's gone now."

"Gone? Where has she gone?" said the wicked old uncle.

"Well, I really couldn't say," said Aunt Ettie innocently.

"But do you mean she has left your employ?"

"Oh, she was never in my employ!" said Aunt Ettie crisply. "She was just—visiting—me—awhile."

"Well, but surely you know where she is gone."

"No," snapped Aunt Ettie, "I don't! Excuse me, I have to make a phone call before it's too late."

She stepped to the telephone on a little table just inside the living room, while the man stood watching her annoyedly.

She called the number the policeman had given her.

"That you, Sam?" she asked nonchalantly. "This is Aunt Ettie. Did you hear? Okay, Sam, it's just as you said. And you might tell them I'll need two pounds more of that nice butter and a pound of good old-fashioned cheese."

"Okay, I getcha. Aunt Ettie! I'll send 'em right up!" chuckled Sam and hung up. His voice was clear and altogether disarming to any criminal that might have been waiting around escaping arrest, but Aunt Ettie had her poise by this time.

"What did you say that girl's name was?" she said as she returned to the former conversation, realizing that it was up to her to keep the suspect around till Sam get here.

"Why, her name was Gillie. That's what we called her. Little runt of a thing. But if she's gone and you don't know where, you can't do me much good. I suppose I've got to go on searching. I've walked miles hunting her. I'm just about all in. I thought surely I'd find her here. I was told very decidedly that I would find her here. I got it from her hospital nurse."

"Oh, had she been in the hospital?" said Aunt Ettie with utmost innocence in her face. "Well, I don't think it could possibly be the same one. But anyhow she's gone."

"How long has she been gone?"

"Well, it's quite a while. I couldn't exactly say just when."

"Did she go in a taxi, or walk? And which direction did she go?"

"Well, there you've got me again. You see I wasn't right here when she left. I didn't see her go. I was pretty busy with a caller. A taxi maybe, if she went by train, though she's awful fond of walking and she mighta went afoot and tuk a bus from the public square. I'm sure I can't tell ya."

The man sighed dejectedly.

"You say you had a caller here when she went? Does she live nearby? Maybe she would remember how she went. You see it's very important that I find her. It has to do with some money and I'm afraid she needs it."

"Oh, what a shame," said the false voice of Aunt Ettie. "But no, my caller was a stranger come to see me on business. He doesn't live near here, not to my knowledge."

"Well, could you direct me to a place where I can get a cup of coffee around here? Is that house next door a boarding house?"

"No, not to my knowledge," said Aunt Ettie, wondering how she was going to detain this person long enough for Sam to get here. "But say, if it's only a cup of coffee you want, I can give you a cup. I've got the pot on the stove now."

"Oh, thank you, that's good, my good woman!" said Uncle Albee. "I'll be glad to pay you!"

"I don't keep a boarding house ner a rest'rant either," said Aunt Ettie, and sailed away to the kitchen with her head in the air, hoping and praying that Gillian and Noel wouldn't turn up from their walk right in the middle of this and spoil it all before Sam got here.

She gave the man her cheapest spoon. You never could tell what a man like that might do, and she handed him a tray with three hard cookies and a cup of coffee. That ought to keep him busy for a few minutes. And then she retired to the kitchen and clattered pans and rattled dishes to keep up with the thudding of her heart. She had never actually been an accomplice to arresting a man before, and it filled her with excitement. Also she was still worried about Gillian and Noel, and yet she hoped they wouldn't come till this criminal was out of the way. Of course he didn't look like a criminal, though his eyes were "some shifty."

And then she got in a panic lest the man might leave while she was making all this clatter out in the kitchen and she wouldn't see which way he went. Maybe he would find the children and spirit them off!

So she came quickly into the living room, and saw the visitor just taking the final swallow of coffee, and slipping the last cooky into his pocket. And just then she heard a step outside, and there stood her policeman as large as life and quite near to the caller.

"You Mason Albee?" the policeman asked in a sharp businesslike tone.

The caller rose precipitately and set down his cup on the little porch table.

"Yes. Y-y-e-s," he answered. "That is, I'm from out west and I'm in search of a niece who has run away. Her mother is nearly crazy about it, and I came in search of her."

The policeman's eyes were looking straight into Uncle Albee's eyes, and somehow he got to stuttering and stammering.

"Oh yeah?" said Sam. "That makes a nice story, but it don't go down here. I happen to know the facts, and you can come along with me and answer the charges made. And while you are about it, you might put on these bracelets before you start."

"But look here, you can't do that to me!" said Uncle Albee with great pain in his voice. "I'm from another state. You can't arrest me here."

"That's all right," said Sam. "We thought of all that before you came and we've got the papers all fixed up. The National Trust Company of Westbrook, Wisconsin is suing you for obtaining funds illegally from your niece's inheritance."

"But look here, my good man," said Uncle Albee, "I can prove to you that's not so. I have papers with me that will show you. I can prove to you—"

"No you can't, not to me. You come along and prove it to the court if you can, but I haven't any time to talk it over with you now. Here comes our car!" With a flourish and a clang of gong the police patrol wagon drew up in front of the door and Sam hustled his prisoner away.

"But—I wanted to tell you something—" pleaded Aunt Ettie as he went down the steps.

"Okay with me," smiled Sam. "See you later, Aunt Ettie," and he was gone in a perfect tumult of noise. For Sandy Haven didn't have many chances for dramatic incidents like this, and they wanted to make the most of it. Especially as the police car was new only a few days ago.

So Aunt Ettie turned the lights down under her coffee pot, and under her depressed looking soufflé, and then went to the back door and surveyed the beach as far as her eye could reach. After that she sat down with her kitchen apron over her head and cried.

Aunt Ettie waited an hour for Sam's return, and when he didn't come, and she could see no sign of him on the street she started out on the beach and walked south a long distance, until she came to a point of land that jutted out as far as she could see, with water on the other side of it glimmering in the distance. Then she turned around and went as far in the other direction. But there also there seemed to be irregularities in the shore line which bewildered her, so she turned about and dragged wearily back to the cottage, trying to persuade herself on the way that she would probably find Noel and Gillian waiting for her on the front porch. The tears were streaming down her hard self-sufficient face again. Never in the whole of her eventful life had Aunt Ettie found anything quite so daunting, that she couldn't meet efficiently.

But when she reached the cottage there wasn't a sign of the Guthries anywhere about. She put on the kettle to make herself a cup of tea, because she felt as if she would collapse, and just as she was getting out her cup and saucer a brisk determined step came on the front porch and there sounded a peremptory knock. Her heart was in her mouth as she hurried to the door. That wouldn't be either Noel or Gillian, not walking and knocking like that. But maybe they had been drowned and someone was coming to tell her.

But it was only a young policeman in full uniform trying to act important and severe. He had a hard young face and no light in his eyes.

"This Aunt Ettie?" he asked sourly.

She nodded, too out of breath from excitement to speak.

"Well, Sam asked me to stop by and tell you he couldn't come back taday. He was assigned ta take that there man back ta Wisconsin. He expects ta be back some time tamorra ur next day, an' he'll stop by an' tell ya all about it. I can't tell ya much. I'm new on this beat and haven't heard the details. Okay?"

"Okay," assented Aunt Ettie, choked between fury and contempt. Think she was going to tell that young squirt about Gillian and Noel? Not she! A lot he could do about it. He was nothing but a tough kid.

So at last as early evening dragged along and it got too dark to see up the beach any longer from the kitchen window, she betook herself to the telephone and tried to get Reuben.

But Aunt Ettie was not very well versed in the art of long distance telephoning. It seemed to take a long time to get that Illinois number, and longer still to find somebody who could tell her that Reuben Remington had gone, already started home as far as they could find out. At last she hung up, thoroughly disgusted with all inventions in general, and the telephone system in particular. Things were going very wrong for Aunt Ettie today and she was fast losing confidence in her ability which had so long stood her in good stead.

It was after that that she remembered to go and get her cup of tea which she had poured out just before the inadequate policeman had arrived, and she found it stone cold. Well, she was too stubborn and too economical to throw it away and and begin over again, so she drank it anyhow and made a face after the last cheerless swallow. Then she sat down in despair and stared about her at the dark windows.

Little lights were twinkling outside, from the cottages about, and occasionally here and there far apart, down near the beach. There was no boardwalk. That had been the charm of the place to them all that there was no boardwalk to make the place a fashionable resort, just plain simple sand and water and nature's own setting. But now it all looked desolate and dreary to the lonely watcher, who did not know what to do. And when would Reuben get here? Would it be too late to find out anything about the lost ones? Would he be very angry with her for letting this happen? Yet what could she have done that she had not done? Telephone the police? Bah! What could they do? If that Sam were home maybe he would accomplish something, fresh as he was, but this little whippersnapper of a kid, he wouldn't know how to find a lost one, not at night in the dark. And anyhow she wouldn't like to send a little squirt like that after her, he might get fresh with her, and Gillian would never stand for that. She would run away. Aunt Ettie had heard a little of Gillian's running away from that uncle after her mother died, and she didn't want to frighten her away again.

And just then she heard a car drive up, and a familiar step on the front porch, and there was Reuben at last!

But oh, what would he say when she told him Gillian was gone? And his dear little boy?

REUBEN walked in smiling and found Aunt Ettie slumped in the big chair weeping. His heart contracted in fear. He had never seen Aunt Ettie in tears before.

"Why, Aunt Ettie! What's the matter?" he said. "Has something terrible happened?"

Aunt Ettie lifted a tear-stained face and nodded.

"Yes," she sobbed. "They're gone! They're both gone!"

"Gone? Who? What do you mean?"

"Gillian and Noel!" she sobbed.

"But how? Why? What happened? Quick! Tell me! Don't waste time!"

"It happened this morning," said Aunt Ettie, all business now as she mopped her excited face. "A policeman came and asked did I have a caller named Albee. I said no, I didn't know him. He told me I'd see him pretty soon, he was coming to hunt for his niece, and he said for me to phone him when he came, an' say 'Okay,' an' then I went to tell Gillian, an' she wasn't there! She musta heard the policeman talk, and skipped out. I looked all around and couldn't find her nor Noel, and then pretty soon that old uncle came, an' I had my hands full, what with phoning that fool police, and trying to keep Albee from gettin' away before the police got here. And then Sam—the police come, an' a red car, an' they took that old uncle away an' I ain't seen hide nor hair of either of 'em since, though the police said he'd come back, but he didn't, and then I didn't know what ta do, so I tried ta phone you like you said, and they said you'd gone home. So then bimeby another police came 'n' said Sam hedta take the old party ta Wisconsin. An' I couldn't tell this young feller, he was too fresh. So I didn't know what ta do. You see I'd went already up an' down the beach callin' and couldn't find either of 'em anywhere, an' I was wondering what else there was to do when I heard your car—" and then she melted into tears again.

"Hush!" said Reuben sharply and strode to the telephone. He called up the police headquarters and told his story briefly, a girl and boy lost. Been gone since morning. He must have help at once. They were the niece and nephew of the old man who had been extradited to Wisconsin that morning. Did Sam really take him or was that a cock and bull story? Yes, they were terribly afraid of the uncle who had made such trouble for them in the past. Would the police please check up on the exact time that Sam had come to the cottage. Yes, the girl was in another room when he came, must have overheard him talking. What trains were there leaving Sandy Haven about that time or after? What buses? Going where? What about the next stations above, or below? What other likelihood was there of escape? What? The beach? Yes, they knew the beach pretty well. They had often walked there. Where? Down the inlet? Oh, you mean that little sort of island that humps up beyond the bathing beach at low tide? Oh! How about the tide there? Does it ever cover that highest land? Sometimes, you say? *Oh, man!* What time was high tide? Now? Oh, no, he didn't think they knew anything about high and low tide over there. They hadn't been near there but once. Yes, I'll go at once. Yes, I have a flashlight, but it's still full moon, isn't it? Yes, I'll take my flash of course. What? What baggage, you say?"

He lifted frightened eyes to Aunt Ettie who was all capability now, and had bustled into Gillian's bedroom, but now returned with Gillian's purse in her hand and a look of awful despair on her pitiful face.

"She didn't take a thing but their coats as far as I can find. She mighta had fifty cents ur so in the pocket of her coat, I dunno."

"They had only their coats as far as we can find out. No, not likely any money unless a few cents in a pocket," went on Reuben talking to the policeman. "All right. I'll meet you at the inlet. I'm starting now. Is there a boat down there? Is it far to swim if there is no other way? Well, what time does the tide turn? I see. Not much time left, is there? Can you come at once? Yes, I'll be there ahead of you. If I'm not in sight you'll see my coat on the beach and you can look for me in the ocean. Good bye. I'm leaving."

He flung his hat off, and the overcoat he had been wearing, caught up a sweater from a chair where Aunt Ettie had placed it, accepted the paper bag of two hastily prepared sandwiches she had scrambled together, and the bottle of cold coffee, the only restorative she could find. Then as he was dashing out to his car she ran after him with a full bottle of milk and a tin cup.

"Don't worry!" he called to her as he whirled his car about and started off at a mighty pace. After that there succeeded for a long and trying silence for poor Aunt Ettie, during which she heard over again the crisp sentences in which Reuben had told the facts to the police. He hadn't stopped to see whether the man was fresh or tough or anything. He had just gone to the point and told all that was necessary for the finding of the two. Why couldn't she have been like that? Why couldn't she had done something early this morning before they had ever got so far? She could have called the police herself and reported her fears, even if they did laugh at her for an old granny? What difference did it make whether they thought her foolish or not? Oh, she was getting old, and beyond her usefulness. She had no business to be out on her own pretending to take care of people. She ought to be in an old women's home, being waited on, and kept out of harm's way.

Then her imagination began to work again, and she thought what would happen, supposing Reuben got there in time before they drowned, and brought them back. She must be ready for anything. She must have hot blankets, and plenty of hot water. She must get the beds turned down, and have hot food that could be easily eaten.

So, with never a thought for herself that she hadn't eaten anything but cold tea all day since breakfast, she set to work. Hot soup. She would have hot soup. There was meat in the refrigerator that she had intended for dinner that night, but it would make wonderful beef tea, and that was easy to swallow and easy to digest. She would boil some potatoes and carrots and onions, for Reuben loved his soup with vegetables in it, and Reuben would be plenty hungry after traveling all day and maybe half the night before to get back. Celery. He loved celery.

She cut great plates of her nice homemade bread, she got out olives and pickles, and a custard pie, in case anybody was well enough and cheery enough to eat dessert of any kind. She filled a pitcher with milk, and put a fresh pot of coffee on. And all the time she was doing this the tears were running a steady stream down her face and she looked a hundred years old at least, blaming and vilifying herself for being an old fool who oughtn't to have any responsibility at all.

Then she turned down the beds and put night clothes to warm. One would have thought to watch her that Reuben himself was likely to come in from this search a physical wreck, for she prepared for his comfort as well as for the other two.

Down at the police headquarters they were busy as bees, preparing for all sorts of possibilities.

"Guess Sam'll be surprised at what he started," said Tim, the fresh young man who had called on Aunt Ettie that morning.

"That's so," said James, an older man who hated a lot of

excitement and liked to carry it off as if he had it all conquered before you told him about it. "Say, Tim, didya see annythin' of this girl they tell about when you went ta interview the old party this mornin'?"

"Naw!" said Tim. "Dont'cha think I'd a told ya ef I had?"

"Well, I see her once," said a man who usually hung around the fire house. "I seen her yestiddy mornin' down ta the newsstand buyin' a paper. She's good-lookin' an' I don't mean just some. Had a little kid with her 'bout five years old I reckon."

"Yep! That's him. I seen 'em too," said the fire chief.

"Shut up!" called the chief of police. "Get on yer job, can't ya? Jeff, you phone up the Coast Guard an' hev 'em take the boats out. Send one down ta the Inlet, we might need 'em. Can't tell. It might be rough out there. Got yer car ready, Tim? Blake got back yet from checkin' them buses an' trains?"

"Yep!" called a sharp-faced man who was pulling a jumper over his head. "Morning trains all gone when Sam called there. Nothin' but the noon train up, and the four o'clock ta the city since. I contacted both conductors, and they both swear no such parties boarded their trains. 'Course they might a gone to Long Neck and tuk a bus south, ur ta the river end an' tuk the ferry, but both Hal and Dan say they ain't seen no such parties. Yes, sir, they's bound ta be at the Inlet ur drowned by this time fer sure."

"Shut up!" said the chief. "Get on yer job! The young fella'll be drownded too ef we don't get a hustle on."

Then two cars went thundering off in different directions from police headquarters, and the men around the fire house settled down in their accustomed chairs, and told stories of disasters they had known.

While back at the peaceful little white cottage Aunt Ettie worked frantically to have a good dinner ready, and mourned meanwhile at what had happened, trying her best to think what Gillian would have done, and where she could have gone.

Gillian had been briskly making her bed that morning when Sam the policeman arrived, and her swift hands paused in smoothing back the sheet, to listen, thinking it might be some word from Reuben. Also, ever since she had come away from the uncle she feared so much she had cultivated the habit of being always on the alert. So now as she paused and heard the name of the dreaded uncle, Mason Albee, she was fairly petrified with fear for an instant, and then she was stung into action. Uncle Mason had somehow heard she was in the east, and he was taking all chances to find her. He was keen to ferret out necessary facts always, she knew, and he would not stop until he had got what he wanted. He was almost cruelly persistent.

She recognized that somehow word had been telegraphed to the police in Sandy Haven that he was on his way down there, from the detective who was trying to trace him. They had found which way he was headed. Well, it didn't matter how it had happened. She was only thankful she had a warning. If only Reuben had been there she wouldn't be so worried, but Reuben hadn't been sure when he could return, and she could not wait for him. She must get Noel into safety at once. Uncle Mason might arrive at any moment. She mustn't even wait to talk to Aunt Ettie, nor to write a note, or pack anything. She could take their heavy sweaters, in case they had to stay out late and it turned cold.

All this flashed through her mind in an instant. She seized her sweater, remembering her little purse was in the pocket, and took Noel's sweater from the hook in the closet, all in one motion. She slid noiselessly out the door into the kitchen as soon as she heard the policeman step toward the door.

On the kitchen table lay a small pasteboard box of crackers. She picked them up as she went by, and slid out the back door to Noel who was building sand cities a little way from the house.

"Come, quick, Noel!" she said, running silently to him and touching him on the shoulder. "Hurry, dear! Don't talk, just come as quietly as you can. We'll run a race down to the beach. There's a reason!"

That was a phrase which had a meaning for them both, for often Gillian had been obliged to leave him without explanations for a time, and so he arose wondering and followed her, taking her hand and running with all his might.

At first they were not thinking where they were going. Just to get out of sight from the cottage was Gillian's first objective. They hurried on toward the sand dunes, where she knew they could be comparatively hidden behind the big hillocks or dunes covered with tall grass.

They came at last to these dunes, and dropped into temporary shelter, till they got their breath to speak.

"What's the matter, Gillian?" whispered Noel, watching her worried face.

"Uncle Mason," she panted. "He's traced us here, it seems. At least the policeman came to tell Aunt Ettie he was likely to come, and she must let them know."

"But Reuben won't let Uncle Mason get me, will he?"

"No, of course not, but Reuben isn't here, dear, and we've got to stay hidden till Uncle Mason is gone."

"But how will we know when he is gone? Will we have to stay here till Reuben comes back and comes to find us and tell us?"

"Oh, I don't know yet. I've got to think about it. You see we don't know when Reuben will come back and it might be several days."

"Oh!" He was thoughtful for several minutes and then he said:

"But won't Mrs. Aunt Ettie be scared, Gillian? Did you tell her you were coming?"

"No, I didn't have time. The policeman hadn't gone yet, and Uncle Mason might have come in any minute. I thought we ought to get out of sight."

There was a long still time when they could only hear the ocean lapping on the beach, the wind waving the grasses about their heads, as they lay nestled in the sand. Then Noel whispered again:

"Gillian, how did Uncle Mason find out where we are?"

"I don't know," said the sister sadly. "I think perhaps he knew the city where father's friend lived, the one who died just after he had recommended me to work in my office. And he has just taken a chance coming to find out where we are. It must be there is still some money left from our father's fortune, and he knows I'll soon be of age. He may have been getting some all the time and not giving us any. And now perhaps he wants me to sign it all over to him."

"You're not going to do that, are you, Gillian?" asked the little boy anxiously.

"No, of course not," said the girl wearily. "But I don't want to face him until I know more about things. Reuben has got a lawyer to look after it and find out if we have anything at all. It may be Uncle Mason just told us a lie about our money and has been using it all the time. It seems as if it must be something about money or he would not bother to hunt for us. But we can't do anything about it alone. We've got to wait somewhere until Reuben gets home."

"But won't Aunt Ettie be terribly scared about us?"

"Yes, I'm afraid she will, but I don't know what I can do about it now. I do not dare go back in the daytime. Uncle Mason might be watching somewhere. Perhaps when it gets dark we could go near enough to see in when the lamps are lighted, and if there is nobody there we might slip in and tell Aunt Ettie. But we've got to have a better place than this to hide. There come some people now. Are they men or women?"

"They are ladies and little girls in bathing suits."

"Well, put your head down as if you were asleep, and when they are out of sight we'll go somewhere else."

"Awright!" said the boy, and down went his head to the sand. Presently he spoke softly:

"Gillian, where can we get something to eat?"

"I brought some crackers. Are you hungry already?"

"No, only a little, but I can wait. Say, Gillian, I know a place where we could hide. Reuben showed it to me one day when he brought me out to walk. It is at the inlet. He said it was a nice quiet place where many people didn't come."

"Where is it? Are you sure you can find it?"

"Oh yes, it is away down that way, almost to that other lighthouse. Don't you know the revolving light Reuben showed us when we were out the other night? Maybe that would be a good place if we had to stay late. It wouldn't be so dark. And I would like to watch the light."

Dear little fellow! He was getting a bit of fun out of even their troubles!

"Well," said Gillian with a rueful smile, "after the people are gone we might walk that way and see how it is."

But there were more and more people coming out to bathe and Gillian got worried, and decided to make their way among the sand dunes. It wasn't easy walking, but soon they got beyond the groups of people and hurried down to the smoother beach, walking very fast and finally running, to get as far away from Sandy Haven as they could.

But at last they rounded a curve in the shore, and there was the lighthouse, standing tall against the sky. It seemed most impressive and Noel stopped and gazed in great admiration. Suddenly he said:

"Gillian, I'm most terribly hungry. Could I have just one little cracker now?"

"Oh, yes," she said. "Suppose we sit down behind this old wreck of a boat, and we shall be hidden."

So they crept behind a small fishing boat, stranded, and bleached in the weather, with broken mast, and a look as if life for it were over. They had three crackers apiece.

"I wish I had a drink of milk," said Noel with a sigh.

"Yes, that would be nice. But perhaps there will be a way to get one before too long. I have my little purse in my sweater pocket. There was some change in that. But we'll have to wait till dark I think, dear. Can you wait and not be too uncomfortable?"

Noel gave a long deep sigh and said:

"Yes, Gillian," and then a little later he spoke again. "Gillian, don't you think we might ask God to send our Reuben right away to find us? It's going to be a long afternoon, I'm afraid."

Gillian choked back the tears that were in her throat and tried to hide her sorrowfulness with a smile.

"Yes, dear," she said, and so Noel bowed his curly head and prayed his direct little petition.

"Dear Heavenly Father, won't You please send our Reuben home to help us, and won't You please show us what to do. If You don't want Reuben to come, won't You please come Yourself and take care of us, and don't let Uncle Mason ever get us again. For Christ's sake we ask it, Amen."

And then he made Gillian pray too, and her heart was helped and strengthened by the child's faith.

"Now," said Noel, "I think we better go over there behind us to that inlet. Reuben said that was a nice place. It's a long point out into the water where you can see the sun rise on one side and set on the other, and perhaps there'll be a moon there and it will be nice. Reuben knows that place, and maybe he'll come to find us. Then we can lie down and go to sleep. I am very tired, sister."

So they rounded the dunes, and walked out on the long point of land. They found a nice high place where they could lie down behind a lot of piles driven into the sand for the water to break against.

"This is nice," said Noel. "Even the lighthouse people can't see us when they come out of their door down to the beach. Only I guess their light can reach over here, because it's up so high."

So Noel nestled against his sister, and very soon he was asleep. And Gillian, feeling very secure, and utterly worn by the happening of the morning and the long walk and anxiety, lay down beside him, and soon she herself was fast asleep.

Then the sun began to slide down to the west and cast long shadows on the sand, and a rosy glow over everything. It sank lower and lower till it touched the ocean's rim, and took a dip into its bright waters. And then the sea began to take notice, and switched its tides. Slowly, slowly, step by step, the little foamy edges of the sea crept up higher and higher on the point of land where they lay.

And over on the other side where the sun had been that morning a silver moon came looming up, a silver thread at a time, until it was a whole round disc casting a silver path out across the water, as if it would lure travelers that way.

But Gillian and Noel were lying with their backs that way and did not notice, for they were still fast asleep. And now the darkness furtively crept along, like a great veil flung everywhere, until the waters grew so bright that the land was illumined also except in hidden places.

And then, the revolving light from the lighthouse was suddenly flung out and whirled long pointing fingers of gold across the heavens. They searched out the darkest corners, and touched lightly the eyelids of the sleepers to warn them on either side, lit with silver on the one side and crimson and gold on the other. Creeping up closer and closer.

The darkness was all about them now, like a pall, and there were no noises to disturb them except the soft subtle swish of the water, and a dull roar like a distant menace breaking high and near, ever nearer.

The child stirred restlessly in his sleep, kicking out, and stretching, turning his cramped limbs. At last he came awake.

"Gillian! Gillian!" he cried. "Where are we? Reuben, are you out there in the night? Gillian! Oh, you're there! Gillian, I'm cold! So very cold!"

Gillian stirred.

"Cold, darling! Oh, why, put on your sweater! Where is it? There it is, here under my hand. Put it on quick, dear! Why, it's night! Have we slept so long?"

"I'm hungry, Gillian! Will there be enough for me to have another cracker? Where is your box of crackers, sister? Oh, here they are. But the box is wet, Gillian. How did it get all wet? And the crackers! They are wet too! And Gillian, I'm afraid of those funny long fingers of light. It hurts the blackness it is so sharp!"

"It's just the light from the lighthouse, Noel. Have you forgotten how you brought me here?"

"Oh, yes, I remember. But Gillian, my foot is all wet and cold. And the water is making a funny sound like a big wave when Reuben lifts me up. Oh, Gillian! There's a big wave

coming! Look! How did we get away out here in the ocean? And there's waves on your side too!"

Gillian sprang to her feet and looked about her bewildered and saw by the light of the long bright fingers across the sky that they were indeed in the midst of the waters.

"What is it, Gillian? Has something happened?" asked the terrified child.

"It's the tide, I suppose, Noel!" said Gillian in a trembling voice that sought to be controlled.

"But didn't God hear us when we prayed?" asked Noel.

"Yes, God always hears," said the sister casting frightened eyes about. "He holds the sea in the hollow of His hand, the Bible says. You mustn't be afraid. We'll just trust in Him."

"Then do you think Reuben will be coming pretty soon? Will our God send him to help us?"

Gillian mustered all her courage and said tenderly:

"Yes, Noel, I'm sure He'll send him, or else—He'll come Himself!"

"Oh—wouldn't that be wonderful!" said the child. "I'd like that. But I'd like Reuben to be here too, wouldn't you, Gillian?"

"Yes, that would be nice," said Gillian, as she cast her eyes almost hopelessly about her in the darkness. "Come, Noel, we must try to get back to land! We must walk away from the lighthouse. We will try first to find the little wrecked boat where we sat down a while. Then we can sit down and look toward the lighthouse and get our bearings. Come. Take my hand so we won't get separated in the darkness!"

So they started out. But no matter what way they walked they kept coming to the water, and after they had gone about and about they realized that there was water all around them, and it was coming nearer and nearer, with the great thundering waves rising tempestously every now and then.

Suddenly Noel looked up at his sister, with a watery little smile.

"I guess it will be God that comes, Gillian. But don't you think it would be nice to eat the rest of the crackers while we wait for Him? I've got an awful funny empty feeling in my tummy."

"Why, yes," said Gillian, suddenly rousing from her horror and realizing she must not let the child suffer. "Let's eat the crackers. You may divide them, but don't give me but one at a time, I like to eat slowly."

"Yes, we will eat slowly," said Noel, and he handed out a soggy cracker.

And so in the strength of that bread they went on with their hopeless walking and each minute the water seemed to be drawing nearer, inch by inch.

AS Rueben spun along the smooth white road the moon was coming up, and the long rays from the lighthouse searchlight shot across his path. He could envision a picture of that long narrow point jutting out into the sea. Even now perhaps the water was rolling in and covering it from view. And those two he loved, were they out there in peril?

Oh, would it be too late when he got there to do any good? Would they have been washed into the sea? How could that frail girl stand against the buffeting of the waves? And the little child! The brave true little boy! He would be blown away with a breath from that monster, the sea. His body was not strong enough, even though his courage was great, to withstand the shock of even one of those waves. Gillian would have to hold him, and she was not able! How could the two brave the fierceness of the incoming tide?

If he only hadn't gone to that wedding! If he only hadn't gone to the Glindenwold affair before that, and had stayed with the two whom God had sent him to protect! The memory of those two gatherings he had attended would stay with him always as something that did not belong in his life.

As he thought back he fairly seemed to grudge those times spent away when he might have been with the two he had come to love so keenly!

These thoughts tumbled through his mind in wild disorder as he drove furiously through the silver night, with those long lights slashing out into the darkness, seeming to point at him mockingly.

Then far behind him he heard the sound of a motor. The police were coming. At least he was doing all he could, and if the ones they sought were not here, and were not in the sea, then where else could they search? Would the police have any other possible suggestions?

Vaguely back in his mind he wondered if they had done anything about that worthless uncle who had made all this trouble, but he brushed the thought away as he might have a fly who annoyed in this breathless struggle with death for life of the two who were beloved.

Then he came to the old ship, where they had sat down to rest, and there he stopped his car, for the water was not far away. There was something dark at the far end of that old boat, hanging over the edge of the gunwale, waving lazily back and forth. He stooped to feel it, and lifted it as its shape grew familiar. It was an old brown sweater that he had seen Gillian wear sometimes. Was he deceived? This was only moonlight in which he was seeing it! As he lifted it something seemed to weigh it down. It jingled as he raised it higher. He put his hand in the pocket, and there was Gillian's little change purse. He had seen it many times in her hand!

Frantically he flung it into the car. There at least was proof that she had been here! And then he dashed into the water before him, flinging off his own sweater and shoes as he went. He plunged through the water with great strides, deeper and deeper, around to the right where he knew that long point of water jutted, feeling his way in the darkness, waiting now and again for the long fingers of light to come his way, and make the distance more clear.

Suddenly as he drew nearer to where he thought that inlet might be he heard a voice soft and sweet and clear even above the wildness of the waters:

Step by step I'll follow Jesus,
Hour by hour I'm in His care,
Day by day He walks beside me,
Through the years I'll know He's there.
He can still the mighty tempest,
He can calm the troubled sea,
He the waters trod, He's the Son of God,
He's the One who always walks with me.

That was Noel's voice, and that was the strange little chorus he had sung that first Sunday when they had had their Sunday School together. The tune had stayed with him, some of the words too, and he found them echoed in his memory!

He swam along heavily, hampered by his garments, wet of course to the skin but his face was wet with tears, whose saltness was bitterer than the sea. The little child who had led him back to God was out there somewhere in the water, singing to guide him to him.

And was Gillian there too?

A few more strokes, strong and nerved by hope, brought him to their side, as they stood in water that already reached almost to the child's neck. Gillian was there beside him, with her arms firmly clasped about him! Praise God, she was still alive! Would he ever doubt God again!

And then the child's voice changed from song into glad rejoicing.

"He's come! My Reuben's come! God sent him. God didn't need to come Himself just now. He's sent my Reuben! I knew he'd hear our prayer!"

And then Reuben lifted himself up on the shelf of sand beside them and raised the child to his shoulder, with the other arm about the swaying girl, who was almost overpowered with the mighty physical effort it had taken to keep the little boy from drowning. She had known she could last but a moment or two longer for she felt her limbs trembling, and to withstand another shock of waters coming like a torrent above her, and keep that darling little head above them seemed a physical impossibility.

And then suddenly this strong arm about her! Had the Lord come Himself to take them both Home to Himself?

Her head fell back against Reuben's shoulder, and the lights were suddenly blacked out. The waves and the sea itself was gone, and there was only this strong arm, and the sense that Noel was somehow safe!

Then Reuben himself began to pray, and to wonder just how he was going to save them both without help. He could not leave either one, and come back for the other. Gillian was limp now in his arms, and Noel would be beyond his depth if he tried to put him down.

And then he called aloud, out of the midst of his prayer, "God, Oh, my God, hear my cry! For Thy Son's sake save us all!"

It is doubtful if the life guards understood that prayer, but they heard the voice of distress calling for help, and they were out there not far away with their boat, obedient to the telephone call. Straight to the place of need their boat came as if guided from above.

The police arrived just as the coast guards brought them all to land. They wrapped Gillian in blankets from the guard house, and administered restoratives. They bundled Noel in another blanket. But Reuben put on the sweater he had shed when he plunged into the water, and said he was all right, he wanted to get his people home. He would come back and thank the coast guards the next day.

At last they were on their way home, too dazed to realize that the terror of the sea was gone, and they were safe in Reuben's care, safe because God had sent him to care for them.

Then poor Aunt Ettie, her dinner just at the spoiling point, heard a car outside, in fact two cars, and came trembling to the door, to watch two forms sheathed in blankets being brought in by several men.

It was Reuben who strode up the steps with Gillian in his arms, and commanded Aunt Ettie to spread out something thick and warm on the bed so that he could lay her down.

But it was Aunt Ettie who took charge immediately, and put them all out, giving Gillian a thorough rubdown, and putting her into a hot nightdress and bathrobe, and then into a warm bed. But Reuben had gone at once to Noel, as he knew Gillian would want him to do, and gave him all the care he needed. At last he was warm and dry and clothed in royal comfort. Then in his little new bathrobe he insisted in going out to thank the policemen, and to tell them about that long time of waiting "before our God answered our prayer, and sent our Reuben to help us, and then sent the boat you telephoned for, just in time to get us away before we drifted out to sea. We think he is a good God."

And more than one of the rough policemen as they listened brushed tears away from their eyes. They watched the child and thought God must have sent a little angel down when he sent Noel to earth.

Then Aunt Ettie bustled around and got cups of coffee and doughnuts for the men, and fed Gillian and Noel and Reuben with hot soup and all the good things she had got ready for them.

It was while he was feeding the soup to Gillian that their glances met, hers with a shy sweet smile in them, his glance very tender.

Suddenly he laid down the spoon and bowl on the table by the bed, and bringing his face down very close to hers he said tenderly, "Oh, my dear! My precious love! Thank God you are safe!" and then suddenly he laid his face against hers and kissed her reverently.

"Gillian, I love you, dear! I think I've loved you ever since I first saw you. But I never had thought much about it until I went away from you out to that wedding. Then I understood. It was while the wedding march was being played I saw the bride coming slowly up the aisle, and I suddenly saw your face, and I knew that you were the one I love. There could never be anybody else for me. There were bells in the music, bells on the church organ, wedding bells, and I felt as if they were ringing in my heart! And then I came rushing home to tell you and I found you gone! Oh, my darling! I shall never cease to thank God that you are alive!"

His face went down to hers, and her hands came up shyly, hesitantly to touch it. Then she put her arms close about his neck, and drew him to her.

"Oh!" she breathed softly, "this is wonderful! To think that you should love me!"

Their lips met in a long sweet kiss.

Then Reuben lifted his head and looked into her eyes.

"Do you think that Noel will be glad about it?" he asked shyly. "Will he want me for a real brother, and be happy in our home?"

"Oh, he will!" said Gillian. "It will make him happier than anything else on earth could do. He loves you intensely."

"And I love him," said Reuben fervently. "He is the dearest child I ever knew. He has done me good."

"And you won't feel that he is in the way?" said Gillian hesitantly. "You know I must care for him."

"Of course," said Reuben with a ring of joy in his voice. "And it shall be my dearest joy next to caring for you, to look out in every way for the dear boy. It is as if he were my own, both for your sake and for his own. I love him too."

"Oh, Reuben! There is no one like you! I never thought such joy could ever come to me!" and Gillian suddenly drew him down and held him close for a long moment.

Then all at once a calm sarcastic voice broke in upon their ecstasy:

"Well, if you two can stop mooning long enough, perhaps you could spare time to tell that poor sleepy boy good night! He wants to see you Reuben, so you'd better hurry up or he'll fall asleep before you get there. But it's just what I expected. I never thought you were a liar, Reuben Remington, but it's turned out exactly as I knew it would. You said she wasn't your girl, but it certainly doesn't look that way now, not as far as I can see! But it's all right with me, Reubie! You've gotta have a girl sometime, I suppose, and I like her a lot, so go ahead. Only say good night to Noel or he'll be padding in here in his bare feet, an' catching his death o' cold, so hurry up."

"That's the talk, Aunt Ettie! I thought you'd come around. All right, I'll go!"

"But I am coming too!" said Gillian, springing up.

"Oh, but you shouldn't!" said Reuben putting out a protesting hand.

"I'm quite all right, and it won't hurt me a bit," she said slipping her feet into the slippers that were beside the bed.

Reuben's arm was about her, supporting her, and they walked into the other room to Noel, their faces serenely happy.

"Shall we tell Noel tonight?" he asked, stooping down to say it in a low tone.

"Yes," she said with shining eyes. "He will be so very happy!"

Aunt Ettie stood beaming on the side lines, watching them and rejoicing.

So they marched together to Noel's bedside and he looked at them with a startled wonder at the glory look in their faces.

"Well, fella," said Reuben, "I'm taking you over for good. We're going to have a wedding. You're going to be my family after this. How'll you like that?" asked Reuben, as they stopped at the child's bedside.

"Oh, truly? And you won't have to go away any more? Oh, goody, goody, goody! We have a good God, haven't we, Gillian?"

He climbed out of his cot and flung himself into their arms.

Then after he had hugged and kissed them, he was tucked back under his blanket again.

"Will there be wedding bells?" he asked eagerly from his pillow.

"Yes, wedding bells," said Reuben. "Wedding bells, and you may ring them. I'm not so sure but you started them ringing long ago. Wedding bells in all our hearts! What do you say, Gillian, may it be soon?"

"Soon as you please," said Gillian smiling.

"Well, how about tomorrow morning?" said Reuben grinning. "Aunt Ettie, do you think you could get up a wedding breakfast in time?"

"Well, it's a little soon, but I guess I could scrape something together. I wouldn't want ta be the one ta delay things."

"We'll have to take time to get the bells!" shouted Noel joyously. "Aunt Ettie, I'm going to ring the bells!"

"Ain't that grand!" said Aunt Ettie, beaming.

"Yes," said Reuben laying a loving hand on the boy's head. "I guess you're in tune all right." And then he gathered the child close. "Little brother!" he murmured, and kissed him softly.

About the Author

Grace Livingston Hill is well known as one of the most prolific writers of romantic fiction. Her personal life was fraught with joys and sorrows not unlike those experienced by many of her fictional heroines.

Born in Wellsville, New York, Grace nearly died during the first hours of life. But her loving parents and friends turned to God in prayer. She survived miraculously, thus her thankful father named her Grace.

Grace was always close to her father, a Presbyterian minister, and her mother, a published writer. It was from them that she learned the art of storytelling. When Grace was twelve, a close aunt surprised her with a hardbound, illustrated copy of one of Grace's stories. This was the beginning of Grace's journey into being a published author.

In 1892 Grace married Fred Hill, a young minister, and they soon had two lovely young daughters. Then came 1901, a difficult year for Grace—the year when, within months of each other, both her father and husband died. Suddenly Grace had to find a new place to live (her home was owned by the church where her husband had been pastor). It was a struggle for Grace to raise her young daughters alone, but through everything she kept writing. In 1902 she produced *The Angel of His Presence, The Story of a Whim,* and *An Unwilling Guest.* In 1903 her two books *According to the Pattern* and *Because of Stephen* were published.

It wasn't long before Grace was a well-known author, but she wanted to go beyond just entertaining her readers. She soon included the message of God's salvation through Jesus Christ in each of her books. For Grace, the most important thing she did was not write books but share the message of salvation, a message she felt God wanted her to share through the abilities he had given her.

In all, Grace Livingston Hill wrote more than one hundred books, all of which have sold thousands of copies and have touched the lives of readers around the world with their message of "enduring love" and the true way to lasting happiness: a relationship with God through his Son, Jesus Christ.

In an interview shortly before her death, Grace's devotion to her Lord still shone clear. She commented that whatever she had accomplished had been God's doing. She was only his servant, one who had tried to follow his teaching in all her thoughts and writing.